Journey
along the
Galsang Road

www.royalcollins.com

Journey
along the
Galsang Road

Dang Yimin

Books Beyond Boundaries

ROYAL COLLINS

Journey along the Galsang Road

Dang Yimin

First published in 2023 by Royal Collins Publishing Group Inc.
Groupe Publication Royal Collins Inc.
BKM Royalcollins Publishers Private Limited

Headquarters: 550-555 boul. René-Lévesque O Montréal
(Québec) H2Z1B1 Canada
India office: 805 Hemkunt House, 8th Floor, Rajendra Place,
New Delhi 110 008

ISBN: 978-1-4878-1164-8

To find out more about our publications,
please visit www.royalcollins.com.

In July, An Ning quietly set out alone. She was going to Xizang.

She went to marry herself off to someone in a distant place, and the other person didn't even know it. Even her parents didn't know it. It wasn't that she didn't have time to tell them; she just didn't want to.

In An Ning's luggage was *One Man's Plateau*, a sample of photo book that had been planned for publication. The cover was very eye-catching, depicting a woman with a bare back. Standing amid an endless field of green grass full of galsang blooms, she faced a tall snow-capped mountain. An Ning was going to give this book to the person she was going to marry. The woman in the photo was not herself, though. It was her sister, An Jing.

An Ning did not tell her parents about her marriage, and she did not tell the man who was soon to become her husband. She did tell her sister, though. She had to tell her sister. Before her father had that woman, An Ning and her sister always lived at home. Each time she put on her sister's clothes or makeup, she told her sister. This matter was so much more important than clothes or makeup. Of course she had to tell her sister.

An Jing had gone overseas three years earlier. She had gone to work for a British music company.

Anjing meant quiet, but her sister was not quiet, not at all. It wasn't that she didn't want to be quiet, but that others would not allow her to be. When she was a child, the adults liked to tease her, and when she grew up, there was always a circle of men around her. As soon as she got home, the home phone was busy; it kept ringing. And if it was not phone calls, it was text messages.

It was because An Jing was beautiful. Hers was not ordinary beauty. She was extraordinary.

Beautiful An Jing, like any other pretty girl, did not have just one cell phone.

The more phones she had, the more secrets she had, and she often had to change her phone number. Each time she changed numbers, she deleted another round of boyfriends. An Jing didn't have all that many phones, just two. One was public, the other private. When she was upset and didn't want to be disturbed, she switched off the public one, so that only An Ning and a few close friends could find her.

In fact, An Ning was quite pretty too, but her bust was a size smaller than An Jing's. That meant fewer men's eyes on her. Fewer eyes meant less trouble, so An Ning's life had always been quieter, more peaceful, and that didn't change until she met Li Qingge. Looking at her sister's bust, An Ning was both admiring and jealous. An Jing liked to sleep naked at night, and in the morning, she liked to stand naked in front of the mirror, turning here and there, posing.

An Ning always scolded, "Shameless!"

An Jing didn't care. She just smiled and said, "Who told you that was my nickname?"

The two sisters had had a good relationship since they were children. There were no secrets between them; even the most private things were brought into the open. After they moved from home to school, they grew even closer, as they felt a little dependent on one another. They studied at the same university, An Ning majoring in Chinese and An Jing as a graduate student in the art department, studying Tibetan music. Looking back later on all that happened, it seemed that it all came back to An Jing's passion for Tibetan culture and music.

They left home because An Jing and their mother had caught their father off guard in a hotel room. Of course, there was also a woman. Or, to be more precise, a girl. She was the same age as An Jing, and two years older than An Ning.

An Jing was always very cheerful. But when An Ning called to tell her of the marriage plans, An Jing did not say anything for a long time. An Ning knew she was crying. When she cried, she did so silently, never making a sound. An Ning could imagine An Jing's big, beautiful eyes, the tears falling.

After a while, An Jing's voice came over the line. "Congratulations! I wish you happiness."

Then she added, "Give my best wishes to Li Qingge."

Before they hung up, An Jing suddenly remembered to tell An Ning that she might be returning to China soon and that she planned to hold a *Galsang Blossoms* concert in Chengdu. She had spent the past two years preparing for the concert.

Aside from An Jing, there was only one person who knew of An Ning's plans, her boss, Yuan Ye, editorial director of the *Rongcheng Daily*. Yuan Ye had served as a soldier in Xizang for three years. When he was discharged, he went to the university, then joined the newspaper after he graduated.

Hearing An Ning's plans, Yuan Ye was so excited his face turned red. "That's a great idea! I'll start a column for you, *A Bride's Journey to Xizang*. How about it?"

An Ning said, "It's a deal! But I don't want to let anyone else know before I go. I don't want them to know I'm getting married. It will all be settled by the time I come back. The effect will be better that way. If anyone asks, just say I'm taking a leave of absence."

Yuan Ye agreed to keep An Ning's secret. Guarding the same secret made them feel closer. There was an inexplicable excitement between them. Yuan Ye quoted a line from the film *The Dream Factory*: "You'll never beat it out of me!"

2

The long distance bus set out from Chengdu and traveled westward along the Chengya Expressway, reaching Ya'an in about two hours. It was not yet lunchtime when the bus pulled in and parked in front of a restaurant.

Some of the travelers objected, "What's going on? Why are we having lunch so early?"

The dark, honest-looking Tibetan driver said casually, "It's up to you whether you eat or not. We'll have to climb Erlang Mountain soon, and there's nowhere to stop on the way up, so your next chance to eat will be this evening."

An Ning had seen this kind of thing very often. She knew the restaurant had an arrangement with the driver, and he would get his kickback from this stop. She didn't say anything. Why not eat Ya fish, after all? An Ning had been to Ya'an before and knew all about "the three Yas": Ya fish, Ya rain, and Ya women. Ya fish was delicious, and it only had one bone, shaped like a sword. Ya rain referred to the fact that there was a good deal of rain in Ya'an, and it was always misty when it rained, giving the little town a distinct character. Ya women, of course, referred to the local girls, all beautiful, soft-spoken, and with a great variety of charms in their gait.

"You can't say you've been to Ya'an unless you've seen the three Yas," a reporter had told her when she had come for an interview the previous fall. When he mentioned the Ya women, he looked at An Ning and grinned awkwardly, as if she were a Ya woman.

An Ning ordered Ya fish and a bowl of rice. She didn't know if the fish was the real thing or a fake, but it tasted pretty good, and the portion size was sufficient. She sat across from a mother and daughter who kind of looked like city people, but also kind of looked like rural folk. They were probably from a small town in the county. An Ning noticed them only because they didn't order anything but a bowl of noodles each. An Ning couldn't finish the fish by herself, so she offered some to the mother and daughter, saying, "Will you share with me? Dig in!"

"Thank you, but you go ahead. We aren't used to such fish," the mother said in Shaanxi dialect as she continued eating her noodles.

An Ning thought about it. They didn't know each other; of course they wouldn't want to eat her fish. The mother looked like she was in her thirties. She had a gentle face, but seemed to be assertive. Her expression was melancholy. She lowered her head and ate her noodles, not even looking at An Ning's fish. The girl was eleven or twelve, and she seemed to be well-behaved. Apparently quite hungry, she finished her noodles quietly. When her mother asked her if she wanted more, she shook her head, pushed her bowl aside, and took a small piece of paper from her little schoolbag and started folding it. When she finished folding, An Ning realized she had formed a little paper crane. The girl put the paper crane into her schoolbag and started folding a second one.

An Ning asked, "Who are you folding that for?"

The girl didn't answer, or even look at her. An Ning couldn't be sure it was because she was so focused on what she was doing, or whether she couldn't hear or speak, or perhaps she just didn't want to speak even though she heard. The mother also pretended not to hear. What a strange pair! Bored, An Ning ignored them and turned her mind to what she should write about in her first column. The drive to Ya'an? Eating Ya fish? That didn't seem right. The first shot fired had to have some momentum. An Ning didn't feel she had much to say about Ya'an, and that wouldn't do. As they went on, she would observe. It was best to start from Erlang Mountain.

When she paid the bill, she realized that the restaurant really was ripping people off. She was charged 120 yuan for the Ya fish, nearly double what she had paid for the same dish a year ago. In the past, she would have pulled out her press credentials and reasoned with them, but today, she didn't. She didn't say a word, but simply tolerated it. She could be as stingy as she wanted at home, but that wouldn't do on a trip, and there was still a long way to go. She might encounter anything. Suffering this small loss was nothing. The important thing was to keep her spirits up.

The bus journey continued. Soon, they were climbing Erlang Mountain.

An Ning had an aisle seat. Sitting in the window seat beside her was a middle-aged Tibetan man with dark red skin. His face was cool. She thought he might be a Khampa man. According to Li Qingge, Khampa males were men among men within the Tibetan ethnic group. Each time the Khampa man looked at An Ning, he smiled, making her very uncomfortable as he displayed two rows of white teeth. It was fine when he didn't smile, but the moment he smiled, all the coolness disappeared. An Ning felt sorry for him.

Seated by the window across the aisle were the mother and daughter who had eaten at her table earlier, and on the aisle seat was a young woman. The little girl continued to fold paper cranes. Her mother watched, sometimes helping her fold. Later, the mother vomited, splattering the window with the noodles she had just eaten. Some of them clung to the glass in a disgusting display. The girl put down her paper cranes and patted her mother's back.

The young woman seated next to them frowned, then covered her mouth, like she was about to vomit too. She gagged a few times, but didn't throw up. She stood up and said to the Khampa man, "I'm also prone to motion sickness. Can we change seats?"

The Khampa man was quite ready to help. Without a word, he stood up and changed seats with the young woman. Once the woman was seated by the window, she no longer retched. She made a show of opening the window for a while, but then closed it again. An Ning knew she didn't really feel like throwing up; she just didn't want to sit next to the woman who was vomiting. The mother vomited a few more times, then stopped, most likely because she had nothing left to throw up. She was pale, her eyes were half closed, and her head rested on her daughter's shoulder. The daughter did not fold any more paper cranes, but just sat cradling her mother—to all appearances, mothering her mother. The car circled the road between the mountains, and the ravines were filled with clouds and mist.

The young woman struck up a conversation with An Ning. "You're going to Xizang?"

An Ning nodded.

"Are you visiting relatives or just traveling?"

"Traveling."

An Ning didn't want to tell the truth, but she couldn't be so aloof either. She turned and smiled kindly at the young woman, which seemed to encourage the latter.

The woman was much chattier, saying, "It was bad luck. I had bought a plane ticket to Bangda, but who knew that it would be postponed for a week. I went to the airport every morning at five, and when half of my time off was gone, I still hadn't left Chengdu. I decided to take the bus instead. It's such a long journey. My butt will be so sore by the time we get there. I swear, I won't be going there in my next life!"

An Ning wanted to laugh, but her own butt was sore too. She was more interested in the flight to Bangda. It was the first time she had heard of a flight being postponed for a whole week. She had heard Li Qingge talk about Bangda, where the world's highest altitude airport was located. The Bangda Prairie was not far from Li Qingge and the others. Arriving at Bangda was equivalent to reaching the hinterland of the Sichuan-Xizang Line. Though An Ning knew there was a flight, she did not want to fly, reaching her destination in the blink of an eye, omitting the seductive process. The boring walk up the plateau, step by step, toward the person she loved, that was romance; making the decision to hike up the plateau all by herself—that was doing it right. She was on her way now, after all. If she had taken a plane, she would still be waiting at the airport.

She realized that there might be news there. She asked the young woman, "Why was the flight postponed for so long?"

The woman replied, "It took off three times, but had to turn back mid-flight. One time they said there was suddenly too much cloud cover and visibility was low. Once it was snow. But seriously, I don't get it. Snow in June? The other time, I have no idea why we turned back."

As they chatted, An Ning noticed that the woman was no more than twenty-eight or twenty-nine, and she was very good-looking. As she was thinking this, a song came over the bus's speakers, *Er ah, Erlang Mountain, oh so high.*

The singing sent ripples through An Ning's heart, evoking in her a sense of infinite tragedy and solemnity for her long journey. The bus went around a curve, and a cave appeared before them. A sign beside it read, *Erlang Mountain Tunnel.* A slogan was hung next to it: *The officers and soldiers of the Armed Police Traffic Force pay tribute to the people of all ethnic groups in Xizang!*

The young woman muttered, "What kind of road is this? All the turning back and forth makes me dizzy."

The Khampa man turned and said, "You should be happy. Now that the army has completed the tunnel, it's much easier to travel than before. It used to take at least a day to cross Erlang Mountain, and traffic could only travel one direction on the road, alternating each day. A few years ago, do you know how many cars were overturned on Erlang Mountain and how many people were killed each year?"

The woman was silent. It was unclear whether she just didn't want to respond, or whether she acquiesced to what the Khampa man had said. An Ning glanced at the Khampa man. She had not expected him to speak Mandarin. But whatever she might have liked to ask him, he had turned away and was now watching the girl fold her paper cranes.

The bus entered the tunnel, and the singing was suddenly much louder, as if a reverberation effect had been added. Listening to the long-lost song as they passed through the heart of Erlang Mountain, An Ning was suddenly inspired. She had the title of her first article: *Crossing Erlang Mountain*.

The bus came out of the tunnel and started winding its way down the hill. The singing had stopped, but another song echoed in An Ning's mind:

> My beloved flowers, on the plateau
> Their beauty is seldom seen
> The one I love is on the plateau
> His smile forever pristine

The previous year, this song had come to An Ning out of nowhere when she was walking on the street. The melody and lyrics immediately grabbed her heart, because the person she loved was on the plateau. She committed the words to memory, chanting them over and over in her mind. She had looked for the song, but never found it. If only An Jing were there! She was a music student; she must know the song.

When the bus passed Luding, An Ning noticed that her eyes were a little wet. She missed Li Qingge and her sister.

After a long day on the bumpy road, the bus arrived at Kangding. The driver said to everyone, "We won't leave Kangding tonight. We'll stay here, then continue tomorrow."

As they got off the bus, the young woman asked An Ning, "Would you like to share a room?"

An Ning had no reason to disagree. When they were checking in, she learned that the young woman's name was Guo Hong.

3

That night, Guo Hong told An Ning that she was going to Xizang to get a divorce. One of them was going to get married, the other, to get a divorce. Putting them together was like pairing up an obstetrician and a mortician. It was bittersweet.

As they stayed together, An Ning soon revised the opinion she had formed of Guo Hong on the road. She began to feel that her traveling companion was in fact a good person, and that though there was something low brow about her, she was actually cheerful and not at all hypocritical. An Ning was moved by how much Guo Hong trusted her.

When Guo Hong first told of her divorce plans, An Ning was writing her travel notes in a notebook. She planned to continue writing like this along the way, and then organize the material when she got home, publishing a series of articles in the column *A Bride's Journey to Xizang*. Her editorial director Yuan Ye wanted her to write and send each article back along the way, but An Ning felt it would be too stressful. The road from Sichuan to Xizang was long, and communication was inconvenient. She feared that it would be interrupted in the middle of the project, bringing the whole thing to an abrupt halt. According to Li Qingge, there were often landslides, avalanches, and mudslides on the Sichuan-Xizang Line, and anything could happen along the way. Besides, time was tight on this journey, and the articles would be much better if they were not rushed. She liked to write freely and when she was calm; she could only write when the mood was right. And, she didn't want to put any added anxiety on her romantic journey. How many times would a person get married in their lifetime, and how many opportunities were there for true romance?

While An Ning was writing, Guo Hong came out of the bathroom, drying her hair with a towel. She said, "You still keep a diary when you travel?"

An Ning said, "Just for fun."

"I really envy you. You're young, beautiful, and passionate," Guo Hong said, sighing. "I'm finished. I'm not yet thirty, but my heart is fifty. There's no passion left in my life."

An Ning stopped writing and looked at Guo Hong. Smiling, she said, "You're so young. How can there be no passion in your life?"

"My passion has all worn away. To tell you the truth, I'm going to Xizang to get a divorce."

Taken aback, An Ning wanted to ask why, but she felt it was a bit of a silly thing to say. People divorced for any reason these days, or even no reason. One of her female classmates had married just last year and got divorced this year.

An Ning asked, "He works in Xizang?"

Guo Hong said, "He's a soldier and is there working on the roads there."

An Ning was shocked. How strange that Guo Hong's husband was in the same troop as Li Qingge. She was going to marry one soldier, and Guo Hong was going to divorce another. It made her very uneasy. She put her pen in her notebook, closed the cover, and set it aside.

"I heard you have to get the soldier's consent before you can divorce him, right?"

Guo Hong tossed the towel on the table. "Whether he agrees or not, I'm divorcing him. My mind is set. I must get him to sign the divorce papers!"

"What if he doesn't agree?"

"If he doesn't give me the divorce, I'll make his life miserable. I know him very well. He loves to keep up appearances. Anyway, he was recently made captain, so he has to think about the impact on those under him. Before, when he was at home, he wasn't afraid of being embarrassed, but now that he's in the army, we'll see how he feels when I make trouble for him."

"How long have you been married?"

"Six years."

"Any kids?"

"No." Then she added, "Fortunately not."

"Is it really necessary? Does he treat you badly?"

"I can't say it's good, but I can't say it's bad either. He's a cold person. I've rarely seen him smile in all these years of marriage. Sometimes I suspect that being in Xizang for so long has made him soft in the head. He used to be very good to me, but then he just stopped. We've been fighting for more than a year, but he wouldn't agree and just kept dragging it out. He can afford to do that, but I can't. I'm almost thirty. For a woman, it's over after thirty. I can't let him drag the life out of me like this. You're not married, are you?"

"No."

"You'll know what I mean, once you're married. Some things can't really be explained, but let me give you one bit of advice: don't be emotional when you're looking for a partner; be realistic. I regret that I didn't listen to my mother. Don't fall for a soldier."

The last sentence had stung An Ning. Li Qingge was a soldier, and she was on her way to marry him now. She didn't want to tell Guo Hong. If Guo Hong hadn't just said she was going to get a divorce, An Ning might have told her quite happily. But she would never mention it now.

An Ning asked, "What's wrong with a soldier?"

"Falling for a soldier brings endless hardships. That's why I've suffered every day," Guo Hong said. After a moment, she added, "But I'm not divorcing him because I can't take the hardship. There are other reasons."

As they lay in bed, Guo Hong told An Ning all about her relationship with her husband.

4

Guo Hong was working in a factory when she met her husband, Deng Gang. Later, the factory closed down, and Guo Hong started working with her current boss, Hu An.

Guo Hong's mother did not agree with the idea of her being with Deng Gang. After all, there were so many good boys around; why did she have to be with a soldier? To make matters worse, this fellow's family was from the countryside. And worst of all, he was going to Xizang, a place where even ghosts didn't dare to go.

But Guo Hong just wouldn't listen. She followed Deng Gang like she was obsessed.

In fact, Guo Hong had not liked Deng Gang when they first met. They had been introduced by Guo Hong's middle school teacher, a fellow villager of Deng Gang. Deng Gang had just come back from Xizang for a few days, and his skin was as dark as autumn and he wore casual clothing. He was not at all outstanding, instead looking like the migrant workers on the street. But to keep from embarrassing the teacher who had introduced them, Guo Hong agreed to a second date. She felt very different on that second occasion, and as if by some miracle, she fell in love with Deng Gang.

Guo Hong remembered their first meeting. It happened in a teahouse, and her teacher was with them. They all joined the conversation, but it was nothing out of the ordinary, and after a while, they each went their own way. But on the second date, they spent the whole day together, and even when it got dark, Guo Hong did not want to go home.

Their second date had been at Wuhou Temple, followed by a visit to the Qingyang Palace and Du Fu's Thatched Cottage, and finally ending with a movie. Guo Hong felt it strange, not like they were on a date, but like they were tourists from out of town visiting Chengdu, and Deng Gang was not so much like her boyfriend as a competent tour guide. They spent the day walking, looking around, and walking some more, but at the end of the day, she still was not tired.

When they had first entered Wuhou Temple, neither spoke. They just looked around awkwardly. But as they came to a stone table, Deng Gang stopped and said, "Let's sit here."

He took half a sheet of newspaper from his pocket, spread it on the bench, and said in a very gentlemanly manner, "Please, have a seat."

Guo Hong had not expected him to come prepared with newspaper. She had not imagined that someone who looked so rough would be so caring.

After they sat, Deng Gang said coldly, "I know I don't have a chance with you."

Guo Hong had not expected this. On the way there, she had thought of several ways to start and end, but she had not expected this, and because it was so unexpected, she didn't know what to do. She peeped at Deng Gang, but he didn't look at her. Looking away, he said, "You look down on me. I can tell."

Guo Hong was a little surprised that he was so straightforward. She bowed her head in embarrassment, saying nothing. Not speaking meant agreeing.

Deng Gang said, "It doesn't matter. You're not the first. I've been back on leave for half a month. You're the fourth one, and I failed every time. The first three met me once and didn't want to see me again. You're nice. You gave me a second chance. Thank you."

Guo Hong did not respond.

Deng Gang went on, "The first one was a kindergarten teacher. She looked like a child herself, but everything she said was very practical. She asked if I had an apartment in Chengdu. I said no, and she didn't say anything else. Later, we went to see a movie. I bought the tickets, and the seats were consecutive numbers, but we didn't get to sit together because there was an aisle between us. After the movie, she shook my hand kindly and said goodbye, adding, 'It looks like we're not meant to be, but I wish you the best of luck.'

"The second one was a salesgirl in a store. She asked me how many times a year I come back, and I told her once. She asked how long I stay each time, and I said, thirty or forty days. She said, 'Ever since I was a child, I've always depended on others. I don't think we're suitable for one another.'

"The third owned her own business, a clothing store on Chunxi Road. We met at Yinxing Restaurant, and after the meal, when I tried to pay, I saw her count out seven or eight hundred yuan and give it to the waiter. I didn't feel good about that. I don't like such women. Later, we went to have tea, and she said she had a friend whose husband had been in the army too. He had changed his career the year before and gone into the Industrial and Commercial Bureau. He has a lot of authority now and can help people do a lot of things. She asked me if I would be willing to change my career so I could come back early. I said I had no plans to change careers, and that made her unhappy. After we drank tea for a while, she suggested we dance, and I told her I didn't know how. That was when she said she had an appointment with one of her female friends and needed to go. There was no more contact after that.

"And then there's you. You're the fourth."

He added, "Sometimes I don't even understand myself. I'm from the countryside, and here I am insisting on finding a partner in the city, specifically, in Chengdu. I won't even give a thought about someone from outside Chengdu. My friends and relatives have introduced me to girls from Mianyang, Shuangliu, and Deyang, but I didn't want to meet them. I just want to find someone from Chengdu. Do you know why?"

Guo Hong didn't look at him. She just shook her head.

He said, "I don't care if you laugh at me. The first time I came to Chengdu was on the day I left home to become a soldier. Eight hundred of us recruits spent the night at the Chengdu Railway Station. I had an uncle in Chengdu—not actually an uncle, but a distant relative. My father told me to look him up if I had time. I asked the platoon leader for time off, and I looked high and low until I found his house, but he wasn't home. My aunt was very cold toward me, not even letting me in, but just shooing me away with a few words, as if I were a beggar. My ego was bruised. On the way back, I swore to myself that I would do something. I was going to change things in the future. I would find someone from Chengdu, and I would start a family here."

Guo Hong's heart suddenly trembled, and she looked at Deng Gang.

He said, "You don't have to feel sorry for me. We'll just sit here for a while, then go our separate ways. But I am grateful that you came today."

Guo Hong had hoped to politely meet him briefly and walk away, but now that Deng Gang had told her all this, she was too embarrassed to leave. She suddenly found him very interesting. His face was stern and serious, but there was something about him that she found attractive.

Guo Hong said, "Who said I'm leaving?"

It was Deng Gang's turn to be surprised, but he just glanced at Guo Hong, his face expressionless.

Next, they started wandering around. Deng Gang stopped talking about himself and started to change the subject, but Guo Hong wasn't finished; she wanted to know more about him. If he didn't offer anything more, it was difficult for her to continue to ask questions. Fortunately, she was quickly drawn into Deng Gang's digression.

Deng Gang seemed to have a wealth of knowledge. He knew more about Chengdu's history, features, and human geography than Guo Hong did, even though it was her hometown. He talked as they walked around, first in Wuhou Temple, then on to Qingyang Palace, and finally to Du Fu's Thatched Cottage. Although Deng Gang was quite garrulous, Guo Hong did not feel that he was showing off. She knew he talked so much mainly to avoid the embarrassment of having nothing to say. And anyway, what he said that day felt fresh to Guo Hong. Though she had been born and raised in Chengdu, she was hearing many of its stories for the first time.

It was only later that she learned that Deng Gang did not usually like to talk much. That day was the time she heard him talk most. After that, she never heard him say so much again.

That evening, it was obvious to Guo Hong that she now liked Deng Gang, and even admired him. She had always liked cultured people. Deng Gang had graduated from the military academy with a bachelor's degree. Guo Hong's teacher had told her this, but she still had not expected him to be so cultured. It wasn't that she hadn't met cultured people before; there were even several in her own family. Guo Hong was the least educated of her siblings, only finishing high school. Her oldest brother had a master's degree from the medical university and was now chief surgeon in the provincial hospital. Her older sister had graduated from university and worked in a research institute before going overseas with her husband, who was a doctoral student. But still, Guo Hong found herself very attracted to Deng Gang.

It was already dark when they left Du Fu's Thatched Cottage. They ate at a small shop by the Funan River, then went to the Southwest Cinema downtown to watch a movie. There was no aisle between them. It was a small cinema with leather seats, and they were very close to one another. It was a foreign love story. Seeing the passion onscreen, the couple next to them embraced. Guo Hong hoped Deng Gang would hold her hand or put his arm around her, but he did not. She was a little disappointed, but also a little relieved. Had he done it, she might have been turned off.

After the movie, Deng Gang walked her home through the quiet alleys. It was ten o'clock, the streets were dim, and there were few pedestrians. As they approached her door, Guo Hong stopped and said, "This is my place. You can go back now."

It was such a romantic night, and the dim light was so warm. She really wanted Deng Gang to embrace her, but he did not. He just turned and left.

As she recalled these events, Guo Hong seemed to enter a state of reverie. Looking at the empty wall across from her, she said to An Ning, "I felt so good that day. I stayed awake all night thinking that maybe this was the guy I had been looking for. I decided to marry him. You might laugh at me for jumping into it so fast, but it really was magical at the time. I fell in love with him. It doesn't take much time to fall in love with someone. Sometimes a single glance or a single sentence is enough. But to hate someone—now, that takes time. And the longer the time, the deeper the hatred is."

The couple met several more times after that, mostly for lunch. Guo Hong was working the late shift then, from two to ten. She had time in the morning, but she didn't like to get up early. She was used to getting up early for work, but now that she had the chance to sleep in, she didn't want to let it go. And anyway, how could anyone fall in love at a teahouse or a park in the morning? On top of that, she couldn't let Deng Gang think he could see her any time he wanted. So usually they just met at midday for lunch. Sometimes Deng Gang paid, and sometimes Guo Hong paid. The first time she tried to pay, Deng Gang wouldn't allow it. Guo Hong was unhappy and told him that if he continued to do that, then she would insist that they go Dutch from then on. He did not dare to insist again. He offered to pick her up at night, but she refused. She was too embarrassed to let him start picking her up when they had only just met. And, she wasn't ready for the people in her work unit to know they were dating. So for the time being, their relationship was basically carried out in secret.

One night when she was riding her bike home, Guo Hong felt that someone was following her. She was scared, but she didn't dare to look back. When she came off a bridge, she heard the sound of the other bicycle's tires drawing nearer. She was very nervous, afraid she would meet a shady character, but the other bike quickly passed her and rushed ahead as if out of control. The moment it passed, she was surprised to see that it was Deng Gang. She tried to shout, and he answered, but he did not stop, continuing to rush ahead instead. Guo Hong was relieved, but also wanted to know what the hell he was up to. She accelerated and caught up, then stopped in front of Deng Gang.

"What are you doing, racing like that?"

Deng Gang said, "I didn't mean to. The bike has no brakes."

"Where are you going so late at night?"

Deng Gang scratched his head. Embarrassed, he said, "Where else would I go? I wanted to pick you up from work and accompany you on the way home."

"So you're sneaking around to do it?"

"You wouldn't let me pick you up. I was afraid you'd be angry if you found out."

"You've been doing this every day?"

Deng Gang nodded. Embarrassed, he said, "If it wasn't for this lousy bike, you'd have never known."

"Where'd you get it?"

"I borrowed it from a fellow soldier."

Guo Hong was moved. No man had ever cared this much about her before.

Half a month later, Deng Gang's leave came to an end. The night before he left, as he accompanied her home from work, they passed by a small wooded area. Deng Gang stopped his bike and said, "I want to talk to you about something."

"What is it?"

"Come over here and I'll tell you."

"I can hear you just fine."

She had an idea what he wanted to do, and she was mentally prepared for it. He was leaving the next day, and they wouldn't see each other for another year. She should just do what he wanted, but she was flustered. She propped her bicycle on one side, pretending not to understand what he wanted. She walked over to him and said, "Go on."

"I—"

Deng Gang hesitated, then suddenly, he pulled her to him. He kissed her hurriedly, then touched her breast. She could feel his hands shaking violently. When he had finished, she asked him if it was his first time.

"Yes," he said. Then he added, "Guo Hong, I'll be good to you for as long as I live."

Guo Hong remembered this line. Later, any time they quarreled, she used it to challenge him. Deng Gang just lowered his head when he heard it, saying nothing.

After they were married, Guo Hong asked Deng Gang why he had been so brave that night. He said that he wanted to get it done before he left. He thought if he kissed her and touched her, that would be it; she would be his.

When she heard that, Guo Hong burst into tears. "That would be it? You're so naive. You've been in Xizang too long. You've become stupid. You can't compare with the guys your age in the city. It's like we're from two different generations."

After he left, they mostly communicated by letter. Xizang was so far away that it took a month for a letter to get there. This sort of communication was awkward, but also very interesting. Guo Hong would ask Deng Gang something in one letter, and it would be several letters before she got an answer. Sometimes, she received several letters in one day. From the dates, she saw that the letters had been sent ten days or two weeks apart. She remembered that they exchanged forty-six letters that year.

Guo Hong told An Ning, "I still have those letters. Even though we're going to be divorced soon, I can't bear to throw those letters away. I cherish them very much, and I still read them when I have nothing to do. Sometimes I cry when I read them, wondering where the old Deng Gang went."

The next year, when Deng Gang came back from visiting relatives, they got married. The wedding was held in his rural hometown. He was the eldest son, and according to local customs, that meant the wedding had to be held at home. Guo Hong understood this very well, and she did not object.

The wedding was grand, but Guo Hong cried that day.

It started with a bedsheet. On the wedding day, Guo Hong's oldest brother and sister-in-law were there. Her sister-in-law was a nurse, and though her own position was not very high, she was rather pleased with herself due to her husband's status. She looked down on everyone and everything. She didn't say anything about Guo Hong marrying a soldier, but it was clear that she looked down on them. Guo Hong worried that something would go wrong, but she had to allow her sister-in-law to attend the wedding. And sure enough, something went wrong. As soon as they walked into the new house, her sister-in-law said, "What's that on the bed?"

Guo Hong saw that it was a coarse homemade cloth sheet.

"What year is this? Do you still buy such things and treat our Guo Hong like a maid?"

Guo Hong was very angry. She hadn't expected Deng Gang's family to behave so shabbily or be so stingy, embarrassing her in front of her sister-in-law. The tears welled up all at once.

Her sister-in-law advised, "Don't cry, don't cry. This is a joyful occasion. Crying on the wedding day will bring endless suffering in the future."

It would have been better not to persuade her at all. The more they persuaded, the more Guo Hong cried.

Deng Gang later told Guo Hong that the coarse sheets had been specially woven for them. It wasn't that they couldn't afford bedsheets, but they were a symbol his mother's good wishes for the newlyweds. His mother was in her sixties and had not woven in years. She had specially borrowed a loom from his uncle so that she could weave the sheets for them, moving it from ten miles away and spending the entire summer spinning and weaving. His mother had said that the coarse sheets were good for the body.

Once he had explained, that was it. Guo Hong was very moved when she heard this, and she felt bad that she had shunned her mother-in-law's kindness.

The problems in the couple's relationship came later. For the first two years, Deng Gang was very good to her. After they got married, they did not live in their own house, but stayed with Guo Hong's parents, brother, and sister-in-law. Deng Gang was very diligent when he came back each year during his leave, doing the laundry and cooking, and sometimes even helping to wash her brother and sister-in-law's sheets and curtains. As soon as he came back, the neighbors teased Guo Hong's mother, asking, "Is your washing machine back?" Guo Hong's mother didn't like Deng Gang at first, but later she discovered that he was a good person. He didn't talk much, and he was quite hard-working. She gradually came to acknowledge these things.

The problem was Guo Hong's sister-in-law. She didn't care what Guo Hong thought. What she cared about was that they were married, but still lived at home. One night, she said to Guo Hong's brother, "What is wrong with her? The girl is married, but she still stays at home."

Her husband whispered, "Can you talk quieter?"

Instead, she raised her voice. "I'm talking in my own house, and I have to worry about who hears me?"

Guo Hong and Deng Gang both heard it. They were watching TV, and Guo Hong's brother and sister-in-law were speaking in the bedroom with the door open, perhaps intentionally letting them hear everything.

That night, Guo Hong cried as she lay in Deng Gang's arms.

Deng Gang said, "I'm sorry." Then he added, "How about we rent a place?"

Guo Hong said, "Rent a place? You only come back once a year. You mean, you won't worry if I live alone for 320 out of 360 days a year?"

Deng Gang stopped talking.

It had been two years like this. Later, the army assigned Deng Gang a house in the Chengdu Family Courtyard. Though there was only one bedroom and a living room, Guo Hong was very pleased to have a home of their own. The days to come should have been happy, but things were not as simple as she imagined.

5

She just wanted to live and work in peace. And living was in fact peaceful enough, but work ... well, she did not have a job anymore.

The factory closed down, and Guo Hong was laid off. Before the closure, the factory manager took his mistress and 2 million yuan in cash and prepared to flee. He got all the way to Guangzhou before he was arrested and sentenced to prison. With no more job, Guo Hong lost her identity, and before she knew it, she was just "family."

In the military, an interesting thing happened to the word "family." It was not used to refer to soldiers' parents, siblings, or children, but only to their wives. When the women in the family quarters talked about Guo Hong, she was not Guo Hong at all, but "Deng Gang's family." At first, she was not used to it. She thought, *I have a name and a surname of my own. It's like I'm an accessory belonging to Deng Gang, and without him, I wouldn't even exist. Before, he relied on me to get into the city, but now, it's the other way around. I have to rely on him for my home here.*

She had no job, no status, and now, no identity. The sense of loss was overwhelming. She was like a kite with a broken string, floating through the air without falling. She was very depressed. The biggest problem was finding a new job. She was so embarrassed by the layoff that she didn't even tell her family. When she married Deng Gang, her parents had been reluctant. Now that she had come to this point, she could not face her family and tell them her bad news, and she certainly didn't want to listen to her sister-in-law scoff. Each time she went to her mother's home, Guo Hong pretended to be happy, talking and laughing all the while. As soon as she returned to her own empty house, she couldn't help but cry. Even when it had been half a year since she was laid off, she didn't tell Deng Gang. She wanted to find a job on her own. She went to dozens of companies, looking for a job, but it was hopeless.

It was not until Deng Gang returned home for his leave that she saw the first glimmer of hope. Deng Gang knew a deputy county magistrate on the Sichuan-Xizang Line, a fellow named Liu Zhi. Liu had been a small section magistrate in Wuhou District, and he went to Xizang to become a deputy county magistrate in the county where Deng Gang's troops were stationed. Liu had returned to Chengdu on leave at the same time as Deng Gang. Liu had been offered a post when he left, and he would be offered another post after working in Xizang for three years, and along with that would come a three-bedroom apartment. Deng Gang and the others had been working in Xizang for more than ten years. They were not given three-bedroom apartments, and they could not be promoted in advance of their posting. They were all the same, but they received different treatment. Local cadres who aided Xizang were heroes, but soldiers who stayed in Xizang for many years did so out of devotion and to fulfill their obligations. Guo Hong felt off balance inside herself, and she begrudged the injustice to Deng Gang and others like him. Even so, she was very happy to hear that Liu Zhi could help her find a job. Deng Gang built roads in Xizang throughout the year, but when he returned to more civilized areas, he looked like a fool.

Liu Zhi was a good person, very loyal, and willing to help Deng Gang. He said that his old classmate was now the director of the sub-district office, and he was sure this friend could come up with a plan. A few days later, Liu Zhi called to say he had set up an appointment to meet his old classmate that night. He told Deng Gang not to talk about the job during dinner, but to wait until later, warning him that this was the rule of thumb with officials.

That evening, Guo Hong and Deng Gang rushed to the restaurant, arriving early. They ordered several dishes, then sat and waited. Liu Zhi arrived first, and Deng Gang handed him the list of dishes they had ordered.

Liu Zhi hesitated a moment, then in a tone more suited for a negotiation, he said, "Should I add a few more dishes? My classmate is pretty particular. He's tried everything that flies, swims, or crawls. I mean, *everything*."

Obviously, the food they had ordered was not good enough. Deng Gang was embarrassed. When they had ordered the food earlier, he and Guo Hong had put their heads together and ordered what they thought were the best dishes, but it still didn't seem to be up to standard.

Blushing, Deng Gang said to Liu Zhi, "I don't know anything about food. It's totally up to you. Have a look."

Deng Gang asked the waiter to bring a menu for Liu Zhi. Liu Zhi turned and said, "Cancel the mandarin fish and bring the sturgeon instead. Add sea cucumbers, and sharks fin and rice too. That should be fine. Count me out when serving the shark's fin. There's nothing much to it. That's mainly just to make it look good."

Deng Gang said, "What do you mean? Are you just trying to embarrass me? All shall be counted in. It's easy to host a banquet, but it's hard to entertain guests. He's agreed to the invitation for your sake. I'm already very grateful."

Liu Zhi didn't insist anymore. He went on, "Just drink Wuliangye. This fellow doesn't drink other liquors. He'll only drink Wuliangye."

The appetizers arrived and the wine was poured, but after a long wait, the director still had not shown up. Guo Hong and Deng Gang were anxious, worrying that he wouldn't come. As the middleman, Liu Zhi was anxious too. When he couldn't wait any longer, he called his classmate's cell phone.

"They're on their way," he reported when he had hung up.

After waiting for a while longer, the director still did not arrive. Liu Zhi called again.

This time, he was a little embarrassed. "He was dragged to another restaurant on the way. He's always like this. He has to go to several different places each day. But his wife and daughter will be here soon. He told us to start first, and he'll join us when he gets here. Let him deal with matters over there first, then he'll be right over."

After a while, the director's wife and daughter arrived, and the five of them started to eat. The director's wife and daughter both had a sophisticated manner at the table, and it seemed they frequented this high-end restaurant. Before the guest of honor arrived, Liu Zhi started to feel a little sorry for Deng Gang, so he extended a warm invitation for everyone to eat, as if he was the one hosting the dinner.

When the waiter served the shrimp and crab, he brought a glass bowl of water with a few slices of lemon floating on the surface. Not knowing what it was for, Deng Gang picked up a spoon and took a sip. The director's wife pursed her lips and laughed. Deng Gang didn't notice. He scooped another spoonful and was about to slurp it when Liu Zhi stopped him.

The director's daughter said, "That's for washing your hands. You don't drink it."

Deng Gang's face turned red, and he laughed awkwardly. Guo Hong's nose itched, and tears almost started flowing, but she held them back.

The shark's fin was served. Five bowls came out first, and the other bowl would only be served when the director came. Guo Hong and Deng Gang had never eaten shark's fin, but when it was served, it looked like nothing more than a bowl of thin rice noodles. Since they had never eaten it, it was natural that they were not sure how to do so. Deng Gang was preoccupied, toasting Liu Zhi. Guo Hong didn't know what to do, so she urged the director's wife and daughter to eat, partly to be polite, but also to see how it was done. The director's wife had great skill. She added coriander and vinegar, stirred it with a spoon, and took a few bites. She then added rice into the shark's fin and continued eating. So that was shark's fin rice. The director's daughter was only a teenager, but she was as sophisticated as her mother. It seemed they ate shark's fin quite often.

Guo Hong's feelings were easily summed up: low self-esteem.

The meal took a long time, most of it spent waiting for the director. When he arrived, he smelled of alcohol, and he staggered a bit as he walked, but he said he was fine, and he went on drinking. The three men drank another bottle of Wuliangye. The shark's fin was served, but the director didn't touch it, saying he'd eaten earlier and couldn't eat another bite. The shark's fin sat there, wasted. It continued to distress Guo Hong for many days after the meal.

Deng Gang got drunk, and Guo Hong settled the bill. She was taken aback when she saw the total. Not counting anything else, the shark's fin was 380 yuan a bowl—or 2,280 for all six bowls—plus two bottles of Wuliangye, in total more than 4,000 yuan. That was equivalent to five month's salary for her.

A few days later, when Deng Gang asked Liu Zhi if there was any news, Liu said he had not heard anything yet, so he would ask for another dinner. Half a month passed, and the director did not schedule an appointment. He was very busy and had many social engagements. Liu asked Deng Gang to wait patiently. Deng Gang's leave was coming to an end, and he grew anxious, but it was no use being anxious. That would only turn others off, so he had no choice but to wait patiently.

A few days later, Liu Zhi called to say that they could meet that night, but the director had other appointments and didn't have time to eat. They could go to the bathhouse instead.

A trip to the bathhouse wasn't for the purpose of bathing; it was to look for girls. Deng Gang knew this was no good, but it couldn't be helped. If he wanted to find a job for Guo Hong, he had to go.

According to what Deng Gang later told Guo Hong, he did not go in that night. He waited outside while the others went in to bathe, and he fell asleep in the main hall. During the second half of the night, Liu Zhi woke Deng Gang and said the director had already left and it was time to settle the bill. Deng Gang was in a daze when he paid, and he spent more than two thousand yuan, plus a *hongbao* that had been stuffed into the director's hand earlier in the night, so another four or five thousand in total. But Deng Gang was very happy. When he went home, he said to Guo Hong, "It's done now. He ate, he bathed, and he received the *hongbao*. I guess that should do it."

Sure enough, Liu Zhi called the next day to say everything was settled. He asked Deng Gang to take Guo Hong to the office to see the director. The couple was so happy. They had not expected it to be so easy.

But in the end, they were disappointed by the results. What was "settled" was that Guo Hong would be given a temporary job in the office, and the salary for the temp position would only be six hundred a month. And her pension and medical insurance wouldn't be covered. What kind of job was that? Guo Hong was ashamed and didn't want to go to work, saying it was not as good as the job she had found for herself before. Deng Gang felt incompetent, and he felt sorry for his wife.

Guo Hong said, "No, you're not incompetent. I am. Don't worry about my job. I'll figure it out."

Deng Gang didn't tell Liu Zhi what had happened. It was over, and there was no point saying anything. It would only embarrass Liu Zhi. His heart was in the right place, and they couldn't blame him. Liu Zhi asked about it several times, and Deng Gang always said, "It's all settled. Don't worry about it. Thank you for your help."

Before long, Deng Gang returned to Xizang. After he left, Guo Hong stood at the window, feeling sad as she watched the flow of people coming from or going to work. She said to herself, *I'm still young. I can't live like this. I need to study so I can rely on my own skills to find a job.*

But what should she study? It was probably most useful to study finance and accounting, as it would be easy to find a job if she had an accounting certificate.

No sooner than she decided, she started her studies. A few days later, she signed up for a training class at the University of Finance and Economics. Six months later, she received her accounting qualification certificate. She soon found a job as an accountant in a company's financial department, earning 1,200 yuan a month. She was very satisfied with her job.

It was only later that Guo Hong discovered that the company did not hire her because of the accounting certificate, but for other reasons.

But that was not something she shared with An Ning as she told her story. Instead, she ended by saying that she had found a job based on her own abilities.

An Ning only came to know about the other reasons later, and of course, that was only because Guo Hong told her.

For now, Guo Hong continued talking about Deng Gang's parents. It was because of them that conflicts arose between her and Deng Gang.

6

During Spring Festival that year, Deng Gang came home on leave, bringing his parents with him from the countryside. Guo Hong knew that Deng Gang was a dutiful son, and she did not look down on her in-laws because they were from the countryside. If she despised such things, she would not have married Deng Gang. But the awkwardness arose mostly from their different living habits, and they were living together now.

Her mother-in-law was as diligent as Deng Gang, and she always wanted to help Guo Hong with the housework, but she always ended up getting in the way instead. For instance, when Guo Hong was cooking, her mother-in-law helped wash the vegetables. Guo Hong loved cleanliness, always insisting that the vegetables be scrubbed several times before they were rinsed under the tap. But her mother-in-law only scrubbed once, and by the time Guo Hong realized this, they had already been cut, and it was too late to wash them again.

Guo Hong gently persuaded her mother-in-law, "Ma, don't be so frugal. Water isn't that expensive."

Her mother-in-law responded seriously, "No matter how small the amount, money is money. The water in our hometown has to be pulled from dozens of miles away by oxcart. We use a single basin of water to wash the faces of everyone in the family."

Guo Hong said softly, "But this is not your hometown."

Her mother-in-law said, "But we can't waste. I feel terrible when I see the water flowing away for nothing."

Guo Hong said, "Not for nothing; for washing the vegetables."

Her mother-in-law fell silent. Guo Hong regretted saying it so bluntly. She worried that her mother-in-law couldn't accept it and would be angry. But to her surprise, her mother-in-law said, "I'm just used to the other way. I'll scrub them twice in the future."

But after that, her mother-in-law continued doing the same thing. Left with no other choice, Guo Hong tried to keep her from helping with the housework. But her mother-in-law was always restless. If she had nothing to do, she grew anxious. She would walk around the house, or she stood on the balcony looking downstairs, where there was a mess hall catering to officials or leaders, where the food was not cooked in one huge communal pot as it was in the ordinary canteen. The higher ups had come to inspect the area, and the local leaders accompanied them to eat at the officer's mess. After eating, the local leaders left, picking their teeth as they walked, as was their habit. When Deng Gang's mother saw this, she was very envious. She turned around to Deng Gang and said, "If you do a good job, that's enough. I don't expect you to be a high-ranking officer. When will you be like them? If you could just poke your teeth with a stick after meals, I'd be content."

Deng Gang and Guo Hong both laughed.

One day, the instructor came to visit Deng Gang's parents. He was an old comrade, a captain, and Deng Gang had always had great respect for him, and the instructor had always been very supportive of Deng Gang's work. The two got along very well.

After the instructor left, Deng Gang's mother asked him, "What kind of officer is the instructor?"

Deng Gang said, "An officer like me—no bigger than a sesame seed."

His mother asked, "Who ranks higher, you or him?"

Deng Gang said, "We're the same rank. Just like you and Pa are both parents of our family. He and I are the parents of our squad. Who would you say ranks higher?"

The old woman seemed satisfied. She did not ask any more questions.

But the next morning, when Deng Gang got up to get dressed, he found an extra star on his epaulette—he'd gone from lieutenant to captain just like that. He didn't know whether to laugh or cry, but his mother very sensibly said, "If you two are the same rank, how come he has three stars and you only have two?"

Deng Gang explained for a long time before she finally understood.

Guo Hong's father-in-law did not talk much, which made him easier to get along with. But he got up very early every morning, even Sunday, making it impossible for Guo Hong to sleep in. He did not say anything when he got up, but he coughed nonstop. Though she could hear that he covered his mouth with his hand, it still woke her up. And not only did he wake her, but he also moved about the kitchen making tea. She had a very good stainless steel pot, and he boiled his tea in it, turning it as dark as an autumn night, so that the tea itself was like black water. But this was the sort of tea he liked to drink. He also liked to smoke, which was unbearable for Guo Hong. He didn't smoke the cigarettes Deng Gang bought for him, but insisted on smoking those he rolled himself, which filled the whole house with smoke and the unpleasant smell of tobacco. There were no ashtrays in the house, so he knocked his tobacco onto the ground or even on the legs of the new coffee table, leaving several burn marks on it. What was even more incomprehensible was that, instead of sitting on a stool when he ate, he took off his slippers and squatted on the seat. Guo Hong complained about this to Deng Gang out of the old man's hearing, but Deng Gang urged, "You can take an old fellow out of the countryside, but you can't take the countryside out of an old fellow. He's had these habits for decades. You can't change him overnight. Besides, how often can they come? Can't you just put up with it?"

Guo Hong didn't feel good about it, but she couldn't really say anything.

Her father-in-law, though, was very particular about certain things, and it embarrassed Guo Hong. For instance, he never wanted to use the toilet at home, but went to the public restroom to relieve himself, because he could not settle his business on a sitting toilet. The day they arrived, he went out early in the morning. Guo Hong made breakfast and waited for him to come back. Fearing that his father would get lost, Deng Gang went out and looked everywhere, and he finally found his father at the door to the public restroom. Displeased, the old man said to Deng Gang, "The city is not good. They charge you money to go to the bathroom here. Back at home, I couldn't just do it on someone else's field."

Deng Gang knew his father was worried about the money, so he coaxed, "People will only accept your money when they don't know you. I'll go talk to them, and they won't charge you in the future."

The old man didn't believe it. Deng Gang said, "You're my pa. Could I lie to you? Go on, and I'll go talk to him."

Deng Gang watched his father turn and leave, then he walked up to the old man who was in charge of the public restroom, took out a ten yuan note, and handed it to him. Pointing at his father's back, he whispered, "When my father comes to the restroom, don't charge him. Tell him it's free for the soldiers' family members. Take this money, and if it's not enough, I'll make it up to you later."

The old fellow did not understand what Deng Gang meant.

Deng Gang said, "My old man is worried about the money."

Understanding, the old fellow sighed. He gave Deng Gang a thumb's up and said, "You're a dutiful son."

Deng Gang later told Guo Hong that his father's insistence on using the public restroom was not just a matter of habit. Mainly, it was feudal ideology that was to be blamed. His father was unwilling to share a toilet with a woman, especially his daughter-in-law.

But even all of this was not really the issue. What annoyed Guo Hong the most during that holiday was that Deng Gang went everywhere with his parents, including Dujiangyan, Qingchen Mountain, the Giant Buddha at Leshan, Mount Emei, and even Doutuan Mountain in Jiangyou. Guo Hong was not bothered about the money, but about the time Deng Gang spent on them. The couple was only reunited once each year, and this perfect holiday was ruined by his parents. Guo Hong had wished upon every star—and the moon too—that Deng Gang would come back, and now that he was home, he was away from home all day every day. How could she be happy about that. Irritated with the circumstances, she lost her temper with Deng Gang. But no matter how angry she got, he kept his temper under control.

Deng Gang said, "Can you keep it down a little?"

Guo Hong knew that he avoided the quarrel not for her, but mainly because he knew his parents would be angry if they overheard. In fact, she could appreciate this part of Deng Gang; she liked a man who respected the elderly. If a man treated his parents poorly, she certainly couldn't expect him to treat her well. The problem was that his filial behavior sometimes went overboard.

One example was the trip to Mount Emei. Guo Hong had never been to Mount Emei, but Deng Gang wanted to take his parents there. His father was a bit strange about it, too. The old man said that he had to go to Mount Emei. He could miss other places, but Mount Emei was a must. The problem with that was that he had already been to all the other places, so there wasn't much point in saying he didn't mind giving them a miss. Spending the money to go to Mount Emei was not a big deal; the real issue was that Guo Hong felt that Deng Gang didn't care about her. Later, he explained that they were like hitchhikers that day, and there were not enough seats to hold them all. He said the two of them would go another time. But he did not say so in the moment, which made her a little angry. If he had asked her to go on that day, it did not mean she would have gone. Like everyone on Mount Emei who fought over a breath of fresh air and the Buddhas there who fought over an incense stick, Guo Hong was fighting for just a single word from her husband.

When they set out early in the morning, Guo Hong did not get up. She felt so bad she could not help but stay in bed crying. She cried the whole day, not because she didn't get to go to Mount Emei, but because of all the other grievances she harbored inside as well. Mount Emei was a rope. Once it was pulled, all the other grievances came out with it.

When Deng Gang went into the room to get his things, he saw Guo Hong's head shaking. He lifted it up and saw that she was crying. Deng Gang was startled, unable to comprehend what was wrong. He asked over and over why she was crying. Guo Hong did not speak; she just cried. He asked again, and she suddenly sat up, and all the grievances she had been harboring over the previous days poured out of her. Afraid that his parents would hear, Deng Gang quickly closed the door and tried to comfort her. But she was half out of her mind by that time and couldn't listen to anything. The more he coaxed, the sadder she grew. When it was almost time to leave, she was still crying, and he couldn't get away.

He said, "I'm begging you, don't make this any harder. My parents are finally here. Please just let them enjoy themselves for a few days. I'll make it up to you when they're gone."

Guo Hong continued crying.

Deng Gang said, "Do you want me to get on my knees and beg?"

Then he burst into tears.

Guo Hong had never seen him cry. Men did not cry easily when they were sad, especially not a man like Deng Gang. Guo Hong tried to restrain herself. She stopped crying.

After returning from Mount Emei, Deng Gang told Guo Hong that when he got to Mount Emei, he understood why his father had insisted on going. The old man had wanted to burn incense for his son and daughter-in-law. He had heard that troops often died while sent out on construction projects in Xizang. His parents couldn't even sleep at night, they were so worried about him. Deng Gang's father said that with so much incense enshrouding Mount Emei, it must be very effective.

Hearing this, Guo Hong did not say anything. But from that time, there was a rift in their relationship. The rift grew bigger and bigger, until finally, it was beyond healing.

Guo Hong felt that Deng Gang had changed then. It was his second trip home after they were married.

7

Guo Hong told An Ning that the following year when Deng Gang came back, she found that he had changed. It was only one thing that had changed; everything else was the same. When Deng Gang came home for his leave, he busily did housework and took care of Guo Hong as attentively as before. These actions had moved Guo Hong before, but now they made her suspicious of what was really going on.

Though there was no other change, Deng Gang had definitely changed in bed. Women were always most sensitive in this area. It was the barometer for the relationship between husband and wife. If a man changed in bed, a woman immediately noticed. In the past, Deng Gang had always been very active, especially on the first few days after he came back, being very demanding and constantly pestering her. But it was different this time. The first night he was back was like their wedding night, with him sweating profusely. On the surface, he was serious and diligent as he went about it, but Guo Hong could tell that he was performing perfunctorily, just making himself get the job done. Deng Gang could tell that she was not satisfied, and after finishing, he touched her apologetically and kissed her. Seeing him like this annoyed her even more. It was only when a man was doing something wrong outside the home that he would show extra enthusiasm with his wife, in an attempt to cover up his own infidelity.

In the days that followed, Guo Hong carefully dropped hints that Deng Gang pretended not to understand. When he had to do the job, he did it reluctantly, showing no passion, as if he were doing something very painful. And when he did it so reluctantly, Guo Hong did not sense any pleasure at all. This sort of sex was like chewing wax, or like drinking watered down wine. At first, Guo Hong thought perhaps he wasn't feeling well, having just come down from the high altitudes of the plateau. When it kept going on like that, she eventually decided that it was not a physical problem at all, but a psychological one.

When it came to something like this, no matter how smart a man was, he could not hide it from a woman.

Guo Hong burst into tears as she talked about it. An Ning found a tissue and handed it to her. Wiping away the tears, Guo Hong said, "I'm a woman, and it had been a year since he left. I thought of him, I missed him, and I couldn't wait for him to come home, and then he treated me like that. How could I not be sad? It was an unspeakable feeling. You can't possibly understand."

Guo Hong went on to describe how suspicious of her husband she was when she one day discovered that he had deceived her. She had gone to work that day and forgotten to bring her keys. When she went back to get them, she found that Deng Gang had gone out, even though he had previously told her he was not going out that day. Where had he gone? It was possible he was just buying groceries or running some other errand. At first, she didn't bother, but while she was at work, she suddenly began to feel uneasy, so she called home to see if Deng Gang had returned. No one answered the home phone. She called several more times during the day, but no one picked up. Guo Hong had not given the matter too much thought at first, but when she got home at night, she grew suspicious.

When Guo Hong walked in the door, Deng Gang had already finished cooking dinner. Guo Hong asked casually, "Did you go out today?"

Deng Gang said, "No."

"You didn't go buy groceries?"

"We still had food. I plan to go buy groceries tomorrow."

"Aren't you bored at home?"

"Where else would I go?"

Liar! Guo Hong was so angry she wanted to expose him on the spot, but she controlled herself, managing to refrain from having an outburst. She would wait for a while, and maybe he would eventually bring it up on his own. But after this event, Guo Hong began to pay more attention to where Deng Gang went. She discovered that as soon as she left for work each day, he went out. She wanted to take a day off and follow him, but she felt that was too pathetic. If he found out, there would be no coming back from that. To tell the truth, she still loved him very much.

It wasn't until the day she discovered a text message sent from a woman to Deng Gang that she really knew that he had cheated on her.

That night, when Deng Gang was taking a shower, an alert for a message came in on his phone. He had left his phone on the coffee table, and Guo Hong was sitting beside it, watching TV. Had this happened before, Guo Hong would not have turned his phone over and looked at it, but now, she had her suspicions, and she couldn't help but look.

The name Feng Xiaoli was displayed on the screen. She clicked, and a message popped up. *When are you coming back? Don't forget to bring me some Xiaohushi sunscreen.*

Guo Hong felt a little dizzy. God, there was another woman. No wonder he wasn't interested in her anymore. She lay on the bed and cried.

By the time Deng Gang came out of the bathroom, she had finished crying and her expression had returned to normal, as if nothing had happened at all. She had been stubborn since she was a child. She knew how to keep her composure in the face of trouble.

Who was that woman? She had to understand the situation before taking action.

But in fact, she took action that day—not to find out about the woman, but to meet a man. She felt uneasy about things, and she just wanted someone to talk to, so she could pour all the bitterness inside her out. Guo Hong told Deng Gang that she needed to work overtime, and she went out alone. She came back very late that night.

Where had she gone? In the Kangding Hotel. She concealed this part from An Ning, and An Ning understood. Everyone had secrets. They would tell you if they trusted you, and if they did not tell you, that was to protect themselves.

For the next few days, Deng Gang continued to sneak out during the day. Guo Hong kept an eye on him, but the woman named Feng Xiaoli never surfaced. The night before Deng Gang left, Guo Hong found some Xiaohushi sunscreen in his bag. She was suddenly confused. Was this Feng Xiaoli in Chengdu or Xizang?

After Deng Gang left, Guo Hong found out about the woman named Feng Xiaoli. She was an engineer in Deng Gang's brigade, 24 years old, and single.

Guo Hong said to An Ning, "I'll see her this time. I want to see what she's like."

8

That night, the two women chatted for a long time. When they had finished, it was as if a heavy burden had been lifted from Guo Hong, and now, she suddenly relaxed and went to sleep.

An Ning did not sleep. She wrote in her diary. She told herself she had to finish writing each day's diary before going to bed. After graduating from college and working as a reporter for two years, An Ning often went to do field interviews, and she had developed this habit. She had not expected to encounter so many things on the first day of her journey. She was excited and a little worried, all at the same time. The fact that Guo Hong was going to get a divorce felt ominous. She was going to Xizang to get married, but her fellow traveler was going to get divorced. It made her feel uneasy.

After listening to Guo Hong's story, though An Ning sympathized with her, on an emotional level, she did not want to believe Guo Hong's husband would have an affair. Judging from the experience An Jing had told her about the trip to Xizang, the soldiers she met along the way, and the Li Qingge she knew, she was sure the soldiers constructing the roads in Xizang would not be like that. It could be something else. It could simply be a misunderstanding. When they arrived, Guo Hong would see Deng Gang and the engineer Feng Xiaoli, and then she would know for sure.

An Ning wrote in her diary, and the title of her second article jumped out at her: "I Want a Divorce."

Of course, the matter had not been fully clarified, and it still wasn't certain that they could get a divorce. Even if everything was clear, she would have to get the consent of all parties before she could write articles about it and publish them in the newspaper.

By the time she finished writing in her diary, it was midnight.

An Ning suddenly remembered that she had not turned on her cell phone all day. She wondered if there were any text messages. As soon as she turned on the phone, it beeped, and eight messages came in all at once. Four were from classmates and friends, just random jokes. One was sent by the editorial director, Yuan Ye, wishing her a safe journey. The other three were all from her mother.

The first had been sent at 8:32 that morning. *I had a bad dream last night. I was very worried about you. I called, but your phone is off. Where are you?*

The second had come in at 1:20 that afternoon. *Why is your phone always off? Your work unit said you're on leave. What are you doing? Where are you? Please reply soon. Do you want your mother to be worried sick?*

The third had come in at 10:56 that night. *I've called many times, but your phone is off. I'm really worried about you. Can you reply as soon as you see my message? I know I haven't been good to you, but you shouldn't punish your mother like this.*

Reading the messages, An Ning was surprised. Her mother didn't contact her often, especially not by text message. Why was it that the first time she made a major life decision, the moment she put it into action, her mother felt it? Was it really a mother-daughter connection? An Ning's heart suddenly softened, and she wondered if it was too much—it was her own mother, after all. Her sister had left for the UK without saying goodbye. She had run far away to marry someone without so much as informing her mother. Were they being unfair? They may have been looked down on in their mother's home, and even though their mother had paid them little attention in recent years, it was, after all, their father's fault. Their mother was a victim, for god's sake.

Thinking of this, An Ning got up and walked into the bathroom. She called her mother's cell phone. Even this late, her mother's phone was still on. As soon as the call connected, she heard her mother's anxious voice on the other end of the call.

"An Ning, is that you? Where have you gone? I've been looking for you all day and haven't been able to find you. I'm dying here."

When An Ning heard her mother cry, she couldn't keep her own tears from pouring out. She tried her best to restrain herself, not wanting to let her mother hear that she was crying.

"I'm fine. You worry too much. I made plans to go out of town with a few classmates. We reached Kangding today. I'll be back in a few days."

"Then why didn't you answer your phone all day?"

"It was out of battery. I just charged it. Okay, my classmates are asleep. I don't want to wake them."

"I don't know why my eyelids twitched so much today. I had a bad dream last night. I'm always so worried something will happen to you."

"Don't worry. There are a few of us together. We'll be fine."

After the call, An Ning lay in bed, but she couldn't fall asleep. Her mind was full of thoughts of her sister and her parents. She knew it would be a sleepless night.

9

Her parents had divorced because of a girl named Wang Jue. Wang Jue was just two years older than An Ning and the same age as An Jing. At first, An Ning didn't know that her name was Wang Jue, until An Jing told her.

But it had not been An Jing who first discovered that their father was having an affair. That had been An Ning.

One Sunday, An Ning had invited her classmates to go for tea on Fuqin Road. Just as she was reaching the door to the teahouse, she saw her father's car parked out front. Oddly, it was not the driver who was driving that day, but her father. An Ning was just about to walk over when a girl got out of the car. An Ning stopped. Her father was the director of the Cultural Affairs Bureau, and he knew a lot of people, so there was nothing unusual about him drinking tea with a girl. The problem was that his hands were in the wrong place. As they walked into the teahouse, An Ning saw her father's hand on the girl's shoulder and the girl's arm wound around his waist. An Ning was stunned, her mind a complete blank.

She did not go for tea, but instead left in a hurry—not just to leave, but to escape, as if she had done something unseemly. For the next week, she fixated on one question: should she tell her mother? In the end, she did not tell her mother, but she did tell An Jing.

An Ning did not expect things to become so turbulent after that, and she regretted telling her sister. Perhaps there were other ways to resolve matters, like hinting to her father, or talking to him directly. Maybe he would have been shamed into breaking up with the girl. Or perhaps she could have talked to the girl, warning the girl not to have any more contact with her father, not to destroy her family. She could even beg the girl. Even that would have been better than how things actually turned out. But she did not think of any of these things at the time. She only thought to tell An Jing.

An Ning had not expected An Jing to tell their mother, and she had not expected the two of them to furtively follow her father. They cornered him in a room at the Jinjiang Hotel. When An Jing and her mother showed up in front of her father, he was stunned.

An Jing was equally stunned. The girl was her classmate, Wang Jue.

Wang Jue came from a remote county town. An Jing and Wang Jue were the beauties of the school. Because they were both beautiful, they tended to stick together. The two girls became very good friends, and they often went around together, arm in arm, brightening the landscape of the campus and making the boys' eyes dart after them like shuttles on the loom. Needless to say, a group of suitors followed them, but An Jing was not interested in boys her own age, saying they were too superficial, too simple, and too weak. Sometimes when she couldn't avoid them, she'd accept their invitations to go out for things like dinner, dancing, or a movie, but that was all. Anyway, she was going to take the postgraduate exam after graduation, so she did not have the energy to talk about something as mundane as love.

Wang Jue was different. She had several torrid love affairs, and she always liked to tell An Jing who had kissed her, who had touched her, who was willing to spend money, who was stingy, and everything else. She also told An Jing that she didn't actually like any of them; they were just something a way to pass the time when she was bored. When she was about to graduate, Wang Jue came and asked if An Jing's father could help her find a way to stay in Chengdu, ideally by landing a job in the Cultural Affairs Bureau. Seeing as she had been classmates for four years, An Jing took Wang Jue out for a meal with her father. Later, he managed to help her stay in Chengdu, working at a radio station. An Jing never imagined that the relationship between her father and Wang Jue would subsequently develop to this level.

An Jing walked over and slapped Wang Jue.

Their mother quietly went to the Disciplinary Committee to report their father. He was punished and demoted, relegated to the post of deputy director. Three months later, he quit his job and opened a cultural company.

After the incident with her father, An Jing moved into quarters at the school. Feeling it was all her fault, An Ning felt guilty, so she didn't do anything at first, just studying at home. But she never spoke to or looked at her father. He knew he was in the wrong, and when he came home, he had lost all stature, not saying a word no matter how mercilessly his wife scolded him. She was a middle school teacher, and normally very quiet. She seldom cursed. But at this time, she became a completely different person. She swore and cursed, heaping all sorts of insults on him. At times, An Ning even felt that her mother went too far. Eventually, her father's returns home were increasingly infrequent, and he was almost always very drunk when he did come home. When he was drunk, he dared to return her mother's scolds. Sometimes, these two cultured people even scuffled. It became impossible to stay at home, so An Ning also moved into the school dorms one Sunday.

Six months later, their parents divorced. They had been college classmates, a couple envied by others, married for 25 years. And just like that, they divorced. Sometimes love and marriage really were fragile—disappointingly so.

Before long, their father and Wang Jue get married. An Ning had not expected that. Perhaps their mother had pushed their father completely into the other woman's arms. An Jing had inwardly cursed Wang Jue, calling her a bitch and accusing her of taking advantage of their father, but the girl had actually married him. This was a matter of even greater embarrassment for their mother, but it was an embarrassment for An Jing as well. For this, An Ning rather admired Wang Jue. As for the divorce, An Ning most hated her father, which outpaced even her mother's hatred for him. The two of them who had colluded to ruin her happy home.

On the day of their father's wedding, An Ning and An Jing went to a pub in Yulin. They got quite drunk and they cried in each other's arms.

The following year, their mother moved in with a divorced civil servant who worked for the district government. They had intended to get married, but the man's daughter didn't agree, so they could only live together and try to gradually work things out. Bai Ling, the civil servant's daughter, was sixteen years old. Spoiled since childhood, she was very overbearing. In that household, An Ning's mother was basically a glorified nanny. The sisters did not want to go to their father's house, and after a few visits to their mother's, they stopped going home at all. Each time they tried to visit their mother, they were bullied by Bai Ling. The civil servant sometimes reprimanded them, saying they were older than her and should let her be. Once Bai Ling even waved a finger in their faces, saying, "This is my home! Get out of here, and don't come back!"

Their mother seemed to need to rely on others, so she did not say a word. The two sisters never went to either home after that. But their father did come to visit them at school, and he gave them some money. An Ning accepted it, but An Jing did not, saying, "I won't ask for his money, even if I'm reduced to working in a dance hall."

An Jing later met Chen Kai and moved in with him. He was ten years older than her. Though An Jing told An Ning that she had moved in with Chen Kai because she loved him, An Ning could not help but feel that she was actually doing it to get back at their father.

Once, when An Jing and Chen Kai were having dinner at Hongse Niandai, they saw her father and Wang Jue. An Jing said to Chen Kai, "I see one of my acquaintances over there at the bar. Let's go say hi to them."

Chen Kai didn't know it was An Jing's father. If he had, he would not have followed her over. An Jing walked up to her father and said, "Director An, it's been a while since I saw you. It looks like life has been good to you."

Her father stood there awkwardly.

"Let me introduce you to someone," An Jing said, pointing at Chen Kai. "This is Chen Kai, my boyfriend. As soon as he gets divorced, we'll get married."

Her father's face flushed all the way to his collar, even his ears turning red. He did not know what to do.

Wang Jue stood up and smiled gracefully. She raised her glass and said, "Then let me congratulate you!"

An Jing looked at Wang Jue, and a single word popped out of her mouth. "Bitch!"

Wang Jue was not angry. She continued to stand. She said magnanimously, "An Jing, don't be so rude. You should call me Ma."

An Jing threw her glass of wine in Wang Jue's face and walked away.

10

An Ning had pondered many times whether, if she had accompanied An Jing that night instead of conducting surveys with her classmates, things might not have happened as they did later. But life was life. There was no such thing as what if.

Early in the morning of An Jing's twenty-second birthday, An Ning went out. On her way to meet her classmates, she called An Jing. "Hey, sis! Happy birthday! I'm really sorry, but I have to go to Pi County with my classmates to do some social surveys. I won't be able to celebrate your birthday with you."

An Jing was still in bed in the dorm. A ray of sunlight had just fallen on her face. By the time she hung up the phone, the sun had disappeared. She was a little sad.

An Jing's phone was on all day. Subconsciously, she was waiting for her parents to call. Even though she hated them, she still wanted to hear their birthday wishes. But she waited all morning and still did not receive a call. Her father didn't call, and neither did her mother. She told herself that if they didn't call by noon, she would turn off the phone so that they couldn't find her even if they wanted to. But twelve came and went, and still the phone did not ring. An Jing thought perhaps something was wrong with her phone. She went to a phone booth and dialled her number, just to ensure the phone was working properly.

Utterly dejected, she turned off her cell phone and walked out of the school gate, then blindly followed the course of the Funan River until she was worn out. She sat on a stone and wept. Passersby turned their heads and looked, but she let the tears flow on and on, as if she were all alone.

She did not go to class that afternoon, but sat by the river until evening. She thought, *They all forgot, but that doesn't mean I can't celebrate on my own.* She went to a nearby shop, bought a birthday cake, and went back to the riverside, where she sat alone, eating cake. She ate and ate, quietly, feeling miserable all the while. Then, she threw the rest of the cake into the Funan River.

She suddenly thought of Chen Kai and wanted to call him. When she had pressed half the digits in his number, she suddenly wondered what she would say. Tell him she was celebrating her birthday, and that she was lonely and needed someone to keep her company? She had left home now. She wanted to live independently. She didn't need anyone to comfort her.

She got up and walked toward Hongfan, thinking she would play the piano there. When she finished playing, she would drink alone—get drunk—and comfort herself.

An Jing was playing the piano in a bar called Hongfan at that time. She played two hours each night, earning fifty yuan each time. This was later increased to a hundred yuan. The money was enough to cover her tuition and living expenses.

Many of the girls in the Art Department went out to work at night, singing or dancing, catching on with one bar or another after school was over. They often performed at several venues in one night, earning eighty or a hundred yuan per venue. There were also some who accompanied guests into the private rooms; they earned more. There was no floor, only a ceiling, and no one really knew much they could earn in a night. But An Jing never went to the dance halls, feeling that they were messy, even dirty. She found a relatively regular gig in a bar, so that she could study during the day and work at night.

When she finished her set one night and was packing her things to go home, the boss came over and said that one of the guests wanted to hear "To Alice." An Jing looked in the direction the boss pointed and saw a man in his thirties. He looked a bit like Pu Cunxin. He came to the Hongfan nearly every night, and he liked to sit in his usual place, drinking red wine. An Jing's boss said the fellow had paid fifty yuan to hear "To Alice." An Jing thought, *Why not, if he's paying? Didn't I come here to make money?* She sat down again, played "To Alice," took the money, and left.

For the next several nights, the man asked her to play "To Alice," always just as she was about to get off from work. Annoyingly, when An Jing played the song for him, he didn't look at her, but just sat alone, drinking. It hurt An Jing's ego. She thought, *What's so great about little extra money?* She didn't want to play anymore. She told her boss, "I'm not playing it again. It's too late. My school will close the gates soon."

Seeing that the man was the only person left in the bar, her boss couldn't say anything. He went over to the man and offered a few words of explanation, then told An Jing to go home.

The Hongfan was not far from campus, about a fifteen-minute walk. There were few people on the street, and only a few empty taxis. An Jing was used to walking alone at night, so she was not afraid, but that night, she could feel someone following her. Her heart was beating wildly. She wanted to run, but she didn't dare. If it was a shady character following her, running would show him that she was afraid, making the situation even more dangerous. She didn't run. Instead, she slowed down, adopting a deliberately carefree pace, but she was still scared.

When she reached a stretch of road that was well lit, she abruptly turned around. It was the man from the bar, the one who asked her to play "To Alice."

She called to him, "Why are you following me?"

It seemed he wanted to hide, but he did not. Standing five or six paces from her, he said, "I wanted to make sure you got home safely. You're a girl. The streets aren't safe."

"With you following me, they're not," An Jing said. "Why do you ask me to play 'To Alice' every night, you pervert?"

For some reason, An Jing wasn't the least bit afraid of him. She spoke harshly.

"I like 'To Alice,' and you play it well."

"I won't play it anymore, especially not when you're sitting there alone."

"What's the point of that?" He smiled. "I want you to teach me to play piano, to play 'To Alice,' okay?"

"No! I've never taught adults. Who knows what scheme you're cooking up?"

"If you don't teach me, I'll keep going to the bar and asking you to play, unless you stop working there."

"Oh brother! You're such a jerk."

The man did not get angry. He took out a business card and handed it to An Jing. "Call me when you've thought it over."

With that, he turned and walked away, looking very cool.

Back in the dorm, An Jing took out the business card and saw that the man's name was Chen Kai. He was the president of a computer company in Moziqiao. The next day, she called the company to confirm, asking if the president, Chen Kai, was in the office. The girl on the phone asked her to wait for a moment.

Chen Kai picked up the phone and said, "Hello. Who is that?"

An Jing said, "It's me. Let's get this straight, for the sake of the money, I will teach you, but my price is high—a hundred yuan an hour."

Chen Kai said, "I'll be a good student. You can come to my office on Saturday afternoon."

"Don't you work for a computer company?" You mean, you have a piano in the office?"

"Not a problem. I'll buy one."

On Saturday afternoon, An Jing went to Chen Kai's office and saw a piano in the spacious room. She was very formal, taking out her student ID and showing it to Chen Kai. He earnestly took it in hand and inspected it carefully. "You're still a graduate student in the Art Department," he said.

An Jing continued to play in the Hongfan every night, and she went to Chen Kai's office every Saturday afternoon for an hour-long piano lesson. She continued to be wary of Chen Kai. Each time she went to his office, she took An Ning with her. After the lesson, Chen Kai sometimes invited both of them to have dinner or tea with him. They all had a good time together.

After a few months, An Ning grew impatient. "I think he seems quite honest. You shouldn't think everyone is bad. You can go by yourself in the future. I don't want to be a third wheel. It's a waste of time."

One day after the lesson, An Jing went to the ladies room. When she came back, Chen Kai opened a can of soda and offered her a drink. The warmth in his eyes roused her suspicion. Worried that he had spiked the soda, she didn't drink immediately.

She said, "I've got something I need to do. I should go."

Chen Kai said, "What's the hurry? Have a drink first."

His persuasions made her even more suspicious.

"It's late. I'll take it with me and drink it on the way." With that, she opened the door and left.

Back at the dorm, she called An Ning and said, "I suspect Chen Kai drugged a soda. I'm going to drink it now. You watch, and if anything happens, take me to the hospital."

An Jing's expression must have frightened An Ning. She asked, "Will you report it?"

"No," An Jing said. "I just want to know if he's out to harm me."

An Ning nodded solemnly. An Jing drank the soda, then lay on her bed, as if making a heroic sacrifice, waiting for the drug to attack her. But she lay in bed for a couple of hours, without incident.

An Ning said, "You're so paranoid. I put off studying for my English exam for this."

After that, An Jing was at ease when it came to Chen Kai. He persuaded her to stop working at the Hongfan and stick to just teaching him, increasing the pay by three times.

An Jing said, "Friends are friends, and pay is pay. I won't quit my job, and I won't ask you for a penny more."

Chen Kai said nothing. Instead, it was the owner of the bar who increased her pay, from fifty yuan a night to a hundred. He said it was because her playing had brought business to the bar, and she deserved a raise for that. An Jing later learned that part of the increase was privately compensated by Chen Kai. This hurt her ego, and it led to their first real fight. They were already together by the time she found out.

On her birthday, An Jing walked into the bar, and she immediately saw Chen Kai, sitting in the same old place. For some reason, seeing him made her suddenly feel sorry for herself. Pretending not to notice him, she walked straight to the piano.

Being in a bad mood, she played several sad songs that night. Two hours passed quickly, and when she stood up, Chen Kai waved her over. She hesitated, then walked to his table. She had wanted him to call her over, and she would have been disappointed if he hadn't. She sat across from him, and he waved to the bar and said, "Music!"

"The Birthday Song" burst out all over the bar, and the bartender brought over a cake with exactly twenty-two candles. Chen Kai looked at An Jing, his expression sincere, and said, "Happy birthday."

An Jing had not expected Chen Kai to be like this. A tear fell down her cheek.

Later, she asked Chen Kai how he had known it was her birthday. He told her that he had taken note of it when she showed him her ID. Once again, she was moved.

That night, they drank a good deal of red wine, until just the two of them were left in the bar. An Jing was dizzy, but she felt a joy and happiness she had never known before.

When Chen Kai helped her into the car, he asked, "Back to school or home?"

Full of alcohol, An Jing said, "I don't have a home, and the school gate closed long ago. Just take me wherever you want to take me."

Chen Kai took her to the Minshan Hotel.

An Jing told An Ning that she was not drunk out of her mind that night. When Chen Kai had wished her a happy birthday, she knew what would happen before the night was done, so she had intentionally gotten drunk. In the hotel room, as Chen Kai slowly undressed her, she had continued the drunken charade.

The next morning, Chen Kai knelt before An Jing and said, "I'm sorry. I shouldn't have done it while you were drunk."

An Jing said coolly, "I was willing. From now on, you're my family."

Over the next six months, aside from visits to the hotel with Chen Kai, there were no changes in An Jing's life. She continued to work at the Hongfan, and she continued to go to Chen Kai's office for piano lessons. But she refused any gift from Chen Kai. Any time he tried to give her money or a gift, it made her very unhappy.

"Please have some respect. I'm not your mistress."

An Jing knew Chen Kai had a wife, but she never asked, not even a hint. The more she was like that, the more Chen Kai felt sorry for her and the nicer he was to her.

An Jing told An Ning, "I don't care about anything else. As long as he treats me well, I'm happy."

But after some time, An Jing found it a little annoying to have to go to the hotel and get a room. Once, while the two of them were still in the room, housekeeping knocked and said it was time to make the bed for the night, and the housekeeper gave An Jing a contemptuous look on the way out. An Jing couldn't stand it anymore. As soon as the housekeeper left, she lost her temper with Chen Kai.

"I don't ever want to come to a place like this again. It makes me feel like a whore."

Two weeks later, Chen Kai picked her up at school and told her he wanted her to see something. They went to the Zongbei Housing Estate and walked into a two-bedroom apartment. Chen Kai took a key from his pocket and handed it to her.

"It's a gift. Please take it."

It was done, and there was no point refusing. And anyway, she couldn't go on visiting a hotel room forever, always living in fear. So from that day on, they officially began to live together.

If An Jing had not gone to Xizang, she might have married Chen Kai early on, and her life might have been different. But that summer, the school organized a group of arts students in the campaign for the popularization of knowledge in culture, technology, and public health in the rural areas and sent them to perform for the road construction troops on the Sichuan-Xizang Line. When they returned from Xizang, An Jing had changed.

While she was away, Chen Kai was finalizing his divorce. Before An Jing went to Xizang, he told her he would be free when she returned. They agreed that they would get married as soon as he was divorced. He kept his promise, and by the time she returned, he really was divorced.

An Jing, however, did not want to get married. Privately, she told An Ning that she had discovered that she did not really love Chen Kai.

11

When she got up the next morning, An Ning caught the scent of rain. When she opened the curtains, it was raining, making Kangding much brighter. Looking up, she saw a touch of white on the mountains in the distance, the snow that had fallen the previous night. In July, it rained in the lowlands and snowed in the peaks. This sort of scenery could only be experienced on the Sichuan-Xizang Line.

An Ning had not slept well the night before. She had only dozed a bit before dawn, and her eyes were blurred now. Guo Hong had gotten up earlier, and An Ning had heard splashing from the bathroom. Guo Hong came out of the bathroom now, combing her hair as she complained, "It's going to be a hell of a rain. Such bad luck!"

"That's how it is on the Sichuan-Xizang Line. It's still snowing on the mountain," An Ning said, as if she had traveled the Sichuan-Xizang Line many times.

Guo Hong walked to the window. When she saw snow on the mountaintop in the distance, she exclaimed, "Damn! No kidding. I heard we were going to climb the mountain today. Can we do that if it's snowing?"

"Yes, sure. We're going to have good luck today."

An Ning turned and asked Guo Hong, "Have you ever traveled the Sichuan-Xizang Line?"

"No."

"You've been married for five years, and you haven't gone to visit him even once?"

Guo Hong shook her head. "I wanted to go before, but he wouldn't let me. He said there were often mudslides, landslides, avalanches, and things like that, so it was too dangerous. I used to think he was looking out for me, but now I know he was just afraid I would find out about him and that woman."

An Ning didn't want to talk about such unpleasant things so early in the morning. She turned to Guo Hong and said, "Have any of the other wives been there?"

Guo Hong said, "There have been some. Some women really miss their husbands, so they go up with their children for a summer vacation, but it never goes smoothly. It is good when the Bangda flight is regular. That saves a lot of time. But when it's not regular, bad times happen, like for us now. It's the rainy season on the Sichuan-Xizang Line now. Very few planes are on time, and the delays often last several days. So every time a woman gives up the mountain, all the wives come to see her off. It's very grand, like a soldier going out on a mission."

She continued, "One year, one of the wives went to see her husband. When she was about to arrive, she encountered a landslide, and the road was damaged. She waited there for a week, but the road still wasn't cleared. Her time off was coming to an end, so she had to turn around. She was gone for twenty days, and she still didn't get to see her husband.

"Another of the wives took her child up there. The family was reunited, but when they were about to come back, there was a mudslide on the mountain. They were trapped there and couldn't come back. In the end, they had to go around to Lhasa and fly to Chengdu from there. School had been open for two weeks by that time, and they wouldn't accept the child's late registration. Someone from the military organization had to take care of the paperwork before the child was finally admitted. So am I wrong? Isn't it a bad idea to marry a soldier?"

A loud noise from outside interrupted them. Someone shouted, "Let's go! All passengers to Lhasa must board the bus!"

Guo Hong said, "I'll get our seats. Hurry!"

Saying that, she picked up her luggage and hurried away. An Ning had not washed her face yet, so she ran into the bathroom and wiped it quickly. Not bothering to put on any makeup, she rushed out of the room, bag in hand.

An Ning was the last passenger to arrive. "Hurry up! If everyone were as slow as you, we'd never reach Batang."

The bus was full of people. Guo Hong sat next to a Tibetan man, clearly not having managed to save a seat for An Ning. Guo Hong looked at An Ning helplessly, indicating that there were almost no seats left. Some of the familiar faces were absent from the bus, and some new ones had been added. The Khampa man was gone. Perhaps he worked in Kangding and wasn't Khampa after all. The long-distance buses going into Xizang were different from those in the interior, more like city buses, with people getting off and on at any time, and with no assigned seats. As An Ning was looking for a seat, she noticed someone in the last row waving at her. It was the woman who had vomited in the bus the day before. An Ning walked over, and the woman pulled her daughter to one side, making room for An Ning to sit. An Ning thanked her and sat down next to the girl.

As soon as An Ning sat down, the bus started moving in the direction of the snow-covered mountain. An Ning only then recalled that she had not eaten breakfast, so she took out some crackers, chocolate, and an apple from her bag. She took out a piece of chocolate and offered it to the girl, who looked at her mother.

The woman said, "If the nice lady wants to give it to you, you can have it."

The girl took the chocolate. After what had happened with the fish the day before, she had not expected them to accept her offer, so she was grateful when they did. An Ning took out another apple and offered it to the woman, but the woman said, "Thank you, miss. I don't dare to eat it. I'm afraid I'll throw up."

An Ning said, "Apples are fine. They're full of vitamins and can make you more resistant to sickness."

The woman smiled and shook her head.

Her daughter said, "My mom didn't dare to eat anything at all this morning. She just took motion sickness medicine."

An Ning was surprised. "How can you do that? The body can't take it. It's such a long journey ahead of us."

The woman said, "It's fine. I feel much better today."

An Ning finished her crackers and apple. She talked to the mother and daughter and learned that the woman's name was Yu Xiulan, and her daughter, Wang Xiaoxue, was ten years old. The girl finished chocolate and started folding paper cranes again.

An Ning asked, "Xiaoxue, why are you folding so many paper cranes?"

Perhaps it was because of the chocolate, that Xiaoxue was not as quiet as she had been the day before. She whispered, "They're for my dad."

"What does your dad do?"

"He's a soldier."

"Where?"

"Xizang."

An Ning understood.

"Are you and your mom going to visit your dad?"

Xiaoxue nodded.

Xiulan said, "Her father is on this road."

An Ning asked, "Is he also with the armed police traffic force?"

Xiulan nodded.

"How long has it been since you saw each other?"

"A long time."

How long was a long time? An Ning didn't follow up on her questioning. If someone didn't want to talk, it was useless to keep asking. Xiulan looked out the window into the distance, as if her husband were there.

An Ning didn't like feeling so awkward. She asked Xiaoxue, "Do you miss your dad?"

"Yes."

When she said it, she suddenly started crying. Xiulan turned and pulled her daughter into her arms, her own eyes now red. An Ning had not imagined that her questions could make both mother and daughter so sad. She felt like she had really messed up, and she didn't know how to comfort them.

The bus was climbing the mountain. A thin layer of snow covered the slopes, and the road was narrow and winding. The bus circled back and forth, gradually gaining altitude. An Ning felt a tightness in her chest, but after an hour or so, the bus reached the top of the mountain and began descending again. Before long, the grassland appeared, and the road became straighter and wider, but there were fewer people than before.

They occasionally passed several Tibetan-style houses along the roadside. Each house was like a bunker, with two or three floors, and with strong, thick white walls. There were small black windows with narrow frames on each wall, like the lookout of a bunker when seen from a distance. Highland barley was being sunned on some rooftops, while other rooftops remained bare, aside from the colorful prayer flags that flew atop every home. An Ning remembered Li Qingge saying that Buddhist scriptures were printed on the prayer flags, alongside the biographies of eminent monks and sages of earlier generations. These were the lifeblood of the pious Tibetan spirit. The prayer flags flapped in the wind, virtually chanting Buddhist scripture on behalf of the home owner.

As the bus passed, several dark faces appeared in the narrow black windows. When the passengers in the bus smiled, they saw white flashes—the teeth of the returned smiles. Some of the residents ran out and waved at the passing bus. Some children ran after it for a while before stopping in the dust raised by the vehicle and gradually turning into fuzzy black spots.

An Ning felt that they had truly arrived in Tibetan territory.

The bus passed the Ya River and reached Litang at noon. It stopped for a while in front of a small restaurant, allowing the passengers to have a quick meal before continuing their journey.

When they continued, it wasn't long before the bus broke down in an open meadow. The driver lay under the vehicle for a long time, fiddling around, then stood up and said he needed to go back to Litang to buy spare parts. He told the passengers to wait here and he would be back soon, then he hitched a ride back in the direction they had come from.

The passengers scolded and cursed, but eventually felt that was no use. Instead of cursing, they clustered into groups of several people and chatted. In this place, with no village or shop anywhere nearby, relieving themselves became a problem. The men could deal with it easily enough, carelessly walking a few paces away and turning their backs to everyone else. It was likewise quite convenient for the Tibetan women to get away from the crowd and, trusting to their long robes to shield them, find a spot to squat and solve the problem.

The Han women were in a more delicate situation. They still felt uneasy, even after walking some distance away, so turned and called to those nearby, "Can you see me here?"

"Yes."

They moved a little farther away, turned back, and asked again, "How about here?"

The Han men smirked and called loudly, "Yep."

Finally, the women couldn't be bothered anymore. They just pulled down their pants and squatted, settling the matter where they were. Once, someone cat-called and sang a familiar song, "I see you, I see you, I ... see ... you ..." The woman who was squatting was not An Ning, but she still blushed, as if she had been seen.

A flock of white sheep moved in the distance, where the sky met the earth, like a cloud descending. The Tibetan shepherd waved something in his hand and called as if in greeting, "Hiya! Hiya!"

Among the distant rolling hills was a high peak covered with snow. It sat like a white-haired old man squatting next to his young sons, all of them watching the misfortune of the passengers on the broken-down bus from the spot where they squatted together in their own doorway. The few white clouds in the sky hardly looked like clouds, but like traces left by someone who had swept the floor, but not cleaned it. Some type of gorgeous flower bloomed in the grass, swaying in the wind. An Ning later learned that it was called the galsang, the flower featured in the well-known song. The surrounding scenery was beautiful, an ideal place to take pictures. Someone pulled out a camera, and they started taking photos of one another. An Ning took out her camera and took a few pictures of Guo Hong and of Yu Xiulan and her daughter. She asked Guo Hong to take two pictures for her as well, one sitting and one standing. The grass was soft, and the smell of grass surrounded them. Feeling good, An Ning sat, not wanting to get up right away.

She suddenly thought of her sister. A few years earlier, An Jing had traveled this same road. It was the same road, but the sisters traveled opposite directions on it. One went up from Chengdu, and the other came down from Lhasa. The direction was different, and the feeling may have been too—who knew? An Ning had just begun her journey, and she felt no particular emotion. But she knew what An Jing had felt back then. When An Jing told her about the experience, she had sensitively captured the mystique of it. This sort of feeling had haunted An Ning for years, making her long for Xizang—an inexplicable excitement.

An Ning thought of An Jing now for no other reason than the grass before her now, which called to mind An Jing's photo—the nude photo printed on the cover of *One Man's Plateau*. It was evident the image had been shot in grass just like this. In the photo, An Jing sat facing away from the camera, legs crossed, on the grass. She faced snow-capped mountains in the distance, and she was surrounded by galsang blooms. Her smooth back highlighted the curvaceous beauty and youthful vitality in the sunshine of the plateau.

When she returned from Xizang, An Jing was a different person. She was always excited. When she talked about Xizang, she was so excited that she would start showing everyone her photos. But the nude photo was only seen by An Ning, and later by Chen Kai. An Ning really admired her sister's frankness and courage. She enlarged the photo and hung it in the house where she and Chen Kai lived together. Strangely, Chen Kai expressed no opinion. Intuition told An Ning that the photo must have been taken by a man, and any man who could take such a photo of her was definitely not an ordinary man. That's not to say he himself was someone amazing, but that his relationship with An Jing was definitely out of the ordinary.

But An Ning did not ask An Jing who the man was. There was no need to ask. An Jing would tell her. And sure enough, An Jing later told her that the man was Li Qingge.

12

An Jing met Li Qingge in Lhasa. When she told An Ning of that time, what made the greatest impression was that one night, in the middle of the night, Chang Na saw the Living Buddha in her room.

When An Jing had gone with the others to Xizang, they flew direct from Chengdu to Lhasa, and then traveled on to the Sichuan-Xizang Line. All seven members of the performance team were girls, one of whom was called Lu Wei, a cadre from the Youth League Committee who had just stayed on to teach at school after graduating the previous year.

When the performance team was formed, one of the directors came and said frankly, "The performance team does not need boys, just girls, and they must be beautiful."

Everyone was stunned when they heard that, thinking they must not have heard correctly. The director seemed to have anticipated this reaction. Ignoring their surprise, he explained calmly, "Our troops who are building roads in Xizang are all men, and they rarely see women. It doesn't matter how well you sing or dance. If you just walk around among the troops, it will boost morale."

They were picked up at the Gonggar Airport by a twenty-five-or-six-year-old, tall, broad-shouldered lieutenant. His face was dark and shiny. It was only later that An Jing learned that he had not always been dark-skinned, but had been tanned by the ultraviolet rays of the plateau. Li Qingge and the others called the dark shiny look of his face "hidden light."

As soon as he saw them, the lieutenant introduced himself. "My name is Li Qingge," he said, and went on to note that the characters used to write his name were the same as those found in the name of Golmud, Qinghai.

An Jing whispered, "What kind of name is that?"

Though she said it softly, Li Qingge heard her. He smiled and explained, "I was born in Golmud, Qinghai. That's how I got my name."

An Jing said, "It sounds like we're all calling you 'ge,' as in 'big brother.' I hope you're not going to take advantage of such familiarity!"

With a blush of embarrassment, Li Qingge said, "Don't blame me. Blame my dad."

He shot An Jing a special look when he spoke. They had just met, and she dared to talk to him like that. It made him feel she was quite a special girl. And anyway, she really was very eye-catching among all those girls. No man would have been impervious to her beauty.

An Jing boldly stared at Li Qingge, and he quickly looked away. She looked at him not because of his name or his face, but because of his shoulders and his physique. She did not bother about a man's appearance, but she did care about his build. She liked men with broad shoulders.

Her first impression of Li Qingge was good. Teasing him, she whispered, "The captain's too old, and the second lieutenant is too young, but this lieutenant's just right."

Not hearing clearly, Li Qingge asked, "What did you say?"

"I didn't say anything."

An Jing looked serious. The other girls gave a cowardly laugh and looked at Li Qingge. He knew she was making fun of him, but he couldn't say anything about it.

It was the first time An Jing and the others had been to Xizang. They were very excited, and they continued to fidget restlessly after they boarded the bus. Li Qingge advised them to be calm, so as to avoid altitude sickness. They ignored him, saying Xizang was nothing special and wouldn't have any effect on them. They sang in the bus:

> I come to you
> Bringing a true heart
> I come to you
> Covered in dust from the road

Li Qingge said, "If you don't stop singing, you'll have a headache before long."

They didn't listen, but just kept singing wildly. As a result, before they reached Lhasa, some of them began to have headaches. When the Potala Palace appeared on the red mountain in the distance, when it would have been appropriate for them to be excited, none of them could muster the energy.

The number of people suffering from altitude sickness increased in the afternoon, and almost all of them were dizzy. The one who had the strongest reaction was Chang Na. The blood drained from her lips and she looked sallow. Li Qingge told her to drink a bottle of Rhodiola, saying he had been the same when he first came up, but with time, he had gotten used to it. He gave An Jing and the others a bottle as well, telling them to drink it. He said they were all to stay in the guest house and rest; no one was allowed to go out.

After dinner, An Jing felt better, so she thought of going to Potala Palace Square to have a look around. The Armed Police Guest House was near Potala Palace, and she knew the palace must be very beautiful at night. She also knew that if she told Li Qingge where she was going, he would not allow it, so she didn't tell him. Instead, she and her roommate Liu Sijia snuck out of the room quietly at night.

When they got to the main gate, they ran into Li Qingge. He asked, "Where are you going?"

An Jing said, "We want to go out and buy some things."

"What do you need? I'll buy it for you."

"Feminine products. Can you get that?"

Li Qingge blushed. Hesitating, he said, "There's a shop next door. I'll take you there."

An Jing thought to herself, *This guy is not easy to deal with.*

But there was nothing to be done but to bite the bullet and follow him. He stood at the door of the store and did not go in, so An Jing and Sijia went in alone. They went in and wandered around for a while before buying a few random items. They did not succeed in their plan, and they ended up spending money unnecessarily. An Jing felt they had been very unlucky.

The next day, everyone's altitude sickness was much better. Even Chang Na had recovered. An Jing and a few of the other girls found Li Qingge and asked if they could visit the Potala Palace and Barkhor Street. At first, he did not agree, wanting them to take another day to rest before going out, but in the end, he couldn't stand to argue with them, and he was left with no choice but to take them there.

When they went out, they visited the Potala Palace, the Norbulingka, and the Jokhang Temple, and they bought a lot of trinkets on Barkhor Street. Li Qingge was an old hand in Xizang, and he knew a lot about the place. He told them about Tibetan customs and shared many stories as he showed them around, and he took many photos for them. Privately, the girls said they were lucky to have the lieutenant lead them around, since he was able to act as guide and take photos, killing two birds with one stone. They all had a great time that day.

An Jing later told An Ning that though Li Qingge had made a good impression on her that day, she had not had time to pay him too much attention. Her eye had been attracted by other things, four of which really impressed her: the five-colored prayer flags that flew everywhere overhead, the long, ancient stone stairway to the Potala Palace, the sheep god in the Jokhang Temple, and the worshippers kowtowing to the deeply pitted bluestone slab in the Jokhang Temple.

But that evening, Li Qingge made an impression on An Jing, twice.

Chang Na was the youngest member of the performance team, and when she woke from a nightmare in the middle of the night, she suddenly sat up in bed and said that she had seen the Living Buddha. Lu Wei was staying with Chang Na, and she woke, frightened. She huddled in the corner of her bed and, voice trembling, asked, "Where?"

Chang Na pointed to the window and said. "There! Look! He's smiling at me."

Lu Wei was supposed to be the teacher chaperoning the team, but she was roughly the same age as them—practically a kid, really. She didn't see anything, but ran out of the room, scared and pale, and knocked on An Jing's door.

"You two had better come here! Chang Na has lost her mind!"

A few of them ran over to see what was going on. Chang Na sat cross-legged on the bed, eyes fixed on the window.

"Look how kind he is."

They were all terrified now. Lu Wei told An Jing to call Li Qingge. He came quickly and asked Lu Wei what was going on. When Lu Wei had explained the situation, Li Qingge reached out and touched Chang Na's head.

"Maybe it was just too tiring for her today, and after seeing the Living Buddha and so many of Buddha's figures all day, she imagined seeing the Living Buddha at night."

Li Qingge told Chang Na to drink a bottle of Rhodiola. Chang Na said she was dizzy and wanted to sleep, and after lying down for a while, she fell asleep. Li Qingge and An Jing were too worried to leave, so they sat together, chatting as they watched over Chang Na. As they chatted, An Jing and Lu Wei learned that Li Qingge was also from Chengdu. After graduating from high school, he had joined the armed forces and was sent to the plateau. Later, he had been admitted to the military academy. Upon graduating, her could have stayed in the Chengdu Corps, but he requested an assignment on the plateau. He said he had not asked to be sent to the plateau because of some high-minded ideals, but because he wanted to assert his own will. He said that suffering was a precious spiritual wealth. He especially liked photography, and there was nowhere more ideal for this hobby than the plateau. His squadron was stationed in Gama Valley, inside the Nujiang Valley, and he was deputy squad leader. He had nothing to do with the girls' performance, but had been temporarily assigned to this detachment so he could take photos. The director of the political department wanted to transfer him to the publicity unit, but Li didn't want that. He didn't like the bureaucratic life, preferring to be stationed in more challenging locales at the grassroots level, where he could really hone himself, and also take good photos. Li said that his father was also in road construction and had worked in Xizang for thirty years before retiring just three years ago. Because he had worked on the plateau, his lungs had become enlarged and deformed, and he had trouble adapting to life in the interior regions. So although the old fellow had retired, he continued living on the plateau and did not dare to return to Chengdu. Li said his father was now on the Qinghai-Xizang Line, his mother was on the base in Chengdu, and he himself was on the Sichuan-Xizang Line. The family of three lived three lives in three places.

An Jing had not imagined that Li Qingge came from such a family, and she was deeply moved by the story.

Chang Na woke in the middle of the night, saying she was hungry for kebabs. Li Qingge went out with An Jing and Lu Wei in search of mutton skewers. Nighttime in Lhasa was very different from that in Chengdu. There were no taxis on the street, so they could only walk. They traversed several streets before they finally found a kebab shop.

Once again, An Jing was moved by Li Qingge. A man who would get up in the middle of the night and run here and there to buy a few mutton skewers for a girl was something that could not help but move An Jing. She wondered whether he would get up in the middle of the night to buy kebabs for her if she were sick.

Oddly enough, as soon as Chang Na ate the mutton kebabs, she was completely well. An Jing and the others wanted to sleep for a while, but it was already dawn by this time.

As soon as the day broke, they continued their journey. Li Qingge showed them to two Mitsubishi buses, and they began making their way to the Sichuan-Xizang Line.

13

The first stop was Mount Mila. There was a squadron stationed there, and it was to be the site of the troupe's first performance.

Although it was summer Mount Mila was still covered with snow, and it was very cold. On the near side of the mountain, the rocks were bare and the vegetation sparse, with only the occasional bush visible, shrinking in the cold wind. Li Qingge said that after Mount Mila, the climate would become humid. True enough, when they crossed Mount Mila and descended to the Niyang River, the air grew much more humid and there was a gradual increase in greenery.

An Jing was surprised that the climate was so different on the two sides of the mountain. One side was like the harsh wilderness of the hinterland, while the other was like the lush gardens of Jiangnan.

Li Qingge said that Mount Mila was the point where the climate turned from north to south in Xizang. In this season, the warm winds from the Indian Ocean that surged up from the Bay of Bengal were blocked by Mount Mila. The warm, humid air flow stagnated here, making the north dry and cold and the south humid and warm. Farther along, they saw dense forests, green grass, white sheep, and gorgeous flowers on the slopes. Li Qingge said it was the galsang flower.

The girls had never seen galsang flowers before. They were both surprised and delighted, and they called out, asking to be allowed to get out of the car and pick the flowers. Li Qingge said the galsang was in bloom all along the way, and they would be able to pick as many as they liked later.

The car turned a corner, and a row of tents appeared ahead. A group of soldiers squatted on the grass, eating their lunch. The bus stopped in front of the tent. Seeing so many beautiful women get out of the bus, the soldiers all stood up and stared blankly, rice bowls in hand.

A captain recognized Li Qingge. Happy, he called to the soldiers, "The college performance team is here."

The battalion exploded on the grass. The soldiers cheered loudly. The captain instructed the cooking crew to prepare more food. Li Qingge told the girls to eat a bit. When they had eaten, they would perform, after which they needed to hurry along if they were to reach 81 by evening. The cooking crew made two pots of vegetables and a pot of rice and placed them on the grass. The girls were hungry after a morning traveling on the bumpy road. They squatted on the grass like the soldiers and started to devour the food. The soldiers stood in the distance, smiling as they watched them finish their meal.

The grass served as the stage. The soldiers sat in a circle around it. The sound of gongs and drums attracted many Tibetan men and women who were grazing flocks or working nearby, and they formed a circle around the soldiers. With it being the first performance, the girls were all serious and diligent, and the performance was a great success, inspiring prolonged applause and laughter from the people seated on the grass. Li Qingge was busy taking photos, far, near, sitting, lying down, so busy that he was out of breath. Later, the soldiers and the Tibetan people joined hands and danced the traditional Tibetan Guozhuang dance, with women in a half circle and men in another half circle, dancing and circling, around the girls. The girls were not able to join them at first, but they picked it up quite quickly.

They reached the town at 81 very late that day, and they set off before dawn the next morning, continuing the journey.

They had slept poorly two nights in a row. An Jing was very tired, and she slept throughout the entire journey along the bumpy road. She wasn't sure how long it was before the bouncing ceased and the bus stopped. She opened her eyes and saw that the sun outside was quite dazzling.

Li Qingge said, "This is the 102 landslide area. Let's take a break. We have to be careful when crossing here."

Li Qingge instructed the driver to check the vehicle, and he walked forward a few paces on his own, looking up to see if there was anything unusual on the hillside. The girls were tired of sitting in the bus, so they alighted and stretched their legs. The 102 area wound back and forth, like chicken guts, halfway up the mountain. The upper slopes were red clay, and there was not a single tree, probably due to a landslide. The other side of the road was badly caved in, and many spots were left dangling in the air, propped up by the trees below. It looked dangerous. Several dozen meters below, the wreckage of several cars were scattered along the banks of the turbulent Palozangbo River. Li Qingge saw that there was no problem, and he said they should resume their journey.

He then got into the bus, sitting in the front to help guide them on the way.

Before the bus had gone far, they heard a rumbling sound and saw smoke and dust in front of them, and there was a sudden landslide. Half the mountain collapsed ahead of them, and in an instant, the mountain road disappeared. The girls were stunned. Li Qingge hurriedly directed the driver to reverse the bus. Frightened, Chang Na screamed so loudly tears dropped from her eyes. Since she was a child, An Jing had always been bold, but even she broke out into a cold sweat now. It was the first time she had encountered a landslide, and she found it both exciting and scary. She thought to herself, *That was close. If Li Qingge hadn't stopped for a rest just now, if we'd just gone straight into the landslide area, we might have been buried.*

Li Qingge did not panic at all. He comforted everyone, saying, "Don't be afraid. We often encounter this kind of thing on the Sichuan-Xizang Line. After a while, someone will come and repair it—one of our troops stationed up there."

Sure enough, it did not take long for dozens of soldiers and two bulldozers emitting black smoke to appear. The girls leapt up in excitement and waved their arms, as if their saviors had arrived.

Two hours later, the road had been repaired. The dirty soldiers walked over from the other side. They were exhausted, but when they saw the girls in the performance team, they were suddenly re-energized. Li Qingge organized a small gathering on the spot. The platoon leader, a man with a shaved head, performed as well, singing "We Soldiers" with the girls. Lu Wei took out the school's little camera and took video of this peculiar celebration.

They arrived at the detachment organization late that night. It was located in the county seat, which was said to be a relatively large town along the Sichuan-Xizang Line. However, An Jing and the others learned the following day that it was not very big, but was instead pitifully small—even smaller than a township in the interior, with just two rows of houses and what barely even passed for a street. The Sichuan-Xizang Highway passed through the city, but a car would have crossed from one end of the town to the other before you could even finish a handful of melon seeds. The military and county leaders came to visit the performance team, and a doctor from the medical crew was arranged to measure their blood pressure and do a general wellness check.

When the doctor came in, she saw An Jing and the others watching the video Lu Wei had taken on the road. The scene from the 102 roadside celebration was playing. As the bald platoon leader sang, the doctor gasped. The girls looked at her and asked, "You know him?"

The doctor blushed. "I don't just know him. He's my husband."

What a coincidence! The girls surrounded the doctor and asked many questions. She told them she and her husband had gotten married on base in Chengdu in March, and they had followed the troops up the mountain a week later. Although they were both assigned to the same line, just a hundred miles apart, it was usually difficult for them to see each other. They had not met in more than three months.

Moved by her story, the girls could not keep from singing "Stargazing." The doctor smiled at first, but as she listened, her eyes turned red. The girls grew uneasy at this, and before the song was half done, they couldn't sing any more.

That night, the troupe performed in the county seat. The town was surrounded by mountains and rivers, and it was a quiet environment, but the activity space was too small. The only place with a lawn was the county government offices. The troops pulled four trucks together to form a makeshift stage in the government offices compound, installing wires to generate electricity. The performance started as soon as it got dark. There were officers and soldiers in attendance, along with local Tibetan people. The military and county leaders sat among the crowd. Tibetan children perched in trees and on windowsills everywhere around them. Standing on this unique stage, the girls panicked, but as soon as the gongs and drums sounded, they got into their roles.

It was said that the atmosphere both on and offstage that night was very lively, and the girls performed well, and no one imagined that something would go wrong. The first thing that went wrong was that there was a sudden power outage, which fried the power amplifier. Understanding what had happened, An Jing did not stop singing, but just went on singing acapella, even walking offstage and moving through the crowd. The atmosphere was even warmer than before. An Jing sang four songs in a row while mixing with the crowd before the amplifier was repaired and the show went on. As soon as she returned to the area backstage, Li Qingge took her hand and said, "You did a great job. Thank you!"

An Jing's entire body softened, and she fell into his arms. Singing for so long all at once had made her suffer from severe hypoxia. Li hurriedly told someone to bring her oxygen as he helped An Jing sit down. She inhaled the oxygen and rested for a while, and she gradually recovered. By this time, the performance was almost over, and it was An Jing's turn to go onstage again. The last show was her solo dance, "All the Way."

Li Qingge said, "If you can't do it, can you just not go on?"

She said, "I'm fine."

Then, she agilely stepped up the bench and table and onto the stage, where she cheerfully jumped up amid applause from the crowd. Just as the show was about to end, something else happened. It was not a big deal, but for An Jing, it was no trivial matter. It may have been from that night that her feelings changed to something she had never experienced before, though she did not fully realize it at the time.

As An Jing was dancing on the stage, she suddenly felt a sharp pain on the bottom of her feet, but she went on to finish the dance and insisted on being a part of the curtain call with the others. But when she got down from the trucks, she plopped onto the ground and could not get up again.

Li Qingge ran over and asked, "What happened?"

An Jing said, "It feels like there's something poking my foot."

Li Qingge grabbed An Jing's foot and turned on the flashlight to have a look.

"Yes. It's bleeding. Your shoe is stained red all over."

Li Qingge didn't say anything else, but after hearing that, An Jing's foot hurt more than ever. Li Qingge took off her dancing shoes and found that there really was a wooden thorn stuck in her foot.

Li said, "Hold still a minute. I'll pull it out."

When the thorn was extracted, tears dropped from An Jing's eyes, but she did not let Li Qingge see them. Li hurried over to the medical crew carrying An Jing on his back. An Jing wanted to get down, but Li Qingge ignored her and kept going forward. She noticed that he did not smell the same as Chen Kai. Chen Kai smelled a little sweet and a little greasy, a mix that was hard to describe. But Li Qingge's smell was pure, like grass. She really liked that smell. It moved her, making her heart hot and her nose tingle. She couldn't help but cry again. She always pretended to be strong, but inwardly, she was actually quite fragile. She wanted to throw her arms around Li Qingge's neck and press her face tightly against his body, but she didn't.

But for a long time after she left Xizang, An Jing could still smell Li Qingge. And with his smell in her mind, she could no longer tolerate Chen Kai's smell.

Because of An Jing's injury, the troupe had to stay for two days at the detachment organization. They only continued their journey when her injury had healed.

Three days later, they reached the squadron. When the soldiers there heard that the performance team was coming, they leveled out a dirt platform outside the camp with their bulldozers and hung a sign above it reading: *A warm welcome to the college student performance troupe.* They also built a women's restroom, calling it a restroom, though it was actually just a crude latrine—a row of wooden slats erected across the cliffs and surrounded by old tents. An Jing told An Ning that it was difficult to use such a toilet, because whenever they released something, there was a long pause before they heard it land.

There was a sudden gale in the valley during that day's performance. The girls' skirts were blown upward by the wind, covering their faces. Fortunately, they had all worn shorts under their skirts, so they were not exposed. Though they were not exposed during the performance, they almost were afterwards. There was an abandoned Tibetan-style house behind the dirt platform. It had no roof, but only a fence about as tall as a man. Standing by the fence, one could see the road halfway up the mountain. The building was made a temporary changing room for the troupe. When the performance ended, the girls ran behind the fence to change their clothes. An Jing saw that a Dongfeng truck suddenly stopped on the highway, and dozens of soldiers stood in the bed of the truck, looking straight at the girls. It was a squadron of soldiers returning to camp after watching the performance. An Jing suddenly understood what they were looking at, and she instinctively wanted to cover herself with her clothes, but she immediately gave up the idea and, pretending not to notice, she changed her clothes. She thought to herself, *These soldiers stay in this isolated place year round. They hardly see a woman at all. If they want to look, let them look. Anyway, they can't really see anything from so far away.*

One day as the sun was going down, the troupe came to river. The bridge crossing the river had been swept away by a flood the day before, and a dozen soldiers on the other side of the river were constructing a bridge from wooden planks. The deep waters rushed, creating a loud sound. Li Qingge cupped his hands around his mouth and asked the soldiers on the other side when the bridge would be ready. The soldiers shouted back that the earliest would be the afternoon of the following day. Li Qingge turned back and shouted to the soldiers to let their squadron leader know that the performance team needed to cross that day, no matter what, and that they needed to find a way to make that happen. One of the soldiers dropped his tools and ran off.

The troupe waited for someone from the other side to respond. There was grass beside the road, and the galsang blooms were particularly gorgeous in the light of the setting sun. The girls rollicked on the grass, not caring whether or not they crossed the river. An Jing thought it would be better if they didn't, since it would so much more romantic to camp in the grass all night. But when she saw Li Qingge anxiously pacing back and forth by the river, looking up and down the banks, she began to worry on his behalf. She wanted to comfort him, but she didn't know what to say, so she didn't approach him at all. Since he had carried her on his back that night, she felt that something inexplicable had developed between them. It was the sort of thing that made her take note of him from time to time, but without really intending it. Maybe it was his smell of grass, or perhaps not. It was not until a long time later that she discovered what it was.

After a while, a loader drove up on the opposite bank, and a thick plume of smoke rose into the evening sky over the plateau. The loader momentarily hesitated beside the river, then drove toward the bank with its bucket raised. As it crossed, the tires—nearly as tall as a man—were completely submerged in the water. Li Qingge waved happily toward the river, jumping up and down like a child. Two wet loaders climbed from the river. Li Qingge told the girls to put their luggage into the body of the car, and then he helped each one of them into the cab. The cab was so small that it could only squeeze four people at a time, so it had to make several trips across the river. Crossing the river in this way was dangerous, but exciting. The girls stood on the loader and cried out in exaggerated tones. Standing on the bank, Li Qingge said, "You're all crazy."

Even so, he took the opportunity to raise his camera and photograph the group of crazy girls crossing the river. From the loader, Lu Wei pointed her camera back and filmed Li Qingge as he receded in the distance. Li was the last to cross the river. The two drivers stayed on the other side. The Mitsubishi buses did not cross the river that day. On the third day, when the bridge was completed, they crossed and caught up with the troupe.

It was midday, and the troupe was to perform for a squadron of officers and men at a construction site. The altitude there was said to be 4,000 meters. It was a show like any other, nothing special. But then, An Jing fell ill, and things changed completely.

14

An Jing's stomach started hurting so much that it made her sweat. The squadron's hygienist could not find the source of the pain.

Li Qingge led the troupe overnight to the next town in the county. He told An Jing to sit in the front seat on the way there, saying it would be more restful than a seat in the back. An Jing wished that she could sit in the back row with him, so that she could lean on him when the pain became unbearable. She seemed fragile, wanting to cry all the time, and always wanting someone to hold her.

She thought of Chen Kai. If he were there, he would hold her. But Chen Kai was not there; Li Qingge was.

Later, An Jing told An Ning, "I really wanted Li Qingge to hold me that day."

The doctor at the county hospital said that she had appendicitis, but with the crude conditions at the hospital, it was not safe to do surgery. Instead, she was given a temporary infusion of anti-inflammatory medication, a conservative treatment.

Wanting to avoid affecting the entire performance itinerary, Li Qingge discussed the matter with Lu Wei, and it was decided that she would lead the performance troupe on while he stayed to take care of An Jing. An Jing was in the hospital for three days, receiving the infusion, and then she was well. Li Qingge found a jeep at the county Party Committee office and set out with An Jing to catch up with the troupe.

There had been a heavy rain the night before, and the road had been washed out in several places. On the way, military officers and soldiers were occasionally seen repairing the road. When they had traveled more than a hundred kilometers, they came across a spot where a landslide had occurred and the road was now blocked and cars unable to pass. A Tibetan driver familiar with roads in the area suggested, "There's a side road on the right side of the mountain there, and it will get you through. It's not an easy road, though, very bumpy. It will take at least two hours to go around that way. If you don't want to put up with the bumpy road yourself, you don't have to take the jeep. You can walk across by a path over the mountain ridge and pass through a meadow. That will take about half an hour for you to bypass the landslide area, and I can meet you with the jeep where the roads cross up ahead."

Li Qingge thought for a while and said, "Alright. She just got well, so I don't want her to take that rough road. We'll walk and meet you up ahead."

When the jeep left, Li Qingge slung his camera over his back, and he and An Jing walked down the steep mountain path, winding back and forth like sheep intestines. At first, he walked in front, and when they came to a place that was difficult to pass, he turned back and helped An Jing. Later, the slope became a bit steeper, and he worried that she would slip, so he walked behind her to shield her. Whenever she couldn't climb, he reached out a hand to help her. Each time his hand touched her, she felt a kind of electric shock, making her heart leap. She liked the feeling.

The sky over the plateau was very blue, so clear that not even a trace of a cloud could be seen. Walking on the ridge, they felt like they were facing the sea. Several mountain eagles flew in the blue expanse, and An Jing's heart soared with them.

Her appendix had long since stopped hurting, but she still pretended to struggle as she walked, wanting Li Qingge to help her again. She wished they could continue to walk like this until they reached the end of the world. But it was not a tall mountain, and they soon crested it. There was a meadow in front of them, full of galsang blooms, with a snow-capped mountain farther ahead.

Startled by the scene in front of her, An Jing cried, "It's so beautiful! It's like a fairyland!"

Then she added, "I don't want to walk anymore. Let's rest for a while."

They sat together on the grass to rest. Li Qingge pointed to the snowy mountain ahead and said, "We're almost there. The roads meet at the foot of that mountain."

An Jing could not see the road. It was like there was no road there at all.

"Are you sure there's a road? Don't lie to me."

Li Qingge said, "You can see it when you walk a little farther. The road is down below, so you can only see it when you get below the ridge."

"You mean we're still on the top of the mountain?"

"Yes."

"God! The top of the mountain is a grassland. The plateau is so broad!"

After they rested for a while, Li Qingge stood up, ready to go, but An Jing did not want to leave. She wasn't tired; she was just reluctant to leave the beautiful meadow. And maybe there was more to it as well.

An Jing said, "I can't walk anymore. Let's sit for a while. The car won't be there so soon anyway."

Li Qingge said, "It looks close, but it's actually still some distance away. It looks like just one kilometer on the plateau, but it's actually three. It will take a while for us to walk this distance."

"I don't care. I just don't want to go."

She was a bit brazen, and a bit coquettish. Even she didn't know what came over her that day. Li Qingge could not do anything. She sat on the ground and refused to budge. What could he do, carry her? He couldn't just pick her up and haul her off.

An Jing suddenly said enthusiastically, "Let's take some photos! Look at this grass. And look at how beautiful the galsang flowers are!"

Li Qingge said, "Ha! So that's why you don't want to leave. You want to take pictures."

"I'm offering to model for you free of charge. That should be just what an amateur photographer wants, but you don't even know how to appreciate it," she pouted.

Without saying a word, Li Qingge smiled and picked up his camera. Suddenly reenergized, An Jing leapt up and ran ahead a few paces, then suddenly turned her head, and Li clicked a photo. It seemed she was a natural model. She sat cross-legged on the grass, her hands clasped together, and her face solemn, looking like a Bodhisattva. Li lay on the ground, choosing his angle, and pressed the shutter. An Jing thought, *This must look great. You can see me against the blue sky when he shoots upward from below like that. I'll look like a Bodhisattva floating in the sky. This guy has a real eye for photography.*

She picked up a sheep skull from the grass, raised it over her head, and smiling, she said to Li Qingge, "Come on, let's take another classic!"

An Jing took up various poses on the grass, and Li Qingge ran forward and backward, snapping shots until they were both exhausted and sat on the grass to rest. In the thin atmosphere, An Jing gasped for breath and fell onto her back on the grass. The strange fragrance was refreshing. It was the galsang flowers. She closed her eyes, content, her chest heaving. When she opened her eyes, she saw Li Qingge staring blankly at her. He blushed the moment their eyes met. Standing up quickly, he patted the grass from the seat of his pants and said, "We should go."

An Jing didn't get up, and she didn't speak. She just looked at Li Qingge, making him even more embarrassed. With feigned reluctance, he sat down again.

"Alright. We'll rest for another ten minutes."

Li Qingge lowered his head and fiddled with his camera, no longer looking at An Jing. But she knew the eyes of his heart were still looking at her. Fiddling with the camera was an attempt to distract himself, forcing himself to ignore something.

The sun was a bit harsh, and it was hot on the face. The snow-capped mountain shone brightly in the distance. An Jing suddenly recalled a photo she had seen somewhere before, and she wanted to take one like it. She got up from the grass, nudged Li Qingge's leg, and said, "There's a picture of four naked men in a row, sitting cross-legged and facing a snow-capped mountain. Have you seen it?"

Li said, "Yes, it's a great photo."

An Jing said, "I want to take one like that."

He looked at her, surprised.

She said, "What are you looking at. Are you really too ashamed to take such a photo here? This is the perfect environment for a nude." She added, "Maybe you would win an award."

Li Qingge blushed and shook his head.

An Jing stood up and looked down at him.

"You're a man. I'm a girl. What are you afraid of?"

Li hesitated, looking around without really thinking about what he was doing. The grass was deserted. Aside from green grass and galsangs, they were alone on the mountain.

"We're not doing anything wrong. Why the guilt? I'm dedicated to your photographic art. If you can't appreciate that, what's the point?"

Li said, "That wouldn't be good ..."

An Jing was angry. She turned and ignored Li Qingge. They were at a stalemate for a while. Finally, Li gave in.

"OK. But not necessarily naked."

An Jing smiled and looked at him. "That's my problem. You just shoot." She suddenly recalled something. Tugging at her long hair, she said, "Is my hair OK?"

Li fiddled with his camera. Without looking up, he said, "It looks great."

"You didn't look. How do you know it's OK?"

"I've looked at it for so many days now. You think I don't know how it looks?"

An Jing said, "But I don't think it looks right."

Li Qingge didn't get it. He had no idea what to say.

An Jing said, "My hair has been permed. In such a wonderful place, there shouldn't be any trace of adornment. We want to shoot natural beauty. How about I braid it? That would be the right feel."

It made sense. What an artistic touch! Her words reminded Li Qingge of something. He said, "If we had a few Tibetan women's accessories, it would be better to decorate your hair with those."

An Jing said, "You finally get it." Her eyes lit up. "How about picking some of the galsang blooms and braiding them into my hair?"

Li Qingge slapped his thigh. "Perfect!"

An Jing picked some galsang flowers and braided them into her hair. She turned her back to Li Qingge and asked him how it looked.

"Great."

Happy, she ran a couple dozen steps, then turned around and said to Li, "Turn your back. I'll tell you when to turn around again. Don't peek!"

He turned around, and An Jing stripped and stood there, naked.

An Jing later told An Ning that for some reason she couldn't quite pin down, she had been very comfortable with Li Qingge that day, not the least bit wary of him. When she spoke of it, her eyes were half closed, as if sinking into a pleasant memory. She said the sun was shining on her skin, and it was warm and comfortable, but she couldn't stop trembling—a trembling born of excitement. With her back to Li Qingge, she faced the snow-capped mountains and sat cross-legged on the grass, surrounded by galsang flowers. Sunlight poured rapturously onto her bosom, caressing her.

When everything was ready, she called loudly to Li Qingge, "Alright, let's shoot."

There were a couple of clicks from the camera behind her. In her excitement, her chest heaved violently, and in an effort to keep her emotions in check, she closed her eyes. The clicking sound suddenly stopped, and An Jing felt her heart leap into her throat. She thought, *What if Li Qingge rushes over here?*

She was a little flustered, and her ears were ringing. For a while, she could not hear any sound behind her, but she could hear her blood rushing in her ears. In the confusion, an image of herself making love with Chen Kai came to mind. If Li Qingge suddenly knocked her over, maybe she would embrace him tightly and make love to him there on the grass in the shadow of the snowy mountain, turning the world upside down and fully satisfying his desire.

But he did not approach her. That day, there on the grass, nothing happened. She felt a slight regret, but also a little happy. If something had happened there on the grass, she might not have been so attached to him later.

An Jing never imagined that just a few days later, she and Li Qingge would be staying in the same room.

15

An Jing later told An Ning that they caught up with the performance troupe that night. The troupe was waiting for them in Bangda, where a squadron was stationed, with a hot spring near the squadron. The girls asked if they could take a bath in the hot spring. It had been half a month since they had had a bath, and they were starting to stink.

Li Qingge called for the squadron instructor. Looking embarrassed, the instructor said, "It's fine for men to bathe in the hot spring, but probably not so appropriate for women."

Lu Wei asked, "Why not?"

The instructor said, "The hot spring is in the wilderness. There's nowhere to hide."

An Jing said, "What are you afraid of? No one will see us in the wilderness."

Looking at Li Qingge, she added, "Let everyone get a bath."

Li Qingge thought for a moment, then said to the instructor, "Let them wash up. Can't you arrange for a few soldiers to stand guard two hundred meters away from the hot spring and keep others from approaching?"

It felt so good to get a bath that day, mainly because it was in the wilderness—it wouldn't have been nearly as romantic otherwise. The girls lay in the warm spring water, looking at the white clouds in the blue sky and listening to the sounds of nature on the plateau. Armed police stood guard in the distance. An Jing later told An Ning what that felt like.

After the squadron had a short rest, the performance troupe continued eastward along the Sichuan-Xizang Highway, climbing more than a dozen snow-capped mountains and seven or eight rivers before they came to Mount Dongda. Mount Dongda was more than five thousand meters above sea level, and its peak was covered with snow year-round. Before they reached the peak, they could see many soldiers working there. From a distance, they looked like mung beans scattered on the slopes. The troupe reached the area, and the girls saw that the soldiers were maintaining the road there. The soldiers were overjoyed when they saw the troupe of girls coming, but they didn't jump up and cheer. They just held their shovels and smiled at the girls. They all had dark faces and white teeth, and all along the way, An Jing saw their unblemished smiles. Because of the arrival of the troupe, the soldiers stopped work early and returned to the squadron with the girls.

The barracks were built on a hill. Getting off the bus, An Jing felt dizzy and breathless, like there was a mass of cotton wool in her chest. Chang Na and Liu Sijia squatted on the ground and vomited. Lu Wei's face turned a little green as well.

The squadron officer said, "You don't need to perform. We're just happy you've come to visit."

Everyone's reaction was quite pronounced, and it really was not possible for them to perform. In the end, the soldiers in the squadron sang a Tibetan song for the girls in the performance troupe.

You are a galsang
I am a galsang
Without the sunshine on the plateau
The flowers are not fragrant
You are a wing
I am a wing
If either wing departs
The bird can't fly

The girls were moved to tears. When they were on the plateau, they became aware of just how easy it was to be moved to tears.

They went ahead, but the road was blocked. It had collapsed at a place called Haitong Gully, and it would take two weeks to repair it. July, August, and September always saw the highest number of natural disasters on the Sichuan-Xizang Line. By this time, it was almost time for school to start. Li Qingge used the squadron radio to ask the detachment leader for instructions. He told them to return to Bangda and fly to Chengdu from there.

On the Bangda Prairie, the troupe gave its final performance. Unfortunately, the squadron's generator was broken, and the soldiers had to hold candles to light the performance team. An Jing later recalled that the performance was very simple and unique. There was no musical accompaniment; they just sang acapella. But in the candlelight, the atmosphere was warmer and more romantic.

On the way to the Bangda Airport, the troupe spent a night in a guesthouse in a small township. The guesthouse was simple, with just two rooms, and the smell of yak butter filled the rooms. After many days of traveling and performing, everyone was very tired and couldn't muster the energy to bother. They just wanted a good night's sleep.

Li Qingge arranged for the girls to stay in one room, and he stayed in the other room with the two drivers. Not long after they had fallen asleep, there was a strong wind, rattling the windows as if someone were slapping them from the outside. Wolves howled in the distance. The girls were so frightened that they covered their heads with the quilts, but the terrifying sounds still dug into their ears. An Jing heard someone crying. It was Chang Na. A few others joined her after a while, Cao Xiaoqing and Liu Sijia. An Jing wanted to cry too, but she held back the tears. In the darkness, she heard Lu Wei say, "Don't cry. Let's call Li Qingge."

Lu Wei shouted for Li Qingge, but her voice was swallowed by the wind, and there was no response from the neighboring room.

Lu Wei said, "I'll count to three, and we'll all shout together."

Lu Wei shouted, "One, two, three."

The girls shouted in unison, "Li! Qing! Ge!"

An Jing said, "How can anyone hear anything in this wind? He might be able to hear if we knock on the wall."

The girls began to knock desperately. Li Qingge finally heard them. He ran out, stood at their door, and asked, "What happened?"

The girls didn't know how to answer. Lu Wei had suggested calling Li Qingge a few moments earlier, but now that he was here, she didn't know what they wanted him to do. No one could explain why they had called him, so they said nothing.

Li said, "Go to bed. We have a long journey tomorrow."

If they didn't say something, he would leave. At the critical moment, An Jing steeled her nerves. She crawled out of bed and opened the door. She said to Li Qingge, "We're afraid. Can you come in and stay with us?"

Li said, "You're all girls. How can I do that?"

Chang Na ran over and grabbed Li Qingge's arm. She said pitifully, "Just ... just come in and stay with us. We're all dressed. What are you afraid of? Please, Qingge."

Lu Wei said, "You can come in."

Li Qingge said, "If anyone found out, I'd be finished."

Chang Na said, "If you don't, I'm going to cry." As soon as she said it, she really did start crying.

An Jing said, "You're impossible! There are so many of us. Do you think we're going to eat you?"

Li had no choice but to agree. He slept at the door that night, like a minor deity protecting the door.

An Jing did not fall asleep for a long time. During the night, she heard Chang Na calling Li Qingge's name as she dreamed, muttering, "Qingge, don't go, I'm scared. I'm scared."

There was no restroom in the room, and no one dared to go outside, so they could only urinate in a wooden bucket. The sound of the girls urinating embarrassed An Jing. Fortunately, it was dark in the room, and no one could see anything. An Jing thought, *If Li Qingge is awake, what does he think of this sound? Even if he were asleep, this indecent sound would wake him up. But there's nothing to be done about it.*

Before dawn, Li Qingge woke the girls. They all got into the bus in a daze and continued the journey to Bangda Airport. The flight was not delayed, but the plane couldn't land due to a sudden change in weather. They could only spend the night at Bangda Airport, the highest and most humble airport in the world. No one slept well that night.

An Jing woke up in the morning thinking about leaving Li Qingge, and it made her very sad. She wanted to say something to him, or make some gesture, but she never found a chance to be alone with him. When it was still early, she heard him wake up and start walking down the corridor. The entire journey, it had always been like this. He got up early to prepare everything, waiting until the last moment to wake the girls so that they could sleep just a little longer. After spending so much time with him, she was familiar with his footsteps. Even when he was barefoot, she could tell when he walked past outside. Sometimes, she didn't even need to rely on her eyes or ears. She knew it was him just by a breath or a feeling. This was a particularly feminine gift, what was sometimes called a sixth sense. An Jing could sense that Li Qingge had packed his luggage early and placed it somewhere in the corridor. As soon as the performance troupe left, he would return to the squadron.

An Jing had shared a room with Chang Na that night. Chang Na had a bad stomach and needed to go to the restroom. An Jing said, "Go out and see if there's a backpack in the hallway."

Chang Na went out and quickly came back in. "Amazing! There is a backpack."

An Jing said, "It's Li Qingge's."

Chang Na said, "Looks like it. How did you know?"

"I guessed."

An Jing suddenly had an idea. She said to Chang Na, "Let's play a joke on Li Qingge."

"How?"

"Go and sneak his backpack in here so that he can't find it later. It will be funny to see him panic."

Chang Na said happily, "Yeah, okay."

She ran out and brought the backpack in. Then, squeezing her thighs together, she said, "I need to go to the bathroom!"

She ran out quickly. An Jing heard Li Qingge ask Chang Na in the hallway, "Have you seen my bag?"

Chang Na said, "No."

Li Qingge said, "I'm sure you hid it."

Chang Na said, "Why would I hide your bag? If you don't believe me, go into my room and look. But I've got to go to the restroom. I can't hold it."

An Jing later told An Ning that she didn't understand why Chang Na said that. Chang Na knew she was still in bed, but she told Li Qingge to go into her room to look for his bag. What was that silly girl thinking? Maybe Chang Na saw her heart, but she swore to heaven and earth that she really had no other intention at the time; she really did just intend to play a little prank on Li Qingge, a little going away prank, as it were. She never imagined what would happen.

As she heard Li Qingge approach the door, An Jing grew nervous. Li knocked on the door and said, "Is anyone there?"

An Jing's heart pounded. She bit the edge of the quilt, not saying a word. Li asked again, but she kept quiet. He walked into the room, and at one glance, he saw the backpack. Just as he was about to take it, he saw An Jing lying in the dark. Embarrassed, he quickly said, "I'm sorry. I didn't know you weren't up."

Li Qingge was about to leave. An Jing had no idea where she got the courage from, but she suddenly sat up in bed, looked at Li Qingge, and said, "Can ... can you give me a hug?"

Her voice shook, not sounding like her own voice. Before Li Qingge could say anything, she had already thrown herself in his arms. Li Qingge held her frantically.

She felt his body shake violently, and his heavy breath sprayed onto her face. Her lips desperately sought his. But Li Qingge pushed her away and walked out.

16

An Ning was sitting on the grass thinking about what all had happened to An Jing when she heard Guo Hong call, "An Ning, come on! It's time to go!"

The bus had been repaired and the passengers were boarding. An Ning got up and hurried to the bus. As soon as she boarded, the bus started moving. Guo Hong waved to An Ning, motioning to the empty seat beside her. The Tibetan man who had been sitting there before had disappeared. An Ning ran her eyes over the faces and saw that he was now occupying the seat in the rear of the bus, next to Yu Xiulan and her daughter, where An Ning had sat earlier. She had no idea how Guo Hong had managed to get someone to move from the front to the back.

After she sat down, Guo Hong asked, "Why were you in such a daze when you were sitting in the grass? Miss your boyfriend?"

An Ning said, "I was thinking of my sister."

"Where's your sister? Is she in Xizang too?"

"No, she's in the UK."

"My sister went overseas with my brother-in-law, to the US. My brother-in-law is a doctor." Guo Hong then sighed for no reason. "Ah, she's better than me! Of all my siblings, I fared the worst."

An Ning said, "What's so great about going overseas? Can they eat *mala tang* whenever they want?"

Guo Hong laughed. "That's true. My sister called and said that she wanted to eat hotpot so badly it was driving her crazy. She asked me to send her the hotpot ingredients, but then it didn't taste right when she made it over there."

They chatted along the way, discussing everything from hotpot base ingredients to Chunxi Road Pedestrian Street, and then on to Beijing's Silk Street, and finally to the concert put on by singers from Hong Kong and Taiwan at the

Chengdu Gymnasium a few days earlier. As their conversation meandered, the sky grew dark, and the bus crawled along the mountain road with its headlights on. An Ning had not slept well the previous night, and as they got to higher and higher altitudes, she began to feel dizzy. Listening to Guo Hong's rambling, she responded wordlessly, and before she knew it, she had fallen asleep. When she awoke, the bus had already reached Batang.

Batang was a small town. Continuing on, the road came to the Jinsha River, and the area after the river was Tibetan territory. But it was dark, and they could not see anything. There was light in the doorway of the small shops and restaurants along the street, but they were all deserted, and there were few people in sight. As soon as the bus arrived, though, many men and women appeared in the light, waving frantically at the vehicle, as if they had been there all along. But the bus did not stop, leaving a trail of dust in its fading lights as it drove past.

When the bus pulled in at the quiet guesthouse, the passengers hurried to alight and check into their rooms. When it was An Ning's turn, the two-person rooms had already been taken up, and there were only four-person, six-person, or eight-person rooms left. An Ning, Guo Hong, Yu Xiulan, and her daughter registered together for a four-person room. After a while, An Ning still did not feel fully awake, but was dizzy and did not feel like going out to eat. At first, Guo Hong wanted to go out to eat, but seeing that An Ning wasn't going, she decided not to go either.

Yu Xiulan said, "I have guokui pancake, a Shaanxi specialty, here. Let's eat and go to bed." She took out some guokui from her bag and invited An Ning and Guo Hong to eat. Each guokui was as thick as a brick. An Ning and Guo Hong had never seen anything like it before, and they found it a little off-putting. Seeing their reluctance, Yu Xiulan took two pieces and shoved them into their hands.

"It's good. It can keep for a month. Taste it and you'll see."

Seeing Yu Xiulan's enthusiasm, An Ning decided to try it, even though she had no appetite. The flavor wasn't bad.

Guo Hong took a bite too. She said, "It's delicious! Really good." Then she added, "But it's a little dry. I'll go get a few packs of instant noodles and we can soak those to go with it."

After taking a couple of bites, An Ning had a bit more of an appetite. She called to Guo Hong, who was walking out the door, "Bring a couple of packets of Fuling mustard greens."

When Guo Hong came back with the instant noodles and mustard greens, Yu Xiulan and her daughter were too embarrassed to eat them and tried to give Guo

Hong money for the food. Guo Hong grew a little anxious and retorted, "Hey, fate brought us to stay together. Why isn't it okay eat my instant noodles, but it was okay for me to eat your guokui?"

An Ning said, "We still have a long journey ahead of us. We became sisters the moment we met. Let's not make things awkward now."

By the time the four women finished their meal, it was late at night. Without so much as washing their faces, they went to bed. It started raining in the middle of the night, but they were tired after such a long day bouncing along the road, and none of them were the least bit bothered by the rain. When they woke the next morning, bad news was waiting at their door.

An Ning had tossed and turned all night, not sleeping peacefully at all, and she woke up several times during the night. When she woke, it was because she felt a man pressing heavily on her, trying to make love to her, waking her with a start. When she opened her eyes, she saw that there was no man on top of her, and the room was dark. It was quiet on the plateau at night, aside from Guo Hong's snoring. Strange! Why did she have such a dream? Was it because she was soon to be married and her sexual desire had been awakened? Later, she determined that it might have been a hallucination brought on by altitude sickness and a lack of oxygen.

The man in her dream was a little vague, like Li Qingge, but also not like him. Once before, she had been shocked when she woke one morning to find Li Qingge leaning over to look at her, and she had been suspicious about what he had done to her when she was drunk. He swore he didn't do anything, but if that was true, why did he blush?

Thinking of Li Qingge, she went back to sleep. She dreamed she was on a snowy mountain with him. He walked in front, and she trailed behind him. She wanted to ask him to wait for her, but no matter how desperately she shouted, she couldn't make a sound. He didn't seem to know she was behind him. She pursued desperately, but the snowy mountain was very slippery, and each time she climbed up to the same spot, she slid back down again. Seeing him disappear over the crest of the mountain, she burst into tears. When she wiped away her tears, she saw her sister An Jing beckoning her to the spot where Li Qingge had disappeared. She shouted again, this time to An Jing. An Jing leaned over, and she tumbled down from the top of the mountain and crashed into An Ning, and then the two sisters continued sliding down the mountain together.

When she woke up, An Ning was covered in a cold sweat. It was bright now, and the rain had stopped. The nightmare was not scary—a dream was, after all, nothing more than a dream. What was scary was the bad news they received in the morning.

There had been a landslide up ahead, at Haitong Gully, and the road was damaged. The women were only now made aware that they would not be able to continue their journey.

They didn't know what to do. Guo Hong anxiously paced the room, cursing both heaven and earth, especially that damned road; Yu Xiulan anxiously went in and out of the room, trying to find more information. Xiaoxue was the only one who wasn't affected. She just sat alone on the bed, folding little paper cranes. Xiulan came back into the room and said it would be at least three days before the road was opened up again.

An Ning didn't want to wait around like this. She said to Guo Hong and Xiulan, "You wait in the room. I'll see if I can find a way."

She walked out of the guesthouse. There were many passengers standing at the door, all of them at a loss, but unwilling to wait forever. An Ning stood with them and listened for a while, but when she didn't hear anything new, she started to walk along the street on her own. There were houses on both sides of the street, some Tibetan style and some Han style, but all of them low and old, and with traces of soot on the doorframes and walls. On closer look, she saw that the buildings were either restaurants or shops; very few were actually residential places. It had been dark when they arrived the night before, and she couldn't see the scene clearly, and that had created a mysterious beauty that hung about the place. Now that it was exposed in the sunlight, it felt more desolate and barren. An Ning didn't want to stand looking at the street scene, but she wasn't sure what she wanted to do instead. As she walked, she saw two soldiers loading items into a Mitsubishi vehicle. One of the soldiers was a veteran, and one a new recruit.

An Ning's heart suddenly warmed, and she walked over to greet them. "Comrades, can I ask you a question?"

The recruit turned to look at her. He held a box of instant noodles in his hands. "What's up?"

Hearing from his accent that he too was from Sichuan, a warm feeling again flooded over An Ning. She immediately switched from Mandarin to Sichuan dialect. "Is the road ahead really damaged?"

"Yes. There was a landslide. Didn't you hear?"

"Yes, I heard. But I'm wondering, when do you think it will be repaired?"

"The armed police are rushing to do the repair work. It will take at least two or three days."

"So long?"

The veteran took the box from the recruit, put it into the car, and said, "This sort of landslide is not a big deal on the Sichuan-Xizang Line. You haven't seen a big one yet. Sometimes half the mountain collapses, and you can't travel for ten days or two weeks. Now, with the traffic force of the armed police protecting the road, it's much better. We should be able to finish these repairs soon."

An Ning asked, "How far is the landslide from here?"

The recruit said, "Not far. Twenty or thirty miles from here, just after the Jinsha River."

An Ning noticed that their uniforms were a little different from Li Qingge's. She asked, "Which division are you from?"

"The Sichuan-Xizang Military Station."

The two soldiers had finished packing their things and were opening the door to get into the car. An idea suddenly came to An Ning. Grabbing the car door, she said to the soldier, "My husband is a soldier too. He's with the armed police who built the road ahead. We family members are anxious to get there. Could you give us a ride?"

The veteran looked at An Ning. "You're married to someone in the armed police?"

An Ning said, "Yes, there are two other wives and a daughter waiting at the guesthouse too."

The recruit said, "We have a good relationship with the armed police—one of us running about while the other builds roads. Like our squad leader always says, we're two gourds on the same vine."

The veteran thought for a while, then said, "We can give you a lift, but we need to tell our commanding officer."

"Where's your commanding officer?"

"At the military depot."

"I'll go tell him."

The old soldier swung his head toward the vehicle and said causally, "Get in, then."

When An Ning went with them to the military depot, she saw that their "commanding officer" was a dark-faced colonel. She took out her press pass and said that she had come to the Sichuan-Xizang Line to conduct interviews, and the two women with her were the wives of soldiers, here to visit their husbands. She did not mention Guo Hong's plans for a divorce, nor did she mention her own marriage plans. If she had said anything about Guo Hong's divorce, the colonel would have been disgusted, and that would have messed up the whole plan. As for her own marriage, there was no need to mention it, not only because she didn't want anyone to know about it, but also because her identity as a reporter was enough. There was no need to add more weight to their case; the real weight was that Guo Hong and Yu Xiulan were wives of soldiers. That was enough. An Ning knew that soldiers felt sorry for military wives, and they wouldn't just sit idly by when something like this happened.

Sure enough, as soon as she finished speaking, the colonel said, "It's no problem to take you ladies there." Then he added, "The problem is, the landslide area is very dangerous. How will you get past it once you get there? How will you move forward from there?"

An Ning said, "Don't worry about that, we know people with the armed police. They'll help us. You can just drop us off there."

In fact, An Ning didn't know any of Li Qingge's men, and she didn't know what would happen once she got there, but she knew the vehicle must have some way to move ahead on the mountain. This was just the sort of person she was—always believing that once she made up her mind to do a thing, she should just do it, and there would be a way to get it done. She had no ideas at all when she woke up in the morning, and hadn't she secured a spot in a vehicle for them now?

Hearing what An Ning said, the colonel was relieved. "Fine, I'll arrange a car to take you there."

When An Ning returned to the guesthouse in the Mitsubishi and told Guo Hong and Yu Xiulan about her idea, the two women were very excited. Guo Hong hugged An Ning, and almost wanted to kiss her. She asked how An Ning had arranged the car. An Ning smiled, but said nothing. Though Guo Hong was itching to know, she didn't ask more. She even seemed impressed by An Ning's mysterious air.

They took a Mitsubishi car to the landslide area, arriving in less than an hour. Once it had dropped them off, the car returned to Batang. It was noon, and the sun beat down on them, numbing their scalps. An Ning and the others picked up their bags and continued down the road. Dozens of vehicles were stuck on the road, including both local trucks and military vehicles. Some people took the opportunity to work on their trucks, while others boiled water on the roadside to cook a meal, using a blowtorch and several stones as a makeshift stove. A few were urinating on the wheels of their vehicles. But most of the men were idle, and the sight of three women and a girl walking down the road was striking.

A man said to them, "The road ahead is damaged. You can't get through."

Guo Hong said, "We'd like to go over and take a look."

A man who stood beside the first whispered, "It must be to see a man. Otherwise, they wouldn't be so impatient."

All three women heard, but they pretended not to as they continued on their way. They felt awkward as they passed the row of male eyes. An Ning thought that if she were alone, she might not have been able to keep walking. But soon the road came to an end; there was no way forward.

It was not actually that there was no road. A dozen or so meters of the road had slid down with the landslide, and that strip was now in the wrong position to connect with the rest of the road. There were dozens of vehicles parked on the other side of the road, waiting to come over, and dozens of armed policemen in camouflage uniforms were rushing to make repairs. Most of them had removed their shirts, revealing red backs. A few bulldozers spitting black smoke shuttled back and forth across the scene. It looked like they were trying to carve out another path on the hillside.

If Li Qingge were here, would he take off his shirt like the other men? An Ning wondered what he would look like without his shirt.

Thinking of this, she took out her camera, chose an angle, and started shooting. Guo Hong and Yu Xiulan were anxious to get across, but when they saw that An Ning was so eager to take photos, they couldn't so anything, they just stood waiting for her.

Seeing someone taking photos, a soldier ran over, shouting, "It's very dangerous here. You need to clear the area now."

An Ning put the camera away. She did not leave immediately, but stood there waiting. The soldier stopped five or six meters away from An Ning. Blushing, he looked awkwardly at her. Li Qingge had said they rarely saw women on the mountain. Sometimes, they would see a woman in a vehicle, but before they could get a good look, the car had passed, leaving only the shadow of a woman.

The soldier talking to her now looked no more than eighteen or nineteen years old, and he looked very immature. An Ning smiled at him. His face turned red, but his demeanor was serious.

"It's not safe here. Please stay back."

An Ning asked, "Will there be more landslides?"

"Very possible. It's always possible," the soldier said.

An Ning looked up the mountain. It didn't seem possible to her. She said to the soldier, "We want to get to the other side."

The soldier said, "No! It's too dangerous."

"You mean your men aren't afraid of the danger?"

"We do this every day. We're experienced."

"Well, since you're so experienced, you can get us across."

The soldier said, "Please go away, quickly. If my superiors see you, they're going to send me back to basic training."

Just as he said this, a lieutenant appeared. The soldier rushed to explain, "Sir, they want to cross to the other side, but I've advised against it and asked them to leave."

The lieutenant looked at An Ning, but before he could speak, she said, "I'm a news reporter, and I've been sent to interview your troops." She pointed to where Guo Hong and the others stood in the distance and said, "They're family, here to see their husbands. We want to get to the other side. Can you help us?"

The lieutenant looked at the two women standing in the distance. He asked An Ning, "Family? Whose family?"

An Ning said, "One of them is married to a soldier in Bomi. I don't know his name. The other is married to a captain in Baima, Deng Gang."

The captain's eyes lit up. "Deng Gang? I know him. He's my old platoon leader."

An Ning was overjoyed. She quickly called Guo Hong, "Hey, sis, come here! He knows Deng Gang!"

Guo Hong came over, and the lieutenant greeted her enthusiastically. "Ma'am, my name is Liu Hao. I used to be a soldier under the captain."

Guo Hong blushed, unsure how to answer. Seeing her embarrassment, An Ning quickly said to the lieutenant, "Can you get us across now?"

The lieutenant turned to look at the collapsed section, then up the hillside. He said, "Alright, I'll take you there. But we've got to move quickly, and you have to keep up."

An Ning thanked him, then she hurried to call Yu Xiulan and her daughter over. The lieutenant beckoned another soldier to him and told the three women, "Give all your bags to us."

The women tried to refuse, saying they could carry their own things. The lieutenant cut off the discussion, grabbing the bags from An Ning and Guo Hong and putting them on his back. The other soldier followed the lieutenant's example, snatching Yu Xiulan's bag and putting it on his own back. The lieutenant took Xiaoxue's hand and said to the soldier, "I'll take the lead. You bring up the rear. And keep your eyes open!"

Then he said to the three women, "You ready? Let's move!"

He pulled Xiaoxue to the front, and the three women walked behind him, with the soldier in the rear. They quickly entered the collapsed area. When they came to a difficult spot, the lieutenant carried Xiaoxue across on his back. The three women looked nervous, but they joined hands and stumbled after him. The soldiers who were repairing the road stopped to watch. The lieutenant shouted at them, "What are you looking at? Come help your squadron leader's family!"

Several soldiers rushed forward and helped each of the women move forward. One of the soldier's asked, "The squadron leader is here?"

"Nonsense! It's the family of Captain Deng. Now shut up!"

The soldier whispered, "I'm just saying she doesn't look like the family who was here last year. I thought the squadron leader must have made a change."

The lieutenant didn't hear what he said. Before long, they had passed through the collapsed area. When they found a safe place to stand, An Ning found that her back was soaked.

The lieutenant said to the women, "That's as far as we can take you. Our rescue mission is on a tight schedule. We can't leave our post. I'm really sorry."

He pointed to the road ahead and said, "There must be some cars up there who are making their way back. You can hitch a ride with one of them and continue on your journey from there. You can get a bus at Zuogong."

An Ning said, "Thank you. Don't worry. We'll find a way from here."

The lieutenant asked Guo Hong, "Do you want me to contact Captain Deng on the radio and ask him to come get you?"

Guo Hong said, "No, I don't want him to know I'm here."

The lieutenant smiled and said, "I see! It's a surprise attack."

An Ning's heart dropped. It was an ambush. She wasn't sure Deng Gang's defenses could withstand the attack. An Ning had some sympathy for Deng Gang, even though she had never met him.

They said goodbye to the lieutenant and went on their way. Before they had gone too far, they came across two Dongfeng trucks that were turning back. They asked and found out that the trucks were headed back to Zuogong. An Ning approached the drivers and negotiated, and it was agreed that the women could hitch a ride, but it would cost a hundred yuan each. The money was not a problem. What was a problem was that the truck could only seat two passengers beside the driver, and there was already one passenger in the front truck, leaving space for just one more. This meant that one of them would be left behind. An Ning spoke up first, volunteering to give up her spot, which would allow Yu Xiulan and her daughter to travel in the back truck and Guo Hong in the front. Guo Hong and Xiulan were uneasy over this arrangement.

An Ning said, "You go ahead. I'll find another way, and we'll meet up again in Zuogong."

Guo Hong and the others left then, leaving An Ning on her own.

The sun was setting in the west, casting long shadows on the hillside. An Ning continued her journey alone. The landslide area receded into the distance behind her, until she could hardly hear the bulldozers anymore. The blocked vehicles were also left behind. From time to time, something moved in the bushes by the roadside, and some birds she didn't recognize flew overhead, their calls unfamiliar. An Ning suddenly felt lonely and afraid. She looked all around as she walked, hoping for some vehicle to come along, but the road was empty. As she walked into the valley, it grew darker, and the fear that she would not find a vehicle before it was dark increased.

As she worried over this, she finally saw a truck approaching from the opposite direction. She was thrilled, as if someone had come to save her.

She raised her hands and waved. The truck stopped, and a young man stuck his head out and asked, "What's wrong?"

It was Sichuan dialect again. Why was it that the Sichuan dialect was heard all along the Sichuan-Xizang Line? She was used to hearing Sichuan dialect, and she never felt anything unusual about it. But hearing it here, now, she felt it had a friendlier sound.

An Ning said, "Sir, the road ahead is damaged and we can't pass."

"I thought it was strange that I hadn't passed any cars this afternoon," the driver said. "Do you know when it will be repaired?"

"I heard it will take two or three days."

The driver hesitated, considering whether to try to go on.

"There are a lot of vehicles backed up at the site. Some have already turned back."

The driver looked at An Ning up and down, then smiled and said, "You mean, you think I should go back too, so you can hitch a ride?"

"You're so smart, sir!" An Ning said. "You could just drop me off in Zuogong. I have friends waiting for me there."

The driver waved and said, "Get in."

17

The driver said his surname was Peng, and he was from Zhongjiang. He had been running on the Sichuan-Xizang Line for five years, specializing in transporting timber. An Ning called him "Master Peng," as was customary with drivers, but he said, "Don't call me that. I'm just a few years older than you. Just all me Peng Liang." So she called him Peng Liang.

Peng Liang was a warm-hearted fellow. He asked An Ning if she was hungry. She said, "I didn't feel hungry while I was walking on the road, but now that I'm settled into the truck and can relax, I am a little hungry."

Peng Liang took a pack of crackers from a pouch and handed it to An Ning. "Have some crackers for now. We can stop for a bowl of noodles when we get to Mangkang."

An Ning didn't like crackers, but she was too embarrassed to refuse, so she ate one. She took some chocolate from her bag and handed it to Peng Liang. "Have some chocolate," she said.

Peng Liang kept his hands on the steering wheel and, looking straight ahead, he opened his mouth, indicating that she should put the chocolate in. Feeling it was a suggestive action, An Ning hesitated, but then decided it was no big deal and stuffed the chocolate into his mouth.

When he had finished the chocolate, Peng Liang said, "Light a cigarette for me."

She knew what he meant. Sometimes when he went out on an interview, the driver would ask her to light a cigarette for him. She asked, "Where are the cigarettes?"

"In my jacket pocket. You can take it."

She took out the packet, Jiaozi brand, and took a cigarette from the pack. "Where's the lighter?"

"In my pants pocket."

Another suggestive action, even more so than before, but it wouldn't be nice of her to refuse to do it. When she took out the lighter, Peng Liang looked at her, smiling slightly, and there was definite heat in his eyes. It made her a little nervous. She put the cigarette in her mouth, lit it, and inhaled, then she coughed. Peng Liang laughed. He took the cigarette from her and took a greedy drag. It was unclear if the greed was born of his addiction, or of the imprint of An Ning's lips on the butt.

As he smoked, Peng Liang said, "I can see at a glance that you're a lady."

A lady. That was very reassuring. He must be cultured, and a cultured person wouldn't hurt a woman. An Ning intentionally complimented him. "I didn't realize you were so cultured."

"Me? Cultured? If I was cultured, I would have gone to university. It was because of my lack of culture that I missed out on the entrance exam by three points and had to become a driver."

From what he said, he seemed to quite enjoy being called a cultured person.

"I think you're very cultured, a quite graceful girl. What do you do?"

"I'm a reporter for the *Rongcheng Daily*."

Peng Liang said, "I knew you weren't an ordinary girl. You wouldn't be traveling alone if you were. There are four types of people I meet on the road: those going to Lhasa for pilgrimage, tourists in Xizang, those going to visit relatives in Xizang, and reporters. Pilgrims wouldn't take my car. They have to throw themselves on the ground as they go, kowtowing all the way to Lhasa, and it takes them six or twelve months to get there. Journalists and tourists take my car, sometimes even foreigners."

It grew dark as they talked. A light appeared ahead, and Peng Liang said they had reached Mangkang. It was a small county town. They stopped and ate a bowl of noodles at a Sichuan restaurant on the side of the road, then continued on their way.

Peng Liang said, "It's faster to travel at night. Running wheels cover longer distances at night, and you can reach Zuogong before twelve."

But as they came over the mountain, the truck suddenly broke down. Peng Liang got out to check.

Swathed in cold air, he said, "The truck has some trouble. We can't go on."

What bad luck! Yesterday it was the bus breaking down, and today it was a landslide. Now that she had finally hitched a ride, this truck broke down too.

An Ning asked, "We're going to have to stay overnight on the mountain?"

Peng Liang lit a cigarette and said, "Looks like it."

Frustrated, An Ning leaned back on the cushion, saying nothing. Peng Liang tried to comfort her, saying, "If we're lucky and someone comes by, we can buy the parts we need and won't have to spend the night here."

But it was pitch black outside. There were no lights to be seen for dozens of miles. Who knew when someone would come.

Peng Liang smoked in the dark, his face appearing intermittently in its flickering light. He stood alone, muttering, "So unlucky! I felt something soft under the wheels when I finished lunch in Mangkang and started the truck. I saw that dead dog I'd run over. Damn! Who knew it would lie there sleeping under the truck. This is the worst thing that can happen to us drivers. I was so nervous all along the way, and sure enough, it didn't go well. There was that landslide, and now the truck is broken down."

An Ning had never been superstitious, but in the mystical land of Xizang, she had seen so many things, and she was beginning to ask herself why. She didn't know how to comfort Peng Liang.

An Ning's head started to hurt, as if a nerve had suddenly been pulled. She asked Peng Liang, "What mountain is this?"

"Mount Dongda."

"What's the altitude?"

"Over five thousand meters."

No wonder she had a headache. She worried she wouldn't be able to handle it if they stayed here all night.

"Turn on the lights. I'm afraid of the dark."

Things had been fine when the lights were off. It was after they were turned on that the trouble started. When the two white beams shot forward, An Ning noticed that there were two black dots wriggling in the white light. Thinking it was the dizziness making her see things, she rubbed her eyes and looked again. The two black dots had grown bigger and were drawing nearer.

"What's that?" An Ning exclaimed.

"Wolves." Peng Liang was not surprised, as if he had known all along that the wolves were there.

"Oh god! What do we do?"

"There are many wolves on Mount Dongda. As long as we don't open the doors everything will be fine."

The wolves came closer and closer to the light, until their green eyes were visible. Involuntarily, An Ning leaned toward Peng Liang. He laughed and put his arm around her. That pulled her out of her state of shock, and she moved away.

Looking at Peng Liang calmly, she asked, "Aren't wolves afraid of light? Why aren't they scared of the headlights?"

Pretending to smoke, Peng Liang withdrew his hand from An Ning's shoulder. "These wolves are always on the road. They're used to seeing headlights, so they aren't scared. But they are afraid of fire. If you don't believe me, watch this."

With that, he picked up a blowtorch and opened the door. An Ning shouted, "Don't get out of the truck!"

He ignored her. Getting out of the vehicle, he lit the blowtorch and walked toward the wolf, blazing torch in hand. The wolves ran away.

He returned to the truck and said, "See, the wolves are afraid of fire, aren't they?"

An Ning admired his bravery. She said, "Yeah, you're a big man, but you don't have to be so reckless."

"I've seen this sort of thing a lot, so I know how to deal with them," Peng Liang said. "But after a while, they'll be back."

He added, "We shouldn't keep the lights on. We won't be able to start the truck if we do."

As soon as the lights were turned off, the darkness pressed down on the mountain, making it hard to breathe. It got colder and colder, making An Ning shiver. She held on, hoping for someone to come. But the world was drowned in darkness, and there was no hope in sight. Her head started hurting again. She huddled there, waiting for her luck to turn.

Peng Liang said nothing, but just smoked one cigarette after another. The sky gradually grew brighter, and a full moon rose in front of the truck. The moon on the plateau was very different from that seen from the interior. It was very large and bright. An Ning had never seen such a beautiful moon. But its beauty was soon destroyed. Two black ears appeared beneath the full moon. The wolves were back. One of them crouched on the hood, staring at the people inside the cab with its green eyes. The other drifted under the truck. An Ning wondered why the wolves on the plateau didn't howl. It was the first time she had been in such close proximity to a wolf.

Frightened, she said in a trembling voice, "They're here again. I'm scared. Drive them away."

Peng Liang lit the lighter, and the wolves fled. An Ning shuddered, her entire body shaking uncontrollably.

"Cold?" Peng Liang asked.

"No."

"You can hardly talk, and you say you aren't cold. Come, move over here."

He pulled her into his arms, touching her chest with both hands.

An Ning struggled to break away. She said angrily, "Don't take advantage!"

"If I don't take advantage, wouldn't that make you think less of me?"

He pulled her to him again. She tried to break free, but couldn't. "You can't do this. I'm a reporter."

"Officials are scared of reporters. I'm not. Last month, I slept with a female painter who hitched a ride."

An Ning shouted, "My husband is an armed police officer with the construction crew up ahead. If he finds out, you can be sure he won't let you off."

Peng Liang suddenly stopped. "Your husband is an armed police officer?"

"He's a squadron commander. He's with the troops up ahead, building the road. To tell you the truth, I came here for our wedding."

Peng Liang suddenly covered his head and said nothing for a long time. After a while, he raised his head and said to An Ning, "I'm really sorry. I didn't know your husband was an armed police officer."

An Ning said, "You look like a good person. I never imagined you would be so bad."

"This is just the second time I've done it. The last time, with the painter, she wanted it too. I'm sorry. I'll never do it again. Please don't tell your husband. Last April, I was blocked by a heavy snow. I was stuck on the mountain for three days and three nights, and the armed police rescued me. They saved my life. Please, promise me you won't tell your husband."

An Ning turned her head away, ignoring him.

"If you don't agree, I'll get on my knees and beg." He really did try to kneel.

An Ning said, "Fine, I promise. But you really can't harass women like this in the future."

"I won't. I wouldn't dare!"

Peng Liang started the truck. It immediately started up.

Surprised, An Ning asked, "Didn't you say the truck had broken down?"

"I lied. I just wanted to take advantage of you."

"You're horrible!"

As they drove, Peng Liang said, "I know I'm horrible, but it's you women who taught me to be so bad." As they went on, he told her his story.

Peng Liang had formerly worked for someone else, a fellow from Sichuan who was in the timber business along the Sichuan-Xizang Line. His boss wasn't very cultured, but he had a good mind and made a lot of money in business. He had a wife and two sons, and he kept another woman in Bomi. The other woman was very young and beautiful. With the boss's money, she had bought two houses in her hometown, Shuangliu, one for her parents who lived there in the countryside, and one that she rented out for the time being, with plans to later live there herself. The boss was good to her, but she was not loyal to him. As soon as he left, she seduced Peng Liang. She was his first. He felt guilty and sorry for his boss, but he couldn't resist the temptation either.

Three years earlier, there had been a flood in Bomi. The boss's timber had floated on the floodwaters. Anxious, the boss tied one end of a fuse from the explosives around his waist, securing the other to a tree, and then waded through the water to retrieve the timber. But he forgot that the fuse was made of paper. When it was soaked, it couldn't hold, and the boss was swept away. He could not have survived, but the corpse was not recovered. The woman didn't cry, and she didn't ask people to keep looking for him.

Peng Liang had assumed that, with the boos gone, he and the woman could be together peacefully. Who would have imagined that she would suddenly take the boss's money and leave one night without so much as a goodbye. Peng Liang came down with an illness and was very sick. When he finally got back on his feet, he put the money he had been saving for years into opening a restaurant in Bomi. Business was good, and he earned more than a hundred thousand yuan a year. He eventually met a young woman named Xiaohong in a karaoke bar. Seeing that she was beautiful and honest, he persuaded her to quit her job in the karaoke bar and join him at the restaurant. She was very happy, and she moved to the restaurant the next day. Not wanting him to worry, she gave him her ID card to hold on to. When he looked at her ID, he saw that her name was not Xiaohong, but Liu Xiang. She explained that none of the girls at the karaoke bar used their real names. She did everything very diligently, and that was how she did Peng Liang too. Peng Liang had never in his wildest dreams imagined she was still a virgin, but when he found out that she was, he was even more at ease. The two planned to go back to their hometown to get a marriage license at the end of the year.

Liu Xiang was very capable, and she managed the restaurant in a very orderly way. Business kept improving, and Peng Liang gradually put the entire business solely in her hands. Maybe it was just bad luck, or maybe if Peng Liang had properly managed the restaurant business himself, things wouldn't have turned out like they did. Either way, he started to feel an itch. He wanted to buy a car for transportation, so he decided to buy a second-hand truck and start up his old business again. At first, it was perfect: the woman ran the restaurant and the man ran the transportation business, and there was income from two sources. Everything was going well.

It was later that things started to happen. It was coming to the end of the year. Peng Liang wanted to make one last run, and then they would go back to his hometown and get married. But when he came back, Liu Xiang was gone. He immediately thought of his former boss's mistress. Would Liu Xiang just leave without saying goodbye, like she had done?

In a panic, he went to the owner of the restaurant next door, and the owner of that restaurant said, "Your place has been closed for several days."

A buzzing sound exploded in Peng Liang's head. He knew something was wrong. He hurried back to check on things in the house. Everything was there, but the bank passbook and the cash were gone. He took Liu Xiang's ID card to the county public security bureau to report the case. The people there told him the ID card was a fake.

Peng Liang said, "Women hurt me. I wanted to show them how it felt."

An Ning did not say anything. Peng Liang had a lot more to say as they drove along, but she did not say a word. Finally, she fell asleep.

When she woke, the car had stopped at the gate of a courtyard. The moon was overhead, and the sky was no longer dark. She thought it must be near dawn.

She heard Peng Liang say to someone standing beside the truck, "She is the family of one of the armed police, can you let her stay here for the night?"

He turned his head to An Ning and said, "This is an armed police maintenance squadron, the same unit as your husband."

The man beside the truck stepped onto the running board and looked inside. It was a soldier.

"Three came in last night, and now one more," the soldier said.

An Ning was overjoyed. "Is one of them named Guo Hong?"

The soldier answered, "I don't know their names. I just heard that it's the wife of Captain Deng."

Excited, An Ning said, "It's them."

18

The next day, the squadron sent a jeep to take them to Baima. The driver was an old soldier with a red badge on his shoulder. His name was Wang Kang, and he had been driving on the Sichuan-Xizang Line for nine years. He was a third level non-commissioned officer.

Along the way, they often encountered soldiers from armed police repairing roads. Each time, Wang Kang slowed and sounded the horn as a way of greeting.

An Ning asked, "Do you all know each other?"

Wang Kang replied, "I know some of them, but not all." Then he added, "But whether we know each other or nor, we all say hello. Don't talk about a comrade-in-arms. In a deserted place like this, I'll even say hello to any rabbit I see. Out here on the plateau, you'll have warm feelings toward any living thing. You'll feel that way too after stay out here for a while."

An Ning already felt that way. She and Guo Hong had hugged each other excitedly when they were reunited, almost in tears. They had only been separated for a day, but they felt like they were being reunited after a long absence. If it had been a longer separation, the reunion might not have been quite as exciting. In the interior regions, there was never any of such feeling. It seemed that the plateau really was a place where people could easily become close.

Wang Kang continued, "It's not just me. All the drivers in the army and the local drivers are the same, always honking to greet the soldiers who are building the roads. It's much harder to build roads up here than it is to run along the route. It can even be life threatening. All the drivers who run the Sichuan-Xizang Line know this. We honk as a way of showing respect."

Though Wang Kang greeted the soldiers along the way, he never stopped. He said he wanted to hurry and take advantage of the good weather, because the Sichuan-Xizang Line was so unpredictable and problems could often crop up. If that happened, they wouldn't reach Baima before dark. Baima was the first stop for the women, because Guo Hong's husband, Deng Gang, was there. The second stop was Bomi, where Yu Xiulan and the daughter were going. The last stop was Dongjiu, which was An Ning's destination. Dongjiu was the end of the section of road that the troops maintained and protected, and Li Qingge was in that squadron.

In the afternoon, they arrived at a place called Bangda. An Ning asked Wang Kang, "Isn't there an airport in Bangda?"

Wang Kang said, "Yes, to the right at the fork up ahead and past the Bangda Prairie. That's where the airport is."

When they stopped to rest, An Ning felt a little breathless. Wang Kang asked them to order food at the roadside stall while he went to refuel at the military station, saying they should eat before they left. Before he left, he warned, "The altitude is high here. Don't wander off."

Bangda was a well-known spot, but it was small, with just a few restaurants and shops. They sat at a Sichuan restaurant and asked for boiled fish and two greens. Strangely, the vegetables were more expensive than the fish. An Ning asked the restauranteur why, and he told her that vegetables had to be brought over from the interior, so of course they were more expensive. There were some that grew in Yehe Gully that were sold by the bucket, so much that you could buy as much as you wanted, and they were, of course, much cheaper. An Ning recalled An Jing once saying they were "fishing in troubled waters," as if they were on the Bangda Prairie back then.

An Jing had told her that the troupe had traveled all the way to the Bangda Prairie squadron and performed there. The squadron had no food at the time, so Li Qingge said, "Wait here. I'll go catch some fish. I'll be back in a while."

Li Qingge grabbed a shovel from the back of the tent and found a plastic bucket, then walked out. Puzzled, An Jing had followed him out and asked, "Why do you need a shovel to catch fish?"

Li Qingge smiled mysteriously and said, "It's my secret weapon."

Curious, An Jing shouted and said she wanted to go with him. Li Qingge had no choice but to let her follow him to a meadow. As they walked along in silence, she began to feel it even more strange.

"You mean there are fish in the grass?"

Li Qingge said, "You'll see when we get there."

He told her that they used to go fishing in the river to improve their diets, Later, when there was a fishing accident, it was stipulated that they were not allowed to fish in the river anymore.

He said the fishing on the plateau was different from that of the interior, where they used fishing rods and caught one fish at a time. Here, they hung more than a dozen hooks on a rope and tossed it into the water, holding the ropes steady by stepping on them. Then, before you knew it, there were a bunch of fish to take back and cook up a big pot of stew, enough for the whole squadron to have a good meal.

An Jing asked, "How come the fish on the plateau can be caught so easily?"

Li Qingge smiled and said, "Hypoxia. The altitude sickness makes them stupid."

After they had walked about a kilometer, a small stream appeared in the grass. It was small and wound like chicken guts, deep in the grass.

Li Qingge said, "We're here. This is it."

He put the shovel and bucket on the grass and started rolling up his sleeves. An Jing squatted beside the stream and looked down. It was a clear, shallow stream. She looked for a hint of the fish, but the water was clear, and there were no fish. An Jing did not believe there were fish in the stream at all.

Without explanation, Li Qingge started to dig in the soil with the shovel. When he had blocked both ends of the stream, he used the shovel to stir the water back and forth until the clear current turned turbid. He then threw the shovel aside and knelt on the ground, dragging his hands through the water.

Hey! That was it! Li Qingge caught a fish from the water. An Jing saw the floundering fish and said excitedly, "Let me get one!"

She rolled up her sleeves and put her hands into the water. She caught one too, and then another. Her cheerful laughter rolled over the grassland. In no time, the bucket was full, but An Jing was not finished; she continued to kneel, hand dragging the water.

Li Qingge said, "Alright, the bucket is full."

Seeing that there was no more room in the bucket, An Jing put the last fish she had caught back into the stream.

Curious, she asked, "At first, there was no sign of the fish. How did you know they were here?"

He said, "Because when it's cold, they hide in the muddy reeds by the stream. When I stirred the water, they became confused and had to run out. It's what we call 'fishing in troubled waters.'"

An Jing and the rest gave a very romantic performance that night. An Ning was very envious as she listened to An Jing talk about it, but now that she had come to Bangda, she couldn't find that sort of romance. All she felt was a headache and tightness in her chest. Was it because Li Qingge was not around?

After lunch at Bangda, it was time to get back on the road. Guo Hong saw a public phone in a roadside canteen and said, "Wait a minute. I need to make a call." And she hurried over to the phone.

At first, An Ning did not give any thought to who Guo Hong was calling. What caught her attention was the fact that there was a phone at such a high altitude.

Wang Kang said, "We've only had a phone here the past few years. Before, it was really difficult to make calls. There were just two phones in Zuogong County, one for the post office and one for the county Party committee and county government to use in the daytime. At night, the phone was for public use, and dozens of people all wanted to call at the same time. It was really difficult to get to make a call, and when someone got the chance, they talked endlessly and it was difficult to get them to hang up. Every night, the squadron leader designated a special person to dial the phone, and he dialed over and over. With all that dialing, they went through several telephones a year. Now with the fiberoptic cable, it's much easier to make calls."

Wang Kang added, "Now there are not only phones. There's also a transfer station, and you can make calls from your cell phone."

"Really?" An Ning said.

She turned on her phone, and sure enough, there was a signal. *Beep beep.* Three text messages came in. At one glance, she could see that they came from the editorial director, Yuan Ye, asking where she had been, what she had learned, and so on, but there was nothing else. She thought there might be something from her mother or father, but there was nothing. There was nothing from Li Qingge either. She felt a hint of disappointment.

She turned off her phone and went to see Guo Hong. It was only then that she noticed that Guo Hong had been on the phone for a while, and she was chatting warmly with whoever on the other end, and her expression was a bit suggestive. She couldn't hear what was being said, but An Ning could guess that whoever was on the phone had something beyond and ordinary relationship with Guo Hong.

After the call ended, Guo Hong walked over, her face flushed. An Ning teased, "What are you so excited about?"

Guo Hong said solemnly, "That was my boss, Hu An."

An Ning sighed inwardly, but said nothing.

The jeep began to climb Mount Yela. There were Marnyi Stone and prayer flags on the peak, and there was a snowy mountain in the distance. The colorful prayer flags were beautiful against the sky, with an air of the sacred. They stopped on top of the mountain to take pictures, and when they looked back, Bangda looked like a leaf.

When they crossed the mountain pass, they were on the famous ninety-nine turns of the Sichuan-Xizang Line. The road led down into the Nujiang Gorge. All the roads they had been on up to this point had been ascending. Here, they would start descending. The road wound down, down, down, and the gorge got deeper and deeper, as if there were no bottom to it. At the same time, the mountain grew taller and taller, reaching into the clouds. An Ning felt like they were descending into the depths of the earth.

After one of the turns, a small Tibetan village suddenly appeared in front of them.

Want Kang said, "This is Gama Valley. There are only a dozen families in this village."

Before An Ning even really caught sight of the Tibetan houses with prayer flags fluttering on their roofs, they had already passed by the village. When she looked back, the small village was above them, and the road continued to descend.

"Do you know what Gama Valley means?"

The woman looked at each other and said, "No."

Wang Kang said, "Gama means 'moon' in Tibetan, so its Moon Valley. It's because the mountains are so high and the valley so deep, so the people in the valley don't see the sun all year, just the moon."

As he was talking it started raining. The window gradually blurred, so he turned on the windshield wipers. After a while, the light rain became a heavy rain. On closer look, they realized it wasn't rain, but hail splashing onto the windshield. An Ning was surprised by how quickly the rain had started. The sun was shining so brightly on top of the mountain a little earlier. How could it have started raining by the time they reached the valley? And how had the rain turned so suddenly into hail?

Looking out through the car window, Guo Hong asked, "Is it okay here? The road won't be damaged again, right?"

Wang Kang said, "It will be okay. This type of weather is common on the plateau, and it will pass quickly. I'm not worried about the rain here. I'm worried about the sun that will come out after the rain."

Surprised, An Ning asked, "Why?"

"The mountain here is brittle and loose. When it rains, the slopes fill with rainwater. When the sky is clear and the sun shines, the rock contracts. That's when landslides happen."

Guo Hong said, "Then don't let the sun come out. But it's never good when the rain is this heavy."

Wang Kang said, "You haven't seen a heavy rain on the plateau yet. It lasts for several days at a time, and the sky and ground are both completely covered. It's like someone poked a big hole in the sky. As soon as a flash flood breaks out, dozens of miles of highway are washed out in the blink of an eye. One year, Squadron 10 spent three months repairing a section of the road, then as soon as the flood came, it was all washed away. All of us stood in the rain crying. Even our squadron leader cried."

He went on, "But I was a little worried about the rain yesterday. It rained all day, and the sun was so bright this morning. So bright—"

Guo Hong quickly cut him off, "Stop! That's enough."

Wang Kang understood. He laughed, but he didn't say any more. Soon, it was sunny again. The road ascended from the left, passed a bridge, and slung up the slope to the right. It didn't take long for them to reach the paved road.

Wang Kang said that the road ahead was being rebuilt. He pointed to a row of wooden houses on the mountain and said, "That's the barracks of Squadron 3. They're responsible for rebuilding this section of the road. Squadron 3 is under charge of the first team. Captain Deng is with that team."

An Ning said, "You mean, we're almost there?"

"We'll be there soon. It's just a few dozen miles after we cross the Nujiang Bridge," Wang Kang said. "But this section of the road isn't easy to travel. It's a well-known landslide area."

The jeep continued its descent. An Ning suddenly saw a cloud of mist rising from the gully ahead of them. Strangely, the cloud was not white, but an earthy red.

"Why are the clouds red?"

Wang Kang was concentrating on driving, and he had not noticed it at first. When An Ning called his attention to it, he noticed the ruddy cloud.

"Uh oh! It may had collapsed up ahead again."

The women said almost in unison, "God! Why are we so unlucky?"

Wang Kang said, "Don't panic. We can only be sure when we get there. It may just be dust from the construction site."

But when they were still a kilometer from the Nujiang Bridge, the car could not go any farther. There was a line of cars backed up in front of them. Wang Kang got out of the car to ask what had happened. Sure enough, one side of the Nujiang Bridge had collapsed just a half hour earlier. What luck! Had they not stopped to eat at Bangda, they could have been caught in the landslide. Just thinking about it was enough to make a layer of cold sweat break out on An Ning's back.

With a gloomy expression, Wang Kang got back into the jeep and said, "It's collapsed again. Looks like we'll have to stay with Squadron 3 tonight."

They turned around and drove back. No one said anything. Before they had traveled far, they saw several military vehicles approaching, full of soldiers in camouflage uniforms.

Wang Kang said, "They're with Squadron 3. They're going on a rescue mission."

When they arrived at Squadron 3, the barracks were empty. Only a few cooks were busy preparing dinner in the kitchen, and a young messenger was on the phone to squadron headquarters. The messenger took the women to a room in a wooden structure, telling them it was temporary housing for family members, and they could stay there for the time being. Without further delay, he hurried back to his phone.

Dinnertime had long since passed. The food had gotten cold and been reheated, but the soldiers who had gone out on the rescue mission had still not returned. The cook made two dishes and brought them to the women's room, inviting An Ning and the others to eat. After dinner, they had no intention of going to bed, but sat in the room waiting for news. Xiaoxue folded her paper cranes, a task that never seemed to end.

At eleven that night, the officers and soldiers from the rescue mission returned. The squadron officer said that the landslide was not too serious. The area had already been fortified, and they should be able to continue their journey the following day worry-free.

When it was almost dawn, an emergency assembly whistle suddenly sounded outside. An Ning got dressed and went out to ask what was going on, only to learn that there was another landslide ahead, this one more than ten times the size of the one the previous day. The troops rushed out again.

19

The next day, the officers and soldiers of the squadron did not come back from their rescue mission. When the cook had finished preparing the meal, he sent it to the front line. When he came back, the cook told the women that this time, the collapse was so severe that half the mountain had tumbled to the Nujiang River, blocking the water's flow so that a lake several kilometers long had formed.

An Ning sent news of the disaster and rescue mission by voice call on her own phone. Then, she wrote in her notebook, *A Landslide, Right in Front of Me*.

The road was cut off, and though he had driven them this far, Wang Kang needed to return to Zuogong now.

The next day, the troops were still out on the rescue mission. The women could not just keep waiting in this spot. That evening, they found the squadron officer who had returned from the site, and they asked them to send a soldier to take them around the landslide area the next day so they could walk to Baima. The squadron officer was in a dilemma. The awkwardness was not because they had no troops to dispatch, but more because he worried that if something happened on the road, he would not be able to explain to Captain Deng. But after repeated pleas from An Ning and Guo Hong, he finally relented.

The next morning, after the rescue team set off, three women, one girl, and one soldier set out on their own mission.

20

Fang Qiang, the soldier who led the way, was a native of Hunan. When they set off, he carried a shovel with him. An Ning wondered why he carried a shovel when they were in such a hurry in their travels. She couldn't guess the purpose of the shovel until Fang Qiang picked up their backpacks and looped them over the shovel, which he then carried over his shoulder.

The squadron could only take them to the bridgehead of the Nujiang River by car, and from there, they had to rely on themselves to hike across the mountain. Walking along the Nujiang Bridge, they heard gunfire from the troops ahead. When they had crossed the bridge and exited the tunnel, Fang Qiang stopped under a cliff, put down his luggage, pointed to a place overhead, and said, "Look up there."

The women looked up the cliff and saw that it was bare. There was nothing, not even a weed.

"Look closer."

Xiaoxue's eyes were sharp. She saw it first. She clasped Yu Xiulan's hand and shouted, "I see it! It's a painting."

An Ning saw it too, then Guo Hong saw it. It was a cliff painting, five or six meters from the ground. They couldn't tell how it had been painted or what it was painted with. The picture was vivid, and very clear. In the center of the painting was a young officer dressed in a uniform from the 1950s, with a turbulent river before him and a cliff behind him. His arms were stretched upward, and he was jumping into the river, like an eagle flying in the sky. Why was there such a peculiar cliff painting in such a remote place? An Ning felt that there must be a story behind it. If not, Fang Qiang would not have pointed it out.

Without waiting for them to ask about it, Fang Qiang began the story. "Anyone who travels the Sichuan-Xizang Line knows this cliff painting. When I joined the army year before last, the instructor brought us here and told the story of this cliff painting. In the early 1950s, when the PLA came to Xizang, they had the difficult task of building the road as they came, and it cost them roughly one soldier per kilometer. It could be said that the Great Sichuan-Xizang Line is paved with the blood and lives of more than two thousand heroes."

Fang Qiang looked up at the cliff painting, his expression solemn. He went on, "I heard that when the Nujiang Bridge was being built, a technician came out at night to inspect the piers where the concrete had just been poured. He slipped and fell into the wet concrete. He tried to shout, but his mouth was filled with the sludge. He sank deeper and was soon submerged in the mire. When his comrades found him the next day, he had solidified into the pier, with only one stiff hand, reaching toward the sky, still visible. He remains embedded in the concrete even today. Later, when the bridge needed to be repaired, the soldiers in the repair crew died one after another, until only the platoon leader was left. Distraught, he jumped into the rolling waters of the Nujiang, following the comrades who had been with him day and night. To commemorate those old road construction veterans, the local Tibetan people used a traditional dye to create this painting, *A Platoon Leader Jumping into the River*, on the rock. Decades have passed, but the cliff painting remains."

It was a very short story, and Fang Qiang's telling of it was quite plain, but it made an impact on An Ning. She took out her camera and photographed the cliff painting. She had the title of her article in mind: "The Story Behind the Cliff Painting."

From there, they left the road and began walking on a foot path. The path bypassed the mountain ahead of them and went into another small valley.

Fang Qiang said, "When we get out of this valley, we'll climb a ridge, pass through an open field, then climb another mountain to reach Baima. If all goes smoothly, we'll reach Baima before dark. Strictly speaking, we won't be in Baima itself, but a little more than ten kilometers from it, but that's where the forward command post of the brigade headquarters is."

Before they had walked much farther, Fang Qiang stopped again. Turning around, he said to the women, "You rest for a while. I'll be gone for a few minutes, but I'll come back."

Fang Qiang put down the luggage and walked up the hillside with the shovel. The slope was covered with galsang flowers. Farther up, there were no flowers or plants, just exposed red rock. The dazzling snow on top of the mountain was like whipped cream on top of ice cream. Fang Qiang stopped in front of a grave and began digging in the soil with his shovel. The three women did not speak, but watched in silence. Xiaoxue picked a handful of galsang flowers on the side of the path and ran back. Xiulan whispered, "Go put them on the grave."

Xiaoxue obediently walked over and placed the flowers on the grave.

When Fang Qiang had finished tidying the soil, the group continued their journey. Several times, An Ning thought of asking Fang Qiang who was buried there, but seeing how quiet he was as they walked, she found it difficult to ask. It was only when they stopped to rest that she finally asked, unable to hold it in anymore.

Fang Qiang said, "My comrade-in-arms." Then he added, "It happened last year, when we'd only been in the army for three months."

Looking at something in the distance, he lit a cigarette. "I didn't smoke before," he said, "but after Lin Fan passed, I started. Lin Fan and I went to high school together, and we were really good friends. We were the stars of our basketball team. He was tall, our forward, and I shot well, so I was guard. We fell short on our college entrance exams. I missed admissions by twelve points, and Lin Fan missed it by just three. I didn't want to go for tutoring, but my family needed me to make some money, so I went for one of those crash courses to prepare for the exam. Later, when the recruiting officers came, I told Lin Fan, 'Let's just go into the army. We can get into the military academy.' He thought it sounded like a good idea, so we went for it. We kept it a secret, only telling our families after we were both selected. By the time they knew, the rice had been cooked, and there was no uncooking it. My family didn't say anything, but his parents wouldn't agree no matter what. His father even slapped him around for it. Lin Fan said he knew his parents did so only out of the best intentions. They wanted him to continue to study and get into university, bringing honor to all his ancestors. But he joined me in the army, and we left. Lin Fan told me on the train that he wouldn't go back if he didn't do well in the army. He wouldn't be able to face his father. After the accident, I felt so bad about it. If I hadn't dragged him into the army, who knows what university he might have been studying in now?"

"I remember, the day of the accident, it was very cold and windy, and we were lined up to build a retaining wall. Then there was a landslide. The guards sounded the emergency evacuation whistle, but because of the strong wind, Lin Fan didn't hear it. A rock hit the ground—hit him. The scene was awful. Even now, when I close my eyes, I see it. We shouted his name over and over, but he had already collapsed in a pool of blood. Half his body had been smashed by the rocks and was left paper thin. After he died, his shadow always lingered in front of me. I couldn't sleep, and I started smoking. When I went to bed, I saw his empty bunk, and I wanted to cry. When I ate, I saw the stool where he always sat, now empty, and I couldn't help but cry then either."

Fang Qiang was in tears as he spoke. The women teared up as well. Standing up, Fang Qiang wiped the tears from his eyes and said, "Let's not talk about it anymore. Talking about it only makes you sad too. Let's go."

The shovel once again came in handy when they were climbing the mountain. Each time they came to a steep slope, Fang Qiang dug out footholds with it, then helped each of the women up in turn. When Xiaoxue couldn't cross a section, Fang Qiang put her on his back and carried her across. When they came over a mountain ridge, they suddenly saw a stretch of green grass before them. A flock of sheep grazed in the distance, and a Tibetan woman stood in front of a tent, looking in the direction of the travelers. It was an idyllic picture of a highland shepherd. An Ning was so excited she wanted to shout, but she was out of breath and didn't have the energy for shouting. It was, after all, a four-thousand-meter-high plateau.

After a short rest, they walked to the shepherd's tent. The whole time they walked, the Tibetan woman waved to them, shouting something. When they got closer, they heard that she was saying, "Jinzhumami," which was what she called Fang Qiang.

When they reached the tent, An Ning could hardly contain her excitement. Before she set out on her journey, though she had read some books about Tibetan customs and knew the tent was made of thread spun from yak wool and woven into pulu, then stitched with cowhide ropes, this was the first time she had ever seen one with her own eyes. The tent was pulled open with wool ropes and nailed to the ground. Cow dung cakes were used to build walls around the tent to keep out the wind. Both tent flaps were pulled apart at the sides, which was taken as the door for entering and exiting the structure.

As they entered the tent, the smell of milk wafted into their nostrils. A wooden pole supported the center. Below it was a mud boat-shaped earthen stove. Behind the stove was a Buddhist altar. In front of the earthen stove was a fire pit with a copper pot on it. The copper pot was so hot it bubbled. There were felt mats and small Tibetan mats all around them on the floor. Their hostess bowed and spread her hands, motioning for them to sit on the mats. She busied herself with the pouring of a soapy yellow liquid from the copper pot into a cylinder with a mouth about as wide as the length from a person's waist to the floor. She then threw a few pieces of wax in as well as started twitching a wooden pestle through it. There was a plopping sound inside the cylinder.

Puzzled, Guo Hong asked Fang Qiang in a low voice, "What's she doing?"

"Making butter tea for us," Fang Qiang said. "There's a brick of tea boiling in the copper pot. She adds the yak butter and salt, then beats it with the jialuo in the dongmo. Then the butter tea is done."

Guo Hong asked, "What are the dongmo and jialuo?"

"The pestle and mortar."

Before long, the butter tea was ready, and their hostess took out several wooden bowls and poured a bowl for each of them. After their long walk, they were very thirsty. Guo Hong picked up a bowl to drink, but An Ning stopped her and signaled toward Fang Qiang. Fang Qiang was very skilled. He picked up the wooden bowl and first dipped his ring finger into the tea, flicked it several times, sprinkling the tea, and then blew lightly against the bowl, blowing away the yak butter floating on top. He then took a sip, and smiling, he muttered a few words to the hostess. The women imitated Fang Qiang, each taking a sip of her tea.

While the hostess was pouring the tea, An Ning whispered to Fang Qiang, "What did you say her to her just now?"

"It was Tibetan. It means that her butter tea is so good that the butter and tea can't be separated. It's Tibetan etiquette."

"Why did you flick your finger three times?"

"Respect for God, respect for the dragon, and respect for the earth."

An Ning suddenly recalled the phrase "suddenly enlightened." When she heard Fang Qiang's explanation, she did feel enlightened.

After drinking the butter tea and said goodbye to the shepherd, they walked several miles and came to a small stream. There was a wooden house beside the stream, and the sound of bells came from the wooden house. Curious, An Ning ran over for a look, but there was no one in the house. The ringing sound was coming from a thick wooden barrel two meters tall. The barrel had a wooden wheel, which was covered with scriptures and prayer flags, along with a string of copper bells. The water from the stream pushed the blades of the wheel, turning the flags and making the bells ring.

Fang Qiang came up behind her and said, "This is a zhuanjing building. They're everywhere. It makes the stream chant scriptures."

Fang Qiang was not very old, but he knew a lot. An Ning thought he was not such a simple fellow. She said, "You've only been a soldier for a few years. How come you know so much?"

Fang Qiang smiled and said, "It's common. If you live all year in Tibetan areas, it's impossible not to learn such things."

"Is there a monastery nearby?"

"Yes!" Fang Qiang said, pointing up the hill. "Do you see it?"

An Ning looked in the direction he was pointing and saw a temple on the horizon. There was a red patch on the hillside in front of the temple. She thought it was flowers, but on closer look, she saw that it was a group of lamas sitting on the slope. The blue sky, white clouds, green grass, red temple, and red cassocks created another picturesque scene. No wonder Li Qingge was so obsessed with photography. She thought of a title for another article: "View of the Lama Temple."

Looking at the lamas on the slope, An Ning asked, "Are they doing yoga? I heard that a snowy mountain is the best place to do yoga."

Fang Qiang was stumped by this question. He didn't know what yoga was, so he couldn't be sure. He muttered, "Maybe! We'll pass by later, so we'll see."

But by the time they climbed the mountain, the lamas had dispersed, and there was no one left on the hillside. As they passed the gates of the temple, they happened to meet the Living Buddha. The Living Buddha had a ruddy face and kind, gentle eyes. When he saw them coming, he folded his hands and took the initiative to greet them.

"Are you one of Captain Deng's soldiers?"

He spoke fluent Mandarin, to An Ning's surprise.

Fang Qiang was also surprised. "The Living Buddha knows our captain?"

"I don't just know him. We are friends. Look." He pointed to the road up the mountain. "Your Captain Deng led his men to build this road. Any visitor is our guest, and that's all the more the case for Captain Deng's people. Please, come in from the cold. You can sit at the temple and have a cup of tea before going on your way."

Fang Qiang saw that it was getting late. He said, "Please don't trouble yourselves. We need to hurry."

The Living Buddha did not insist. Smiling, he said, "Alright. I won't delay your journey."

He suddenly grew very serious. He asked, "I heard that there was another landslide in the Nujiang Valley. Was it serious?"

"Half the mountain collapsed. Our troops are rushing to repair it."

The Living Buddha shook his head and sighed. "The troops are going to suffer again."

Before they left, the Living Buddha recalled something. He called Fang Qiang.

Fang Qiang asked, "Is anything wrong, Living Buddha."

The Living Buddha glanced at the women, and then hesitated before saying anything. Finally he said, "Never mind. I'll go on my own in a few days. Please tell Captain Deng Rinpoche Tenzin sends greetings."

21

When Deng Gang came back from the construction site, he was shocked to find a woman lying on his bed. On closer look, he saw that it was Guo Hong.

She had fallen asleep fully clothed and covered with Deng Gang's cotton coat. It was already dark when he got home. He had been on a rescue mission at a construction site and had not come back for dinner. The messenger, Bai, had started to go to the construction site to get Deng Gang, but Guo Hong had stopped him.

When they arrived at Baima, Guo Hong learned that there was a problem up ahead, in Ranwu Valley, as well on the previous night. There had been an avalanche, and three kilometers of road had been destroyed. In other words, the roads both east and west of them were damaged, and they were caught in the middle. They had finally skirted around the landslide area and reached Baima, but An Ning and Yu Xiulan would still not be able to leave the following day. Moreover, according to Bai, the area to the west was all cliffs, and it was not possible to hike over the mountain. He said that there were avalanches in Ranwu Valley almost every year, and this one was relatively small. The one the previous year had been scary, destroying dozens of kilometers of road and killing fifty-three travelers.

There was nothing for An Ning and Xiulan to do but wait here for the road ahead to be cleared. The cooking crew was washing pots when they heard that the wife of the team leader had come, so they re-lit the fire and started cooking again. The head cook, Hou Qing, personally placed egg noodles before them. As the women ate the noodles, Hou Qing stood by, watching them with a smile. It made them feel a little uncomfortable. Hou Qing did not look like a head cook at all. The stereotype of a cook was a pale-skinned, plump fellow, but Hou Qing was thin and dark-skinned.

After dinner, Bai faced some difficulty. The difficulty was not because of more hardship on the road, but because there were suddenly so many women here, and there was no place to house them. There was only one row of wooden houses for the brigade, and every spot was designated, distributed, and filled based on headcount. There were no spare rooms. Squadron 2 was not far away, and the soldiers there could squeeze into a room, or even half a room, but it was not suitable for the women to stay in those conditions.

Hou Qing pulled Bai outside and asked in a low voice, "Do you know how bears die?"

Not understanding, Bai looked at Hou, "How do they die?"

"Of stupidity."

When he realized that Hou Qing was scolding him, he was displeased. "Well, you're not stupid, so what do you say?"

"Couldn't be easier," Hou Qing said, spreading his hands wide. "Let them stay in the reception room."

Bai glared at Hou. "What's the use saying that? I thought about that already. The problem is that's where the team leader and his work group stay, so I can't put the women there."

"Didn't the team leader take someone up the mountain for inspection?"

"And what do I do when they come back in the middle of the night?"

"It won't be so soon. It's not easy to travel on the mountain road. They won't be back tonight. They're sure to spend the night on the mountain. Didn't you see them carrying their backpacks when they set off?"

"But what if they do come back?" Bai asked seriously.

The old man patted Bai's head. Why so many what ifs?"

The correspondent pulled his head away. "It's not just tonight. What if they come back tomorrow?"

"Worry about that tomorrow. Just let them stay for now. The captain will be back then, and it won't be your problem anymore, will it?"

Bai thought about it. He recalled another problem. "It's still not enough. There are only three beds in the reception room, and there are four of them."

"You really are stupid, aren't you?" Hou said. "The captain's wife is here at last. Are you going to split the couple up?"

"But what about me?" Bai stayed in the same quarters as the captain.

"You really don't know what to do? Step back, soldier! Come stay with me."

Bai whispered, "The single bed is so narrow. Can they sleep like that?"

Hou Qing laughed. "You really are a new recruit, aren't you? You don't know a thing. You and I need a wide bed if we have to share. The two of them don't." He patted Bai's head again.

Bai was annoyed. "Hou, do you dare to pat me again?"

"Hey, you're a fresh fish, I'll pat you again if I want. Anything wrong with that?"

Hou Qing reached out again, but Bai was prepared and got away in time.

Pulling out of reach, he ran off. He stepped into the room, calling over his shoulder at Hou Qing, "You big ape."

Hou wanted to chase him, but was too shy to continue teasing Bai in front of the women, so he had to let the fresh fish get the better of him.

"Big ape" was Hou Qing's nickname, due to the similarity between his surname and the Chinese word for monkey. The veterans all called him that to his face, but the new recruits did not. He was actually very kind, a solid worker, and well-liked, but he was not very educated. If not for that, he would have been promoted long ago. He was one of the most excellent soldiers every year. The men teased, saying that he was always ranked as an excellent soldier because he kept them well fed, while he himself remained as thin as ever. After ten years of military service, the recruits who had once started fires under his stove had all become platoon leaders, but he had remained head cook for the squadron all those years.

Hou Qing had learned Chinese medicine back in his hometown and knew acupuncture and massage. Guo Hong had a lot on her mind at the time, and she hardly noticed Hou Qing at all when they first arrived at camp. She was thinking about what to say when she saw Deng Gang. An Ning, Yu Xiulan, and Xiaoxue were already asleep in the next room, but Guo Hong was having trouble falling asleep. The wooden house was not soundproof, and she could hear faint snores from Yu Xiulan. Guo Hong thought for a long time, but she could not settle on just the right thing to say when the two of them finally met. But the divorce was a must; she had made up her mind about that.

Later, her eyelids began to sink a little, but she forced them open, only for them to soon close again. She had been very tired recently. It was almost midnight, and Deng Gang was still not back. She could not wait anymore. She took out the divorce papers and placed them in the center of the table, putting a teapot on top of them. Maybe that was the way. Just let Deng Gang come back and see it, and everything would be quickly understood, saving her the trouble of saying anything at all.

She put on his cotton coat and curled up on the bed, wanting to take a quick nap. To her surprise, her eyes closed almost immediately, and she fell asleep.

Naturally, Deng Gang was very happy to see Guo Hong. He was about to lean over and wake her when he saw the divorce papers on the table. His face immediately darkened, and his heart sank. The excitement and joy he had felt moments earlier now slid into a dark pit.

Just then, Guo Hong woke up and sat up. Pretending not to see what was on the table, Deng Gang started taking off his uniform. He said, "You didn't tell me you were coming, or I would have arranged to pick you up. You must be exhausted!"

He causally tossed his shirt on the table, covering the divorce papers, and stretched out his arms to Guo Hong. "Come here. I've missed you so much. Hold me."

Guo Hong sat where she was, not moving. She lowered her face, saying nothing. She glanced at Deng Gang, then turned her face away.

Tears fell. Deng Gang sat on the edge of the bed and put his arm across Guo Hong's shoulder.

"What's wrong?"

Guo Hong shook her shoulder, shaking Deng Gang's arm off, and burst into tears. Maybe it was because when she saw how dark and thin Deng Gang was, she realized how difficult he had it, living on the plateau, and she knew that no one would take care of him after the divorce. It made her heart ache, and the tears fell. One day as husband and wife equalled a hundred years of kindness, and they had been married for six years. Perhaps it was because of the hardships of the road that, upon seeing Deng Gang, she felt particularly aggrieved. Perhaps there was no reason. She just needed to cry, so she cried. At that moment, she almost softened, wanting to just cry in Deng Gang's arms, but then she thought of that woman, Feng Xiaoli, and her heart started to harden again, and she hated Deng Gang.

"I didn't pick you up. Is that what's wrong? Okay, don't cry. It's late. It isn't nice to disturb the others."

Deng Gang moved to hug her again, but she pushed him away and jumped off the bed. Picking up the divorce papers from the table, she threw them at Deng Gang.

He knew what they were, but he pretended to be serious. Looking them over, he said, "Look, here it is again! A couple can argue at one end of the bed and make peace at the other. Why does this keep going on and on?"

Guo Hong turned her back on him and said coldly, "Don't try to shrug it off. I'm serious this time. Whether you want to or not, I'm divorcing you. I don't want this to drag on any longer."

"Don't make trouble, okay? What did I do that's so wrong? Why do you resent me so much?"

"You know what you did!"

"I really don't."

"I don't want to say more. If you're a man, you should have a heart and just sign it quickly. Once you're divorced, you can go find another woman."

"Who would take a second look at me, besides you?" Deng Gang said, smiling.

"I guess there's one person who can hardly wait," Guo Hong sneered.

The smile froze on his face. "What do you mean?"

"Stop pretending!"

Deng Gang pulled back and cursed. "What kind of bastard has an affair? You're making this up just so you can get a divorce, aren't you?"

"Think what you want. I don't want to talk about it anymore. Are you signing the papers or not?"

Without realizing it, Deng Gang glanced at the door. He said in a low voice, "Can you be quiet? Everyone just got back from a long day of work. You may not want to rest, but they need to. The troops are out on rescue missions every day these days. We can't affect them or rattle their emotions because of our own affairs."

Guo Hong knew that it was not the right time to discuss the divorce with him. She lowered her voice, but her tone remained hard. "Don't try to scare me by talking about rattling the soldiers' emotions. I want out of this marriage."

Hearing that, Deng Gang grew angry too. "You really want to leave, there's nothing I can do, but we have to wait until the rescue mission is completed. Let's not talk about it now. It's time for bed."

When he had said that, he finished undressing, and without cleaning up, he lay on the other bed. Within five minutes, he was snoring.

It was a long time before Guo Hong fell asleep. She thought, *That heartless guy can fall asleep even when things are in such a mess. There must be someone else. He doesn't care about me at all.*

The more she thought about it, the sadder she became, and the sadder she became, the more sleep eluded her. She thought about all of Deng Gang's good points, and she was a bit reluctant to let him go. But even in her reluctance, she hated him. Her thoughts really were a mess, after being tossed about on the road for so many days. She was exhausted. Eventually, she fell asleep.

When she woke in the morning, Deng Gang was gone. At breakfast, An Ning noticed that Guo Hong's eyes were red and swollen. Having nothing else to do, the three women sat in the reception room chatting, while Xiaoxue sat on the bed folding paper cranes. She was a quiet child, not fidgeting, and that made her quite lovable.

When everyone had gone to the construction site, the camp was very quiet, the only sounds being those of the cooking crew. Guo Hong was worked up, thinking about the quarrel with Deng Gang the night before. An Ning told her they had all heard it. She urged Guo Hong not to mention the divorce while the troops were out on the rescue mission. Deng Gang was in charge of hundreds of men at the construction site every day, and he didn't need to be distracted while undertaking such dangerous work. Yu Xiulan said that marriage was a matter of fate, and if they gave each other a little space, it would all pass.

While they were talking, they heard footsteps outside. Before anyone entered, a voice came in, "Let me see whose occupying my place."

As soon as he finished speaking, a short colonel walked in, followed by Deng Gang and two young officers, one of whom was wearing glasses. Guo Hong had seen this man several times in Chengdu and knew that he was the battalion leader, but he did not know her. She quickly stood up. The battalion leader looked at the women, and looking back at Deng Gang, he said, "Don't tell me. Let me guess which one is your wife."

Guo Hong lowered her head. The battalion leader pointed at her and said, "It's her, right?"

Guo Hong blushed.

Pointing at Deng Gang, the battalion leader said, "You're a good man, but how did you ever get such a beautiful wife?"

Pointing at An Ning, he said, "Whose wife is this?"

An Ning said, "We met on the road. I'm not anybody's wife. I came to Xizang to travel, and I'm just staying here for a few days."

The battalion leader said, "Good, welcome!"

Turning his attention to Yu Xiulan, he said, "What about this one?"

Xiulan hesitated, then said, "Her father is in Bomi."

"Who is it?"

Xiulan said, "He's a soldier. You may not know him. He's a driver."

The battalion leader said, "There's no one in our detachment that I don't know," but he did not ask any more questions. Instead, he comforted Xiulan, saying, "Unfortunately, there's been an avalanche in Ranwu Valley. Your reunion will probably be delayed for a few more days. But the troops are rushing to do the repairs. The road should be cleared soon."

Then he said to all of them, "I admire your courage, coming up here at this time. You are indeed soldier's wives! Some people in the organization have different views on family traveling to the mountains to visit their husbands, worrying that visits from their wives will affect the combat readiness of the troops, but I don't see it that way. Quite the opposite! When you come to visit, it boosts morale. Being a soldier's wife isn't easy. They only get leave to visit their families once a year. No one has a right to stop you from coming. It's good for you to come see how your husband is doing here. You'll have more sympathy for them and be more supportive while they work up here in the mountains."

He teased Guo Hong, saying, "Deng Gang is in such a good mood today, now that you're here. I have an idea. After you go back, you can give a talk to other soldiers' families and tell them how things are up here on the mountain—you know, educate them. How about that?"

Guo Hong blushed, unsure how to answer.

From the moment he entered the door, An Ning did not see Deng Gang smile. Even when the battalion leader joked about him, he didn't laugh. It was like Guo Hong had said—he had a cold face.

At that first meeting, Deng Gang did not make a good impression on An Ning. Hearing what the battalion leader had suggested, Deng Gang said coldly, "Teaching is her forte. She taught me a good lesson last night."

Guo Hong stared at Deng Gang blankly.

The battalion leader didn't catch the tone of Deng Gang's words, but he picked up meanings of his own. Laughing, he said, "Well, keep it up tonight! Keep it up."

Laughing, they walked away. As soon as they left, the door was darkened by another figure, a female lieutenant in camouflage.

She came in and asked, "Which of you is Guo Hong?"

Surprised, Guo Hong looked at the pretty lieutenant. She asked cautiously, "Who are you?"

"I'm Feng Xiaoli. Are you Guo Hong?"

Feng Xiaoli approached warmly, wanting to take Guo Hong's hand. Pretending to say something to Xiulan, Guo Hong turned and avoided it. Feng Xiaoli was embarrassed. Her face flushed, and she didn't know whether to keep walking or stand still.

Just then, a messenger shouted from outside, "Lieutenant Feng, time for the meeting!"

22

The meeting was held in an adjacent room. The wooden house was not soundproof, so the women could hear everything clearly. Guo Hong sulked as she sat by the bed. Though Xiulan did not know the inside story, she could tell there was something between Guo Hong and the female lieutenant, but it wasn't convenient to ask questions, so she moved to one side and helped her daughter fold paper cranes. An Ning knew the inside story, but she was not able to urge Guo Hong right now, so she took out her notebook and sat at the desk to write in her diary.

From the room next door, they heard the battalion leader say, "The situation is very serious, comrades! When I say serious, I don't mean to say it's the worst landslide we'll ever have in these parts. I just mean that this will be difficult enough to give all of you a good taste of what a serious situation really is. The collapse of Nuba yesterday has alarmed the leaders of the Party Central Committee and the State Council, and it's brought attention to the 'general defense.' The commanders at HQ and the political commissar have issued important instructions, telling us to break through within the next ten days. That's an order!

"Yesterday, our comrades from the engineering department went up the mountain to inspect the project and estimate the amount of work that needs to be done. We need at least half a month just to complete opening to traffic, but we have our orders, and they are unmovable. There's no retreat. That's the first thing you need to understand. Second, the water level of the lake that was formed by the landslide is rising every day. If the natural levee can't bear the pressure, the water will overflow when the levee breaks, wiping out the two villages downstream. The consequences of that would be unimaginable! Finally, due to the road damage on both sides, more than five hundred vehicles traveling east to west were blocked along the way. Feeding and accommodating these people will be a problem.

"This being the situation, we need to adjust our original rescue plan. I'll walk you through the new rescue plan and tasks here. The general idea is that we will carry out a two-pronged attack on the Nuba landslide area and put a frontline flat push rescue effort of Ranwu Valley into place. Chief of Staff, you will notify Squadron 5 that they should temporarily withdraw from the Bangda construction site and make haste to the Nujiang Bridge tonight to join Squadron 3. These two squadrons will be optimized to form a mechanical commando unit and a youth commando unit, and they will rotate work on the east side to dig a diversion channel to release the flood waters and reduce pressure on the leave. After the meeting, you are to immediately go around the landslide area through the mountains and get to the Nujiang Bridge, where you will command the troops from the east. The Captain of the First Brigade will lead Squadron 2 out to repair the road in the west. Lieutenant Feng will take the design drawings to the site as soon as possible. For Squadron 1, Captain, your squadron will still be in charge of the front line at Ranwu Valley, and you will be assigned three bulldozers from the Second Brigade, but you won't have any extra troops, not even a single soldier. The instructor from Squadron 2 will be responsible for the service team and roving medical team. Your main task is to address problems for the trapped drivers and the public.

"In summary, on all three fronts, you must complete your tasks before July 21. If you can't complete the mission, I'll take the stars from your shoulders myself. Dismissed!"

As he walked out, the battalion leader said, "Deng Gang, set up a tent at the construction site. Starting today, you'll eat and sleep there."

"Sir, I ..."

"You what? Get to it! Get someone to set it up and go, now!"

After the battalion leader had gone, Deng Gang arranged for someone to set up a tent, and the women heard him call for Lieutenant Feng. An Ning had finished her notes, and she saw that Guo Hong was still angry. Feeling that the atmosphere in the room was too morose, she said to Guo Hong, "Let's go out for a walk."

She said to Xiulan, "Let's all go together."

Xiulan said, "You two go. I'm a little dizzy."

Guo Hong's spirits were low. She said, "This place is a mess. What's the use of a walk?"

An Ning walked over, smiling, and pulled Guo Hong up. "Let's go. You have to keep me company."

Guo Hong had no choice but to go out with An Ning. As they went out the door, Guo Hong felt it was a little cold. "Hold on. I'll go get a jacket," she said, and turned to go into the next house.

An Ning hadn't seen the barracks yet, so she followed her in. As soon as they entered, the two women saw Deng Gang and Feng Xiaoli leaning over the table, heads together, as they looked at a map.

Deng Gang was so focused he did not hear the women enter. He said to Feng Xiaoli, "Look, Xiaoli, if we cut across diagonally through here, we'll shorten the trip by two kilometers."

"No, I've surveyed the place. It's all granite. It won't be easy to dig there."

Before she had finished speaking, she saw Guo Hong, and she quickly walked away from the table, greeting Guo Hong with a hearty, "Sis!"

Guo Hong didn't seem to hear or care. She picked up her jacket and turned away. Deng Gang asked, "Where are you going?"

But Guo Hong had already walked out of the door, angry. Trailing behind her, An Ning called over her shoulder, "We're going for a walk."

The two women walked up the hill behind the barracks. Guo Hong walked quickly, her face even more twisted with anger than it had been before. She did not say a word. An Ning followed, regretting that she had suggested going out for a walk. If she hadn't, Guo Hong wouldn't have gone back into the house to pick up a jacket, and if she hadn't gone into the house, she wouldn't have seen Deng Gang and Feng Xiaoli together. She thought, *Guo Hong is being too sensitive. They're talking about work. What's to be jealous of?*

The slope was not steep, but it was a gradual ascent covered in green grass and flowers. It was a nice place for a walk, but Guo Hong was in a bad mood. As she walked, she couldn't help but scold, "Shameless!"

An Ning wasn't sure if she was talking about Deng Gang or Feng Xiaoli. Probably both.

With the quick pace they were walking, An Ning was a little out of breath. She caught up to Guo Hong and said, "Where are you going? You can't just run aimlessly. Don't forget, this is the plateau. Don't walk too quickly or you won't feel good."

Guo Hong was panting heavily. They sat on the grass. An Ning advised, "Don't worry about it. Maybe it's nothing. They were studying the map."

"Do they need to stand so close to each other to study a map? And what's with calling her Xiaoli? She's his colleague! It's overly familiar. Did you hear how disgusting he was? If he's like that when I'm here, then what's he like when I'm not here? Just imagine how affectionate they are then!"

An Ning smiled. Tilting her face, she looked at Guo Hong. "I didn't expect someone who was about to get a divorce to be so jealous."

"Jealous? Over him? Ha!"

"You can say you're not jealous all you want, but there's so much jealousy oozing out of you I can smell it! There's only one explanation for your unusual behavior here."

"Yeah? What's that?" Guo Hong asked.

An Ning smiled and stared at her. "You still love him."

An Ning's reminder made Guo Hong aware that her behavior really was out of the ordinary. She didn't think this meant she still had feelings for Deng Gang. She hated him.

"Still love him? It's not that. It's just that I hate being played. It makes me sick."

An Ning stopped laughing. She said seriously, "Woman's intuition tells me that Deng Gang is not that kind of person. He seems quite honest."

"It's an illusion! When honest people go bad, it's all the more lethal."

"Maybe it was just a misunderstanding."

Guo Hong was a little confused. Looking at An Ning, she asked, "Why are you always taking up for him?"

An Ning said, "From what you told me the other day, it wasn't easy for the two of you to get together. Wouldn't it be a pity to end it all over a misunderstanding?"

"A pity? There are guys like him everywhere you look. If we ended it today, I could have another one tomorrow, and you can be sure the new one would be better than him!"

An Ning teased, "You're so determined. Have you already found his replacement?"

Guo Hong blushed. Giving An Ning a little push, she said, "Screw you! I'm so upset and you still want to joke about such things!"

An Ning pursued, "Is it your boss?"

Guo Hong was startled. "How did you know?"

An Ning had actually been half guessing, but also half joking. She didn't expect to hear it confirmed. For some reason, she suddenly grew very uncomfortable, and she despised Guo Hong.

"That day when you called him from Bangda, I noticed. So it turns out you've been stepping out for some time."

Guo Hong's face turned even redder. "No, Deng Gang cheated on me first."

That afternoon, sitting on a hillside covered with galsang blooms, Guo Hong told An Ning the story of her and the other man. It began a few years earlier, when she was in tears after seeing the ambiguous text message Feng Xiaoli had sent to Deng Gang. She had acted casual, telling Deng Gang she needed to go back to the office and work overtime, and she left the house, alone.

When she left the house, she didn't think anything would happen that night, but something unexpected happened. For the first time in ages, she spent a long time with a man other than her husband.

It was her boss, Hu An who she spent time with. He was in his early thirties, and he was a typical ideal potential husband. For some reason she could not fathom, he had never been married. She didn't think of him at first, but just wanted to go out for a walk to be alone for a while, mostly out of fear that she couldn't keep her emotions in check at home. She didn't want to paint her marriage into a corner all at once, preferring instead to buy some time for a solution to present itself. But as she walked, she didn't know where to go. Her parents' home was her only safe haven, but she didn't want to go there. She didn't want them to see the unhappiness in her marriage, and she didn't want her sister-in-law to feel sorry for her. Saving face was the most important thing to her. She suddenly felt that she had no space for relatives. Walking alone on the streets, she felt lonely for the first time in her life, and sadness welled up from the soles of her feet and flooded over her. The sadness was like an anaesthetic, making her wander aimlessly and making her legs weak. But she continued to walk the night streets alone.

As she walked, she thought of Hu An. Even now, she couldn't think of what brought him to mind that night. She had been working in his company for a year, but she rarely spoke to him. She was an employee, and he was the boss. It was their habit to just nod and say hello when they met. Even so, she felt that the nod was not just a nod, and hello was not just hello. It was normal for the way Hu An nodded and said hello to others, but it was not normal for her; she wasn't sure what was so unusual about it. She liked the smile Hu An gave her when he greeted her first thing each morning. There was an indescribable feel to it, as if it were particularly warm and kind. Yes, that was how it felt. Maybe it was this feeling that make her think of Hu An as she walked.

Without quite realizing what she was doing, she dialed Hu An's number. She immediately realized how inappropriate that was, and she wanted to hang up, but the call had already connected. She quickly hung up. A moment later, Hu An called back.

"Who is this?"

Guo Hong didn't say anything.

"Who's there?"

Guo Hong's heart pounded, but she still didn't say anything.

Hu An asked in a low voice, "Guo Hong, is that you?"

How did he know it was her? With just that one question, Guo Hong's tears started to flow.

"What happened? Where are you now?"

Guo Hong said, "I'm on South Renmin Road."

Hu An said, "Stay where you are. I'll be right there."

He quickly drove over. When she got into the car, he asked what happened. She just cried, not saying anything. He patted her back, comforting her.

"What happened? Take your time. Tell me everything."

But she didn't want to say anything. He drove three times round the Second Ring Road before Guo Hong finally said, "I'm fine. Please take me home."

After that, things were the same as always. He was still the boss, and she was still his employee, and they still smiled and nodded in greeting, as if nothing had ever happened. Hu An never asked her what had happened; that's the way he was. She liked that about him.

It was not until the eve of the Spring Festival that things changed between them. Each year before the Spring Festival, the company sent New Year greetings to important relevant departments and organizations. In previous years, the director of the financial department bought the things for the New Year greetings, then went with the boos to deliver each one. That year, the chief financial officer had just had a child when the Spring Festival came around, so Hu An asked Guo Hong to handle it. On to Hu An's instructions, she bought nineteen diamond necklaces, each costing 23,000 yuan, and she prepared 23 envelopes with 10,000 yuan each. On New Year's Eve, when all the red envelopes had been delivered and there was just one diamond necklace left, Hu An said, "Let's go find someplace to eat."

He took her to Gingko, a place by Funan River, where he ordered shark's fin soup and wine. When everything had been brought to the table, Hu An was in very good spirits. He looked like a very foolish man, but actually, he was very wise. He put eighty percent of everything he earned back into managing the various relationships he had to juggle. As his accountant, Guo Hong felt sorry for him. She didn't understand why he did this. He said, "It seems that we only clear twenty percent, but if I don't reinvest the eighty percent, even that twenty percent will be lost. That's the secret behind the growth of my business."

While they were at Gingko, Hu An drank too much. He asked Guo Hong to take out the last diamond necklace.

Not understanding what he meant, she took it out and handed it to him. He handed it back to her, saying, "This one is for you."

How could she accept something so expensive? She said, "Mr. Hu, I think you've had too much to drink."

Red-eyed, he looked at her. "I haven't had too much to drink. I bought it with the intention of giving it to you."

"Mr. Hu, you're ... I can't accept it."

Hu An shook his head and said with a wry smile, "I know it's very audacious of me. Let's call it a bonus."

"I still can't accept it. Please respect my wishes on this."

Hu An put the necklace away. "Okay. I'll respect your wishes ... Drink up!"

And so they drank again. They drank and drank, and as they drank, Hu An started to cry. He said the thing he hated most in life was money, and because he hated it, he was so frantic in his efforts to earn it. Guo Hong didn't understand, but Hu An just chattered on and on. She had never seen him beside himself like this. From his chattering, she learned a lot about his earlier life.

Before Hu An had been the secretary for an official in the city government. If not for what later happened, this might have been the path for his entire career. But then, a female typist came into the office. There was nothing wrong with having a female typist, but this woman was very beautiful. Before half a year was up, they were together. It was fine that they were together, but Hu An was very vain, and he liked to take his beautiful girlfriend to various parties to show off in front of his friends. On one such occasion, one of his old friends, an old school mate, developed a crush on Hu An's girlfriend, though neither Hu An nor his girlfriend was aware of it. This friend hadn't gone to college after graduation, and he couldn't find a job, so he started his own business. Almost miraculously, he expanded the business, opening a hotel, and the business grew and became increasingly prosperous. Within a few years, he had become a millionaire.

At the previous class reunion, Hu An had been the loudest about proclaiming his achievements. He was a graduate student and a civil servant. He had a bright future. And he kind of looked down on his classmate.

Now that his classmate had made some money, though, the tables were turned, and he looked down on Hu An. He occasionally invited Hu An out for dinner, followed by a game of mahjong, but only in hopes of meeting the pretty girlfriend. Hu An had not played much mahjong before this, but he was not good at rejecting his classmate, so he went along with it. After several games, he started to win, and as he gained a little skill, he won three or four thousand yuan. He was soon addicted and felt it's not a bad thing to play mahjong. Before long, the stakes became higher, and thousands were on the line all the time. After a few months, he had won seventy or eighty thousand yuan. He bought a lot of jewelry and clothes for his girlfriend. Seeing that the money came so easily, she started to feel uneasy. She urged Hu An, "We can't afford to pay if we don't win. Don't play anymore. What if we lose?"

Hu An said, "My luck is too good for my fortunes to change."

Flustered, his girlfriend said, "Do you think money just falls from the sky?"

He said, "My classmate has got plenty of money. Would he bother about a minor loss?"

He had lost his mind. He wasn't listening to reason at all. He took every single invitation and played every single game.

Hu An's luck eventually ran out. The more he played, the more he lost, with the losses becoming both more frequent and in greater amounts each time. He was unwilling to take the loss, so he kept trying to win it back, borrowing money from his classmate to do so. His classmate was very generous, lending him as much as he asked for. As time went on, he lost track of how much he had borrowed. Finally, one day, face downcast, his friend said he could not borrow any more money, taking out a stack of IOUs and counting. The total exceeded 400,000 yuan. Hu An was dumbfounded. He wouldn't be able to earn 400,000 yuan for as long as he lived. But gambling debts were still debts, and there were all those IOUs, in black and white, and they had to be paid. Hu An didn't tell his girlfriend, and he didn't speak up at his work unit. He quietly borrowed money from every source he could think of, but it was never enough, no matter how hard he tried.

Then his girlfriend found out. She sold the clothes and jewelry, and after everything had been sold, she borrowed money from her parents and classmates. Between them, they had come up with 100,000. Hu An took the money to his classmate. Looking at the money, his classmate said, "You think you can bring such a small amount and we'll be square?"

Hu An said, "It's all I have. I'll pay the rest back, I promise. Just give me time."

His classmate said, "Are you joking? Do you think I'm a fool? Give you time? How long? Didn't you boast about how well you were doing? Where's all the boasting now?"

Ashamed, Hu An said, "I really can't come up with that much money."

His classmate said, "If you'll agree to one demand, you don't have to pay me back. Send your girlfriend to spend the night with me."

That was what really woke Hu An up. His classmate had been setting him up all along.

His girlfriend spent that night with his classmate, and then she disappeared. Hu An heard she had gone back to Shenzhen. He traveled to Shenzhen several times to look for her, but he couldn't find her. In a fit of anger, he quit his job and went into his own business. Eight years had passed, and there was still no news of his girlfriend.

As they talked over drinks, Hu An told Guo Hong that the reason he had hired her over many other applicants for the job was that she looked like his girlfriend. Guo Hong felt sorry for Hu An, but she felt bad, both mentally and physically, to know she was just a stand-in for someone else. She never accepted the diamond necklace.

A month passed. The company was planning to cooperate with a unit in Beijing, and Hu An needed to travel there for meetings. He wasn't going there to discuss matters; everything had already been negotiated over the phone. He was there mainly to send a message to the leaders, so he took Guo Hong with him. Returning to the hotel after dinner that evening, emboldened by the liquor, Hu An knocked on Guo Hong's door. As soon as she opened the door, he fell on top of her. Thinking he was drunk, Guo Hong quickly supported him and helped him inside. Taking advantage of the situation, he grabbed her around the waist and fell onto the bed, rolling over and pressing her beneath him.

Angry, she pushed him away, snapping, "What do you take me for?"

He suddenly grew more alert. Sitting up on the bed, he looked at Guo Hong. "I like you."

She straightened her hair, "It's her that you like. I'm just a stand-in."

Hu An said, "She's been gone for eight years. I really do like you. Can't you feel it?"

Guo Hong said, "I know you're very good to me, and I really do respect you. But I don't like you in that way. It makes me very uncomfortable. I have no money, and my life is very unhappy. But I do have a husband and a family. You just make me feel like a bad woman, so dirty."

She started crying. Hu An panicked, saying it really was because he liked her that he had behaved this way. He promised to never behave this way again.

Guo Hong said, "I'm crying because of myself. It has nothing to do with you."

She poured out all her misfortunes and troubles, telling Hu An everything. They sat for a long time, and Hu An listened to Guo Hong's story, smoking one cigarette after another.

That afternoon, the two women sat for a long time on the hillside behind the camp. Finally, Guo Hong said, "Nothing happened that night. Before he left, Hu An said to me, 'If you get a divorce, marry me.'"

An Ning asked, "Do you really want to divorce Deng Gang?"

Guo Hong said, "Yes."

An Ning said, "So you don't have feelings for him anymore?"

Guo Hong said, "I hate him."

An Ning said, "Hate is a feeling. It means you still have him in your heart. You still care about him."

Guo Hong did not say anything.

An Ning asked, "So, do you like Hu An?"

Guo Hong was silent for a while. Then, looking at the grass beneath them, she said, "I'm not sure about that either."

It was getting colder, and the night came up silently from the ground, gradually covering the sky until there was only a serene emptiness on the horizon. Then the dinner whistle sounded.

23

The troops were still busy with the rescue work. During the day, the camp was very quiet. Aside from the muddy soldiers who came back for dinner at shift change and the few vehicles that brought construction materials, hardly anyone came or went. Only the cook, messenger, and the women remained in the camp.

An Ning wanted to go to the site of the rescue work to take photos, but Deng Gang would not allow it. She had snuck to the site several times, but always failed to enter. Each time, she was "escorted" back by Deng Gang's men before even getting close to the real rescue work.

Yu Xiulan was idle, having nothing of her own to do. She went around collecting dirty clothing from under the soldiers' beds and, squatting in the courtyard, set about washing them.

Guo Hong slept in the room. Deng Gang had come back the previous night, and the couple had quarreled again. Though they kept their voices low, An Ning and Xiulan could still hear them from the adjacent room. The whole argument lasted for more than two hours, but they hardly heard Deng Gang say a word. Xiulan turned over and sighed, and An Ning complained a bit about Guo Hong. She wasn't irritated because the noise kept her awake, but because Guo Hong was so heartless. Even if she wanted a divorce, she shouldn't make trouble like that. An Ning felt some sympathy for Deng Gang. He was busy at the construction site all day, and of course he was tired when he came home in the middle of the night, yet he still had to deal with Guo Hong making a fuss. If it went on like that, it would wear down even a body made of steel. Sure enough, when she got up the next morning, she saw that Deng Gang had dark circles under his eyes.

After breakfast, An Ning wanted to wake Guo Hong up, hoping to prevent her from sleeping all day and making a fuss with Deng Gang all night. But Guo Hong covered her head with the quilt and said she had a headache. She was drowsy and didn't feel well, and she did not want to get up.

An Ning went out into the courtyard to help Xiulan with the laundry, but Xiulan waved her away with dripping hands. "Go write your stuff. I hardly have enough clothes to keep me busy."

Though it was summer, it was still quite cold on the plateau. Their water supply was all snowmelt from the mountain, and it was bitingly cold to the hands. Seeing that Xiulan's hands and exposed forearms had turned red from the cold, An Ning was moved. She suddenly thought, *Deng Gang and the others are better off if they find a virtuous woman like Yu Xiulan to marry.*

Xiulan would not let her help, so An Ning went to see if the cooking crew needed any help. The head cook Hou Qing said he didn't want to bother her, but An Ning hung around. With her and the men working together, the work was not tiring. With a pretty girl around, the cook worked more quickly, and there were occasional bursts of laughter from the kitchen.

An Ning came out of the kitchen with a pot of carrots and was going to wash them at a water storage tank that had been converted from an asphalt bucket. She saw Deng Gang and Feng Xiaoli returning, followed by a few soldiers who carried survey equipment over their shoulders.

Deng Gang scolded Feng Xiaoli as they walked. "How did that happen? I told you to look out for everyone's safety. What happened?"

He stopped and pointed at Feng Xiaoli. "Let me tell you, if anything happens to them, I have no choice but to punish you."

Feng Xiaoli defended herself. "I didn't know there would be a sudden landslide."

Deng Gang grew even angrier. "Aren't you an engineer? Not very competent, are you?"

Feng Xiaoli burst into tears and ran all the way to her quarters, covering her face.

Deng Gang did not let up. "You feel wronged? Looks like it's time for a little self-reflection."

Angry, he walked into the barracks, took out a safety rope, and walked out of the camp again. A soldier followed him out, not daring even to breathe too heavily. The other two soldiers stood in the courtyard, looking at each other.

An Ning didn't know what was going on. She walked over to the two soldiers to ask. They told her that the surveying and mapping team had gone up the mountain to survey the route along the access road, but there had been a landslide. The two soldiers who had taken the lead had disappeared and were probably trapped somewhere on the mountain.

Feng Xiaoli came out then. She had stopped crying. With a tight expression and carrying a roll of blueprints, she hurried out without so much as greeting An Ning.

Back in the kitchen, An Ning told the cooking crew what she had just witnessed. The laughter came to an immediate stop. It seemed that the situation really was serious.

An Ning said to Hou Qing, "Your captain was a bit too much. He didn't hold back at all, scolding Lieutenant Feng in front of all those people."

Hou Qing said, "The captain is like that. He doesn't care who he's talking to when he's angry."

An Ning said, "It's not easy for a woman staying in a place like this. Not only is it a rugged environment, but she also has to endure such harsh treatment from her male comrades. The captain isn't gentle at all!"

Hou Qing said, "You don't understand. The captain's expression is cold, but his heart is better than anyone else's. Everyone in our detachment calls him the Cold-faced Bodhisattva. I've been with him for many years, and I've rarely seen him smile. One of our old veterans was discharged last year, and when the squadron officer asked him what he wanted before he left us, he said, 'I've been stationed here for three years, and I've never seen Captain Deng smile. My only request now is to see him smile before I go.' The officer told the captain, and he really did go and see the old veteran, smiling at him. The old soldier was moved to tears."

An Ning thought that Deng Gang really was an interesting fellow, but she couldn't understand how he could be so harsh toward a woman.

Hou Qing explained, "He's the captain. The weight of responsibility is heavy on his shoulders. How can he keep from getting angry when something goes wrong? And anyway, sometimes Feng Xiaoli is harsh with him too."

"She dares to be harsh with the captain?"

"You don't believe me? You see she's normally very quiet, but when it comes to the quality of the project, even the captain doesn't dare to cross her."

This surprised An Ning. "You mean she has so much authority?"

"You've seen the captain treat her harshly in public, but he treats her better than anyone in private."

An Ning was quite surprised to hear this. It was no wonder Guo Hong was suspicious. It seemed there really was something there, something even the soldiers saw.

Hoping to extract more from Hou Qing, she said deliberately, "Seeing how fierce he was just now, I find that hard to believe."

"If you don't believe me, ask them." Hou Qing said, pointing to the other cooks.

One of the others said, "Everyone knows about it, even the battalion leader."

An Ning was again surprised. The battalion leader knew? It looked like the matter really had gotten bigger.

"What do you mean he treats her well? In what way?"

"Closer than a sister," Hou Qing said. "If the captain scolded Lieutenant Feng, she won't be angry. Just watch; everything will be fine between them tomorrow."

Hou Qing finished cutting the carrots and bent over to choose the garlic sprouts. An Ning had not quite believed anything was happening between Deng Gang and Feng Xiaoli, but now that she'd heard what Hou Qing said, she started to believe it, at least a little. Partly for the sake of Guo Hong and partly to settle her own curiosity, she squatted beside Hou Qing and started picking out garlic sprouts. Pretending to be light hearted, she said, "It seems like there's something going on between them."

Hou Qing said, "To tell you the truth, it hasn't been easy for Lieutenant Feng. After her brother died, she joined the military and came to the plateau. Aside from three years when she studied at Xi'an Highway Institute, she's been on the Sichuan-Xizang Line the whole time. A woman, and exposed to all the elements out here—she's really put up with a lot."

"Her brother died?"

"Nine years ago."

Once again, An Ning was surprised.

Hou Qing said, "He was stationed with the troops in Zhongba, about two hundred kilometres from here. Our squadron was responsible for opening the Eagle's Mouth. Our battalion leader was still a squadron leader at the time. He was leading Squadron 2, and Lieutenant Feng's brother, Feng Wei, was leading Squadron 1. I had just joined the army at the time, and I was assigned to the battalion leader's squadron. The Eagles's Mouth was the key point of the rebuilding project in the middle section of the dam, like the neck of the entire project. It was difficult to carve the road out of the cliff at Eagle's Mouth, a big, dangerous, difficult task. We worked in three shifts every day, and after three months, everyone was exhausted. Both squadrons were doing excavation work, which was very difficult. I remember it was really windy one day, and they were using the pneumatic drill below. Rocks and sand dropped from the cliff from time to time. Sometimes, the stone hit a hard hat, rattling someone's noggin, but they were used to it and didn't bother much. After lunch, it was our turn to be on the line. As soon as we replaced Feng Wei and his men, sand blew into Deng Gang's eye. Feng Wei hadn't left yet, so he turned Deng Gang's face and tried to help him get it out. Whether it was because the wind was so strong or because Feng Wei had been on the pneumatic drill that morning and had sand all over him, Deng Gang's eye became more and more irritated, until he could barely keep it open. Feng Wei told him to go back and have his eye looked at, while Feng took over his duty. So Deng Gang went back and had someone look at his eye while Feng Wei continued on at the construction site.

"Less than half an hour after Deng Gang left, there was a landslide. Feng Wei heard the sound and knew something wasn't right. He looked up and shouted, 'Quick!' And then he ran with the rest of us. One fellow who was working the pneumatic drill—probably half deaf from working the thing all day—didn't hear the instruction, and he just stayed where he was, *tat tat tat tat*, drilling away. Feng Wei went back and pushed him out of the way. Just then, the rocks fell, and Feng Wei was crushed under them.

"By the time he was sent to the Basu Hospital, it was already dark. Deng Gang didn't say anything. He just fell onto Feng Wei and wept. Feng Wei didn't say a word. The doctor told us to pull Deng Gang away so they could work on Feng Wei. I stood beside him as they took Feng Wei to the hospital. Another comrade and I held candles to provide light for the doctors. Basu Hospital was in bad shape back then. There was no electricity, and no generator, so we had to use candles for lighting.

"Feng Wei's internal organs had all been smashed by the stones. Blood bubbled from his mouth and nose. It seeped through the mattress and dripped onto the floor below his bed. The doctor put a washbasin under the bed, and I later saw that it was half full of Feng Wei's blood. I cried the whole time. I was so scared my hands shook. The doctor told me not to shake or he couldn't see clearly. I tried to make myself stop shaking, but no matter what I did, my hands trembled. The wax poured over my hands, but I couldn't even feel it.

"About an hour later, the doctor straightened up and covered Feng Wei's face with a white cloth. He told me, 'Call your leaders.' I knew Feng Wei's life had been sacrificed then. My legs grew weak, and I almost fell to the ground, but I knew I had to go call our squadron leader, the current battalion leader. Deng Gang was the first to run in. He saw the white sheet on Feng Wei's body, and he leapt up, crying. As he cried, he said, 'Brother, you took my place.'

"The squadron leader cried too. He was the top chief there at the time, though, and, not wanting to affect morale, he quickly got hold of himself and told us to take Deng Gang out. When Deng Gang was gone, he grabbed the doctor's collar and said, 'Why didn't you save him? Why?'

"The fellow was just an ordinary doctor who had come from Jiangsu to aid Xizang. With red eyes, he said, 'I did my best, but he was injured too badly. All his bones and organs were smashed.'

"When they dressed Feng Wei, they couldn't get the shoes on. His legs had broken and swollen, so the feet were much bigger than usual. We searched the entire squadron for the biggest boots we could find, but they still weren't large enough. Deng Gang burst into tears and said Feng Wei couldn't be allowed to go on the road barefoot. In the end, they had to cut the heels from his boots and force them over half his foot. Nine years have passed since that happened, and any time you mention it in front of my battalion leader, he still expresses regret over the fact that we couldn't find shoes to fit Feng Wei before he left.

"After Feng Wei's death, it was Deng Gang who went to Feng's hometown in Gansu to deal with matters. When he came back, he brought Feng Xiaoli, who was seventeen years old at the time. We later learned that Feng Wei's parents had passed away long before, and he only had a younger sister left at home. Now that he had died, his orphaned sister was truly alone. A comrade from the Civil Affairs Bureau asked Feng Xiaoli what she wanted to do, and she said she wanted to join the military and be a soldier in her brother's army. That was how she ended up coming back with Deng Gang. Through all these years, Deng Gang has always treated Feng Xiaoli as his little sister."

Hearing the story, An Ning was touched. She found that she had started crying. She had not expected the story between Deng Gang and Feng Xiaoli to be so moving. Guo Hong really had misunderstood the situation!

After helping in the kitchen, she wanted to tell Guo Hong the story she had just heard, but when she returned to the room, she saw Xiulan and her daughter crying and embracing one another. Surprised, An Ning asked them what was wrong. Xiulan quickly wiped away her tears and said, "It's nothing. My daughter misses her father."

Saying that, she went back into the courtyard to do the laundry. Xiaoxue sat on the bed and started folding paper cranes again, crying as she folded. An Ning sat down to comfort the child, putting aside what she wanted to tell Guo Hong for the time being.

24

That evening, Feng Xiaoli was carried back on a stretcher. According to the soldiers who brought her back, they had divided into two groups to rescue the two soldiers who had been trapped on the mountain that afternoon. The battalion leader took a group to the east, where they planned to climb to the top of the mountain to conduct the rescue mission. Lieutenant Feng led them along the waterway, and they borrowed a cowhide boat from a Tibetan villager, planning to approach the cliff from the lake that had been formed by the landslide. The current was too fast, though, and their numerous attempts were all unsuccessful, with the cowhide boat threatening to overturn in the flood numerous times. Lieutenant Feng was not satisfied. She took them around to the north and tried to climb up from there, but the cliffs there were steeper, and as smooth as an ax or knife blade, making it near impossible to climb them. Lieutenant Feng would not be dissuaded. She insisted on going up from there, and they couldn't stop her. They understood how she felt. The two soldiers were trapped on the mountain, and she felt that she was responsible for them. She was also angry with the captain. The soldiers didn't dare to dissuade her any further, so they could only bite the bullet and follow her up the cliff. As a result, when they were halfway up the mountain, she slipped and fell, injuring her face and spraining her ankle.

Hearing that Feng Xiaoli had been injured, An Ning and Yu Xiulan rushed over to see if they could help. Feng Xiaoli was lying on the bed, blood all over her face. The medical staff went to the construction site, and the messenger hurried to call Hou Qing, since he had previously studied Chinese medicine.

Hou Qing ran in, his apron still tied around his waist, and asked, "Where is the injury?"

At one look, he could see that it was not too serious. She was bleeding from a cut on her forehead, and her right ankle was sprained. Hou Qing wiped the wound on her forehead with a cotton ball, and as he bandaged it, he said, "It's alright. Just a flesh wound."

Standing beside the bed, An Ning asked, "Will it leave a scar?"

Hou Qing said, "No. Lieutenant Feng is young. She'll heal quickly."

Feng Xiaoli didn't care about her face. She said to a soldier, "Go ask the captain if they made it up the mountain."

Hou Qing took off Feng Xiaoli's muddy boot and sock and tentatively pinched the foot. Feng Xiaoli grimaced and gasped.

Hou Qing said, "It's not a light sprain. You'll have to stay in bed for at least a week."

When Lieutenant Feng heard that, she grew anxious. "A week? I'm an engineer. How can I abandon the construction site?"

She tried to stand up.

Hou Qing urged, "The world will keep turning without you. If you don't take good care of your injuries, there will be consequences. You might even be lame. Don't say I didn't warn you."

Feng Xiaoli looked unhappily at Hou Qing. Hou Qing said, "What are you looking at me for? You're an officer, and I'm just a soldier, but I'm still older than you, so you have to listen to me!"

Feng Xiaoli patted the edge of the bed helplessly and said, "It's really unfortunate the chain gave way at the worst possible moment."

Hou Qing smiled and comforted her. "Don't worry. With the captain there, what is there for you to worry about?"

He stood up and said, "You sit right here and wait a while. I'll be right back." And he hurried out.

An Ning went to get water for the lieutenant. She saw Hou Qing running toward the snow-capped mountain behind the barracks, and she was very puzzled. His patient was here, so what was he doing leaving her and hurrying up the snow-capped mountain?

Half an hour later, Hou Qing returned, breathless and carrying something wrapped in his jacket. As he entered, he said to Feng Xiaoli, who still lay on the bed, "Quick, sit up. I've got a compress for you."

Hou Qing squatted and spread out the jacket on the ground. There was a pile of ice inside. An Ning suddenly understood why he had gone up the mountain. He pulled Feng Xiaoli's foot over and put the ice on it. After applying the cold compress, he kept rubbing her foot with his hands.

There was a clatter of footsteps outside. The soldiers had changed shifts, and as soon as those returning to the camp heard that Feng Xiaoli had been injured, they ran in to see her. Hou Qing drove them out like a flock of ducks. "Go! Get out! Let Lieutenant Feng rest!"

The dinner whistle sounded. An Ning said to Hou Qing, "I'll take over here. You go feed the soldiers."

Hou Qing left, and An Ning squatted beside the bed to apply the compress and massage the foot. Xiulan helped Feng Xiaoli remove her camouflage uniform and took it to be washed.

Feng Xiaoli said to An Ning, "I'm sorry."

"Don't say that," An Ning said. "To be honest, I envy you. You've got it good here. So many people look out for you. I really admire you. You're amazing!"

"What's to be admired? I can't do anything right."

She was obviously still worried about the two soldiers. She called for the messenger and asked if the battalion leader was back, but the messenger reported that he was not. Feng Xiaoli grew even more anxious. She chatted with An Ning, but her mind was elsewhere. She looked at the door from time to time.

An Ning could not sleep that night. She thought about the stories Hou Qing had told her during the day, about Feng Xiaoli, about Guo Hong and Deng Gang, and about the two soldiers who were still trapped on the mountain. Xiulan could not sleep either. She tossed and turned on her bed, and An Ning heard her sigh softly from time to time. Next door, Guo Hong was very quiet. There was no sound from her at all, which An Ning thought was a little strange. She thought Guo Hong knew about the events surrounding Feng Xiaoli and her brother, and perhaps there was a reconciliation between Guo Hong and Deng Gang. That made An Ning feel relieved. She had planned to tell Guo Hong about it, but if Guo Hong already knew, that would not be necessary.

Xiulan finally fell asleep, probably worn out from washing clothes all day. When she had been asleep for a while, she suddenly cried out very loudly, "Wang Li! Wang Li! Hurry! Run!"

Startled, An Ning sat up in bed and turned on the light. Yu Xiulan sat on her bed, tears streaming down her face as she looked at the door in horror.

"Xiulan, what's wrong?"

Xiulan was trembling. Her expression anxious, she said, "I had a nightmare."

"What kind of nightmare could scare you so badly?"

Xiulan trembled all over. An Ning walked over and put a coat over her and sat down beside her, stroking her shoulder. Xiulan gradually calmed down.

"I dreamed of those two soldiers. They had nothing to eat up there on the mountain, so they ate grass and roots and snow. Their hands and feet were frozen.

Then one of the soldiers suddenly disappeared, and the other one was left alone. He was naked. He walked and walked in the snow, and he suddenly turned into my husband. An avalanche came from the peak, but he didn't know, so he kept struggling to walk here. Just as I shouted for him to run, he was buried in snow."

An Ning comforted her, saying, "The dream is the opposite of reality. He's just fine, so that means the soldiers must be fine too."

"It's so cold at night. I can't imagine what will happen to them up there."

"Feng Xiaoli said they each had a backpack with them when they went up the mountain yesterday. They can't freeze," An Ning said. Then she asked, "You miss your husband?"

Xiulan lay down, saying nothing. An Ning turned off the lights and lay beside Xiulan. The two women lay silently together, not sleeping. Xiulan had not mentioned her husband before, a long-time veteran on the plateau named Wang Li, but now she told An Ning all about him.

She and Wang Li had gone to high school together. She said that though they went "together," they actually only overlapped for a year at school. After the first year, Wang Li transferred to another school more than ten miles away. There was only one reason for him to transfer. All the students in the class knew why, and so did the teacher. Wang Li and Yu Xiulan had fallen in love. Seventeen or eighteen years ago, puppy love among high school students was rare, especially in rural areas, and the couple became infamous throughout their school for the indiscretion. The direct consequence was that they later both failed the college entrance exam. Wang Li became a soldier and was sent to the plateau, while Xiulan went home and became a farmer. Even so, Xiulan said she had no regrets.

Xiulan said that if a fight had not broken out between the two classmates who sat behind her, she might not have ever noticed Wang Li, and they might not have ever fallen in love. But for some reason, the two students who sat behind her suddenly started fighting one day, overturning the table in the ruckus. There was nothing wrong with classmates fighting, and it was not unusual. The problem was that it wasn't a fight between boys or between girls, but a fight between a boy and a girl. That made it a serious problem. All along, in order to keep the students from talking during class, the teacher had deliberately arranged the students to sit one boy, one girl at each table. To the teacher's surprise, there was indeed less talking, but it ultimately led to a thunderous noise amid the silence.

When the teacher asked the two students why they had fought, they were both silent, not saying a word. The teacher had to punish them equally, switching seats for them. Wang Li was the class monitor, so she switched him with the male student.

As soon as Wang Li was seated behind her, Xiulan smelled a nice fragrance, the aroma of detergent. Afraid An Ning wouldn't understand what she meant, Xiulan explained that it was a soapy smell. It smelled so good, and even after so many years, when she thought of Wang Li, she immediately thought of the detergent's fragrance. The other students smelled of soap or bathing foams, even saponin. Only Wang Li smelled of detergent. She later learned that his mother had died when he was very young, and he and his younger brother had been doing their own laundry since they were in elementary school. Their clothes may have had many patches, but they were always clean. What was even more admirable was that he had done much of the patching himself. Wang Li was very frugal, but he was never lax when it came to his laundry; he always used detergent on his cuffs and neckline. His father reprimanded him many times for this extravagance, but it was no use. He continued the habit even after he had been married for many years.

Xiulan told An Ning that she had always liked clean men. It may have been the smell of detergent that made her fall in love with Wang Li, but he was not aware of her feelings for a very long time. Falling in love was both painful and sweet. The greatest pain was when she loved him and he didn't even know it.

When Xiulan said that, An Ning called to mind a well-known saying penned by a female writer in Hong Kong: The greatest distance in the world was not that between life and death, but that between the lover who stands face to face with the beloved, when the beloved does not even know it. Maybe that was how Xiulan felt at that time.

Recalling the line, An Ning mentioned it to Xiulan, but Xiulan said, "I wasn't so stupid. I wanted him to know I liked him."

But she was only seventeen at that time, and not nearly that bold. She had to find out whether he liked her too before deciding whether to tell him how she felt. Women always had a higher EQ than men, and she quickly came up with a solution. During class, she deliberately dropped her pencil, testing to see if Wang Li would pick it up for her. If he picked it up, it meant he cared about her. So, when he picked it up, softly poked her back, and handed it to her, she felt an electric shock and a numbness stab through her. It felt so good! She wanted to try again, to experience the numbness again. The following day, she dropped her pencil again, and Wang Li picked it up again. She tried it three times, but she still couldn't be sure Wang Li liked her. Maybe he would just help anyone pick up their pencil. She couldn't be sure.

The more uncertain she was, the more she longed for certainty. She lost interest in class. She looked at the teacher and the blackboard, but another pair of eyes in the back of her head kept looking at Wang Li. When Wang Li didn't come to school, or when he was late, she was restless and didn't want to study. When he did come to school, she calmed down and concentrated on her work. Her academic performance plummeted over a period of several months. She had previously ranked among the top five in her class, but after the mid-term exam, she had dropped to number twenty. Things couldn't go on like this. She had to tell Wang Li. Once it was out in the open, everything made clear, she would no longer be tortured. So she mustered up the courage and boldly tucked a note into one of Wang Li's books, saying that she would wait for him in the woods by the roadside after school that evening.

As she waited for him in the woods later that evening, her heart pounded uncontrollably. She worried he wouldn't come, or that she would not know what to say when he did come. It felt like she waited a very long time, more than a lifetime. It was actually just ten minutes. When Wang Li came, he told her he liked her too. She was so excited she almost cried. She really wanted to jump up and hug him, but she didn't move, and neither did he. There were three steps between them. It seemed that what stood between them was not air, but solid ice, or a city wall, or a slab of steel. They just stood there, looking at each other in the dark. She couldn't remember how long they stood there or exactly what they said. When they realized it had gotten late, they walked back together, one walked on the east side of the road and the other, the west side, with an empty road lying between them.

Xiulan said she felt good after that. They said they would not let it affect their studies, but once it was out in the open, there was no thought of studying. Wang Li's grades began to decline too. The next semester, he was transferred to another school. But even that was not a solution. Once love had taken root, even a whole team of oxen couldn't pull it out. The school Wang Li went was far away, and it was a tough time for him. He couldn't afford to have a proper meal at school and only paid for half the meal. He would buy a bowl of porridge at school and ate it with two cold buns he brought from home for lunch. He went home to fetch the buns once a week, and Xiulan was always waiting for him by the road before he headed back, giving him a jar of chilli or a can of pickled vegetables. Later, when Wang Li became a soldier, Xiulan always got a warm feeling when she passed the intersection where she had always waited for Wang Li, and she would stop there for a while.

An Ning said, "I wouldn't have imagined you were such a romantic girl."

"I was a very happy, romantic girl. I'll miss that sort of happiness and romance for the rest of my life." Xiulan sighed. "Others endure bitterness to get to the sweet. For me, it was sweet first, then bitter later. Maybe I had too much of the sweetness offered me, and that's why God made me suffer so much later."

An Ning didn't say anything, waiting for Xiulan to go on.

Xiulan said, "When Wang Li's father passed away, he couldn't return from the Sichuan-Xizang Line, and his younger brother, Wang Bo, was working in Guangzhou and couldn't be contacted. I buried the old man myself. As soon as he passed away, I felt that the house was very empty, so I locked it up and went to work in a condensed milk factory in the county. Later, I had Xiaoxue and couldn't work for a few months. By that time, even if I went back to work, they wouldn't want me. So I went to work in a private cotton spinning factory, and I've been there until now. With a salary of six hundred a month, my daughter and I are very frugal, and we manage to get by."

An Ning asked, "Is six hundred enough? Doesn't Wang Li send you money?"

Xiulan was quiet for a long time, then shifted the topic to Wang Li's brother Wang Bo. "Wang Bo later came back from Guangzhou and rented a small house in the county seat, where he ran a cement company, but business was no good. Actually, I knew that half the reason Wang Bo came back was for us. He was much more innocent than his brother. He hardly ever said a word. Who knew that such an honest fellow would be arrested no more than half a year after he came back."

Surprised, An Ning asked, "What did he do?"

Xiulan said, "When the police arrested him, he had no idea what he had done. They accused him of being a gangster. He was taken to a detention center, his head was shaved, and he was locked up for two weeks. I found a relative of one of Wang Li's comrades-in-arms at the Regional Public Security Bureau, and asked him to help arrange for the release of my brother-in-law. When I made the request, I found out that the government branch in charge of development in the west wanted to rectify the investment environment and crack down on wrongdoers. But why would they need to rectify honest people? Wang Li's comrade said that Wang Bo had once played mahjong with a particular person, and it had all been recorded. When there were not enough arrests, he had been arrested too. I said that I knew about Wang Bo playing mahjong and it had been dealt with at the time; he had paid the fine. Wang Li's comrade didn't say anything for a long time, but he finally said that those working for the County Public Security Bureau were meddling in the affair and had broken the law, so sooner or later, something would go wrong. After a year, something really did happen."

"What?"

"The chief of the Public Security Bureau was arrested."

"Why?"

"Collaborating with the gangs. They were told to move in on the underworld. Who knew that the public security bureau and the gangs were two legs of the same pair of pants? They tipped off the gangsters, and many honest people like Wang Bo were arrested in place of the actual criminals."

An Ning said, "I've heard of such things. It seems like it was in the newspapers a few years ago."

"Yes, you're right. It caused a big commotion. It was published in the *People's Daily* and broadcast on CCTV," Xiulan said. "There was another incident in the county that was even more notorious than this one. An escort became a judge— maybe you've heard of that?"

An Ning, "That was also in your county?"

Xiulan said with a wry smile, "My county is a poor county, and it's never been well known. These two things made us suddenly notorious. And both incidents were connected to Wang Bo."

Surprised, An Ning asked, "What did this have to do with Wang Bo?"

Xiulan said, "The escort was Wang Bo's former girlfriend. They planned to get married before my father-in-law died. I said half the reason Wang Bo came back was for me and my daughter; the other half was for that girl.

"Her name was Chunling. When Wang Bo was working in Guangzhou, she was working in the county seat. She said she was working, but her work was done in a dance hall. At first, she just served tea or other drinks to the guests, but when she saw that the escorts made such easy money, she got the itch to try it, and she started making enough to get by on. She was good looking, so she made good money. Once she started earning such good money, she started to look down on Wang Bo. Later, she got involved with one of the county officials who often patronized the place. He rented an apartment for her. She stopped working to be his mistress. She got bored staying at home alone, so she pestered the official to find her a job. The official put together falsified qualifications, and she changed her status, and she became a judge in a neighboring district. Once she became a judge, she didn't know anything, so she would not make decisions on any case, and the cases were better dealt with without her involvement. She didn't know how to write the verdicts, but she figured there were ways around that. She gave her colleagues packs of cigarettes in exchange for them writing verdicts on her behalf. This all came out eventually, and it was in the papers and on TV. The official was dismissed, and the woman returned to the countryside to live as a farmer. She never contacted me, and I didn't know anything until something happened later on. I wanted to call Wang Bo and tell him, but I felt there was no point. Of course, he couldn't marry a broken woman, so I thought it best to wait for him to come back, and I would help him find someone else then. But Wang Bo saw the report in the papers, and he rushed back. The woman couldn't bear to see Wang Bo, so she jumped into the well that night, killing herself."

Xiulan finally turned back to the topic of Wang Li, but she would only talk about his past, never mentioning anything about his present circumstances. An Ning thought it was very strange.

Throughout their journey, Xiulan had always been evasive when talking about her husband. An Ning felt there was much hidden behind her words, but it was a private matter. If she didn't want to bring it up herself, it wasn't nice to pry.

25

When An Ning woke in the morning, she saw that Xiulan was already doing laundry in the courtyard. Xiulan woke up early every day, always feeling that her work was still unfinished. After she finished washing the soldiers' dirty clothes, she washed their sheets and blankets. She washed almost anything she could find to wash.

Guo Hong got up early that day as well, surprising An Ning. Guo Hong did not busy herself with this and that like Xiulan did, but wandered around the camp alone, as if looking for her lost soul. An Ning knew she was worried about Deng Gang. One day for a husband and wife held a hundred days worth of bliss, all the more for now that Deng Gang had not been back for two days and two nights. Anyone would be worried in that situation. On top of that, the two trapped soldiers had still not been rescued.

Not wanting to bother Guo Hong, An Ning went straight to Feng Xiaoli's room. She had mostly spent the past two days taking care of the lieutenant. Though Hou Qing and the messenger were there, and though they were comrades, they were male comrades, making it inconvenient for them to be Lieutenant Feng's caregivers. An Ning climbed the snowy slope behind the barracks nearly every day, chiseled out blocks of ice, and went back to apply the cold compress to Lieutenant Feng's foot. Feng Xiaoli was very grateful for the help. She was three years older than An Ning, and the two had taken to calling each other "Sis." As they got to know each other over the past few days, An Ning had developed a favorable impression of Xiaoli, feeling she was a simple, cheerful girl. She had an even stronger feeling that there was nothing going on between Xiaoli and Deng Gang, and that Guo Hong must have misunderstood things. She tried to find a time to talk to Guo Hong and help loosen the knot, but she never revealed anything in front of Xiaoli, and Xiaoli did not take the initiative to bring it up.

As An Ning and Xiaoli chatted after breakfast, Xiaoli talked about her brother. She said he was 1.8 meters tall and very handsome. He wrote poetry, sang, and played the guitar. Xiaoli really loved and admired her brother. Her female classmates all envied her for having such a good brother. Each time her brother came home to visit his family, she followed him around like a puppy, never leaving his side. Her brother knew a lot, and every time he came back, he told her all about Xizang.

The summer of the third year he had been in Xizang, there was a heavy rain and the house collapsed, trapping her parents inside. After her parents died, she stayed at school, and her brother sent her money every month. He was still studying in the military academy at the time, not working as an officer, so his allowance was quite small. He lived very frugally so that he could send her everything he saved. She harbored a wish to visit her brother in Xizang as soon as she graduated from high school. But before she graduated from high school, her brother was gone.

Talking about it, Xiaoli got choked up and couldn't go on. An Ning cried with her.

When the tears started, An Ning didn't want Xiaoli to talk about such sad things anymore, so she changed the subject and spoke about her experiences when she was in college. Xiaoli's mood brightened up again as they chatted.

An Ning said, "Actually, I admire you female soldiers more than anyone else. When you wear your military uniform and walk down the street, you look so cool."

Xiaoli said, "That's how female soldiers look in the big office. They live in the city, so of course they're cool. People like us, staying in this ravine all year round, we're covered in water and mud, and we look horrible. We aren't the least bit cool."

An Ning said, "It really isn't easy for a woman to stay here."

Xiaoli said, "I don't mind suffering. I'm used to it. Other people who live wrapped in good things won't understand what good is, and we don't really understand what is meant by suffering when we live immersed in suffering. Take showering. It's much better now that the squadron has installed solar water heaters. When I first joined the army, I would go without a shower for ten days or two weeks at a time, and I smelled terrible. I kept my distance from others when I spoke to them, afraid they would smell that awful odor. Construction crews like ours are like migratory birds. Or not quite, actually. Birds move as the seasons change. We didn't care what season it was. Once the road was repaired, it was time to move to a place where there was no road or where the road was blocked. We always stayed in the most difficult places, where there were no roads. People often say that station camps are fixed or unmoving like iron, while the soldiers move all the time like flowing water. But we are the opposite, moving our camps all the time and working as steadily as iron soldiers."

An Ning said, "You don't really understand what is meant by suffering when you live immersed in suffering, and you soldiers in mobile camps really like iron. That's good. Well said, and very deep."

Xiaoli said, "I'm not the one who said it. It was our captain. Look at this wooden house. It's hot in the summer and cold in the winter, but because we're always on the move, it's the only kind of house we can live in. The biggest problem is that it's not soundproof. There are almost no secrets among the troops. If someone's family comes to visit him, those staying next door hear it all. It's most troublesome for the female soldiers. Back when there was no solar power, when we female soldiers couldn't stand it anymore, we would boil a pot of hot water and bring it to my room. We didn't dare to make a sound as we cleaned up, fearing that the male soldiers would hear. When I first joined the army, our squad was working alone in one place. There were nine of us in the squad, and I was the only woman. While the male soldiers went to the construction site, I just made a fire and cooked at the camp. I was alone in the barracks for most of the day. The mountain was quiet, aside from the occasional sound of distant explosions where the male soldiers were opening up the mountain. We were so high above sea level that there were not even any birds. The days were so lonely it almost drove me crazy. Aside from cooking, all I could do was help the male soldiers with their laundry, then sit on a rock and count the explosions in the distance. I was only at ease when the other soldiers came back in the evening.

"But many things were unreliable, like the wooden walls. There were small gaps in the wooden wall between me and the male soldiers, and though I turned out the light before undressing for bed each night, I was always uneasy and on my guard, fearing there were one or two pairs of eyes peeking at me in the dark. I covered the gaps in the wooden wall with newspaper, but after a few days, I found that someone had poked a small hole in it at one spot. I was terrified, so I covered the hole with more newspaper. After a few days, there were other holes in other spots. I didn't know who poked the holes, and to be honest, I didn't want to know. What was the use in knowing? I didn't tell the squad leader, and I didn't complain about my comrades. They were all as young as I was, and they were naturally curious about girls. That was normal. And anyway, I always turned off the light before undressing, so it wasn't like they could see anything. But inwardly, I was still uneasy. It was like there was a thorn growing inside me, and I couldn't sleep soundly at night. During my first few months on the mountain, I don't know how many times my fellow soldiers poked holes in the newspaper covering my walls, and I don't know how many times I plastered yet more newspaper over it. But when I had been on the mountain for a while, I became more familiar with them, and we all felt we were dependent on each other. I was confident they wouldn't hurt me, and that they began to care more and more for me, like they would for a sister, and I was no longer afraid. The next time a hole appeared in the newspaper, I didn't bother to paste over it. After a few days, that little hole was pasted over from the other side.

"And like I said, I was afraid the male soldiers next door would hear me bathing in my room. I didn't dare to hang my underclothes outside to dry when I'd washed them, either, so I had to hang them indoors, out of the sunlight, to dry. Think about it: I was just seventeen or eighteen, and I was living in a house where there was no soundproofing with eight guys. It was so embarrassing! After a while, I started bathing in the daytime, when they were at the construction site. While the rice simmered in the pot, I went in by myself to bathe. I always worried that one of the male soldiers might come back, but it was still better than cleaning up at night. Once when I was bathing inside the house, the firewood fell from the stove and some of the kindling on the ground caught fire. The male soldiers were there, so I frantically fought the fire on my own. I finally managed to put it out before it caused too much damage, but half of my hair was singed."

Once the mission was completed, we went back to the squadron. Deng Gang was deputy squadron commander at the time. When he saw that my head was like that, he got angry with the squad leader. I had never seen him angry before. I told him it had nothing to do with the squad leader, but that it was just an accident. His eyes turned red, though, and he said he would never let me leave the squadron again. He said he would not forgive himself if something happened to me when he owed such a debt to my brother. When he mentioned my brother, I started crying. He really didn't let me leave the squadron again after that, but arranged for me to join the cooking crew. As a girl in a construction team like this, all I could do was cook. When Deng Gang came back from an assignment, he brought me a set of materials I could review to prepare for the college entrance exam, which would allow me to go to the military academy. He said a girl who didn't want to spend her life cooking in the army needed to learn some real skills. I was touched, and I almost cried. If my own brother were there, that's exactly how he would have taken care of me. I wanted to call Deng Gang my big brother, and I wanted to cry in his arms, but I held back my tears. I knew that if I cried, he would be sad too. I didn't want to make him feel sad anymore. For the next few months, I sat in front of the stove, reviewing the material as I kept the fire going. I was admitted to college, but not the military academy. Instead, I went to the Xi'an Highway

College. Deng Gang sent money to me at school every month, just as my brother had done before he died."

An Ning said, "You obviously have very deep feelings for him."

Xiaoli said, "He's always taken care of me like I was his own little sister, and I've always seen him as a big brother. You might laugh, but sometimes I misbehave in front of him or throw a bit of a tantrum, and he never gets annoyed."

"Doesn't it make you angry when he reprimands you like he did the day before yesterday?"

"That's work. They're two separate things." Xiaoli recalled something, and a sort of anxiety filled her eyes. "I don't know how they are now."

They were silent for a moment, then Xiaoli said, "Guo Hong may have gotten the wrong idea. That makes me very sad."

While they were talking, Deng Gang came in, covered in mud. His eyes were red and swollen, and there were blisters on his mouth. His whole face was dirty and peeling.

An Ning hurriedly stood up and said, "Well, speak of the devil."

Xiaoli asked anxiously, "Have the two soldiers been rescued?"

Deng Gang replied, "No." He picked up the jar of tea and emptied it in one gulp. "I've tried everything, but I still can't get up there."

Xiaoli said, "What can we do? It's been two days and two nights."

Deng Gang said, "They'll be fine for now. I saw a fire they lit on the mountain this morning. I've reported to the corps and asked for air support from the Chengdu Military Region. We'll try to rescue them with Black Hawk helicopters. The corps is requesting instructions from HQ. I've come back to wait for the call from the higher ups."

Concerned, he asked Xiaoli, "How is your injury?"

She waved her hand casually. "I'm fine. You go take care of your work."

Deng Gang turned to An Ning. "I'm sorry. This is so much trouble for you."

Then he said to Xiaoli, "You get some rest. I'm heading out."

And with that, he left.

The news that the Black Hawk was energized An Ning. Thinking it was a good opportunity to capture some live action news, she followed Deng Gang out. She couldn't follow him all the way to the brigade, so she turned in at the reception room, waiting to see when Deng Gang would set out on the rescue mission. When she went in, she saw Guo Hong and Xiaoxue sitting on the bed folding paper cranes.

Suspecting Guo Hong had heard what she and Xiaoli had said next door, she said, "Deng Gang is back. Why don't you hurry and find him?"

Guo Hong sat where she was, not saying a word. They could hear Deng Gang on the phone.

An Ning understood. The couple had not spoken yet, and Guo Hong was still under the wrong impression about Deng Gang and Feng Xiaoli. Thinking it was time to tell Guo Hong everything, she tugged at Guo Hong and said, "Come on. I've got something to tell you."

When the pair went into the courtyard, An Ning summed up for Guo Hong all that she knew about the relationship between Deng Gang and Xiaoli.

Guo Hong said, "I heard the two of you talking just now."

"Don't you want to hurry to see Deng Gang? He's lost a lot of weight. I really felt bad for him when I saw him."

There were tears in Guo Hong's eyes. "But ..."

There was still a question in the back of her mind, something she couldn't put into words clearly so that An Ning could understand.

An Ning said, "What's there to be shy about between a husband and wife?"

They were standing in the courtyard, whispering, when Deng Gang walked out of the brigade office. An Ning left Guo Hong and ran over to ask, "Did you get through?"

"Yes. The helicopter will be here in an hour. I need to hurry and make preparations."

An Ning said, "I want to go with you."

"For what? The construction site is dangerous. You can't go there!"

"I'm going to report on it. I'm a reporter. It's my job."

Deng Gang said, "So what if you're a reporter? You're not allowed to go there. Who will be responsible if something goes wrong?"

"I will," An Ning said.

Deng Gang said, "No, absolutely not."

An Ning said, "You have your job, and I have mine. I'm going to do onsite reporting, with or without your approval."

She turned away from Deng Gang and went into the room. Taking her camera, she set out on her own.

Helpless, Deng Gang told the messenger to take a hard hat, caught up to An Ning, and gave it to her. Then he told her sternly, "When we get there, you have to follow my instructions. No running off."

Happy, An Ning snapped to attention and saluted. "Yes, Comrade Captain!"

26

A Black Hawk helicopter circled in the blue sky. On the ground, the battalion leader spoke to command over the radio. An Ning ran back and forth, snapping one photo after another.

The Black Hawk was locked onto the target, but because the top of the mountain was covered with snow, it was impossible for it to land. The Black Hawk seemed to be frozen in the sky over the mountain, its rotor stirred up dust and snow. A rope was lowered from the helicopter, and five or six soldiers descended to the mountain's peak. After a while, a man began ascending the rope, going back to the helicopter. Half an hour later, the two were safely in the helicopter. Cheers rose from the construction site.

An Ning was so excited her hands trembled a little as they held the camera. Watching everything unfold in front of her, she suddenly thought of the American film *Saving Private Ryan*. Wasn't the scene here a true story of China saving its soldiers in Xizang? How many senior generals had been stirred to save these two soldiers? And how many hearts had been touched by the rescue efforts?

The Black Hawk flew away from the top of the mountain, but instead of continuing to fly off onto the distance, it circled and landed on flat ground near the construction site. An Ning ran over with the battalion leader and Deng Gang. The two soldiers were carried out on stretchers and surrounded by several medical workers who had been standing by. A general then descended from the Black Hawk, followed by a colonel, then the rest of their entourage.

The battalion leader hurried forward and saluted. "Reporting, sir! My battalion is on a rescue mission, sir! Awaiting instructions, sir!"

The general returned the salute. "Carry on with the construction works!"

The battalion leader saluted again. "Yes, sir!"

When Deng Gang saluted, the general asked, "Are you Deng Gang?"

Deng Gang said, "Yes, sir. It was me who failed to organize the troops well, sir! Awaiting the general's reprimand, sir!"

The general smiled. "Your battalion leader is here. If someone is to be reprimanded, it won't be you."

The battalion leader said awkwardly, "Quite right, sir."

It seemed he wasn't sure whether he should reprimand himself or Deng Gang.

The general waved a hand. "I came here to boost morale, not to reprimand anyone. How could such a situation be avoided in the midst of such a daunting task? Fortunately, the two soldiers escaped safely, and they are just a bit cold and hungry. Recovery will not be too slow."

Seeing An Ning, the general turned and asked Deng Gang, "Why is there a local female comrade at the construction site? This is ..."

Before Deng Gang could answer, An Ning stepped forward and said, "Sir, my name is An Ning. I'm a reporter with the *Rongcheng Daily*."

"A reporter! Welcome then!" He joked, "It's fine to report on this, but we'll need to review the manuscript. We can't have you leak military secrets."

As the general inspected the construction site, he asked about the progress of the rescue world. The battalion leader reported, "Three kilometers of the access road have been repaired, and more than half of the diversion channel has been dug. According to our estimations, we will complete the task on schedule."

The general said solemnly, "No estimations. I want guarantees. We must ensure that the task is completed on schedule."

The battalion leader shouted in reply, "Yes, sir! The task will be completed on schedule, sir!"

The general asked Deng Gang if any of the troops had been injured. Deng Gang replied that four officers and soldiers had sustained minor injuries.

The general waved his hand and said, "Let's go see them."

Deng Gang led them toward a nearby tent. An Ning followed.

As they walked, the general said, "The things you've achieved so far are not negligible, but the further you go, the more vigilant you need to be. Don't be careless! Judging from the situation at the site, the rescue work is very difficult, an arduous task. You must do the rescue work with one hand and monitor with the other, and both hands must be deft in their work—especially the safety work! That is the key. It can't be taken lightly."

Lowering their heads to enter the flap, the small group went into the tent. One officer and two soldiers lay inside. The officer's arm was injured and had a plaster cast on it. One of the soldiers had a bandage on his head. He said he had been injured by a stone that flew at him. The other soldier was a new recruit. His face had turned a dark blue color from exhaustion and altitude sickness. He had an IV in his arm and an oxygen tube in his nose. The general walked to each one, leaned over to inspect his injuries, said a few comforting words, then stood up and prepared to leave. He suddenly stopped and asked Deng Gang, "Didn't you say there were four injured troops? Why are there only three here?"

Deng Gang said, "The other one is in brigade HQ. It's our engineer, Lieutenant Feng Xiaoli."

The general seemed to be familiar with Feng Xiaoli's name. Surprised, he asked, "She's injured?"

The battalion leader said, "During an attempt to rescue the two soldiers who were trapped on the mountain, she slipped and sprained her ankle. Do you want to go visit her?"

Before the general had a chance to express his view, the colonel said, "Of course we want to visit her."

They drove to the brigade camp and walked into Feng Xiaoli's room. Guo Hong was there, chatting with Xiaoli. Seeing so many people come in at once, Guo Hong quickly stood up. Deng Gang was embarrassed. His wife visiting the team at this time would not make a good impression on the higher ups, but it wouldn't be so easy to hide who she was, so Deng Gang took the initiative to make introductions. Pointing at Guo Hong, he said, "This is my wife."

Feng Xiaoli tried to get up, but the general reached out and stopped her. "Lie down. Don't get up. Didn't you injure your leg?"

Feng Xiaoli said, "No, sir, I'm fine."

Standing to one side, the colonel laughed and said, "What's this 'sir' nonsense? You've got the license. You should call him Dad."

The battalion leader and Deng Gang both laughed, and the battalion leader said, "Yes, you should call him Dad."

Feng Xiaoli blushed, but didn't say anything. An Ning and Guo Hong looked at each other, stunned.

The colonel said, "When will we get your wedding invitations?"

Feng Xiaoli said, "Gao Hu and I only recently registered, but then there was the landslide, and ..."

The colonel looked around and asked Deng Gang, "Where is Gao Hu?"

Deng Gang replied, "He's leading an emergency team in the Ranwu Valley."

The colonel asked the general, "Would you like to have Gao Hu come to meet the commanding officers?"

The general said, "No need for that. Tell him not to come to see me until he completes the mission in the Ranwu Valley."

It was from this conversation that An Ning and Guo Hong finally understood that Feng Xiaoli had a boyfriend, the general's son, and was getting married soon. Guo Hong's face reddened. An Ning shot her a look, by which she telegraphed the message, *See? All a misunderstanding!* Guo Hong lowered her head in embarrassment.

Xiaoli said to the general, "Why did you come up here, with your high blood pressure?"

The general laughed. "I don't just have high blood pressure. My cholesterol and blood sugar levels are high too. I'm almost as swollen as Pavarotti, now that I'm always staying in the capital. For the whole twenty or thirty years I was up here on the plateau, I didn't have any problems. I couldn't get used to things, once I left. It seems that I was born to be on the plateau."

27

On July 18, the road was finally cleared, three days ahead of schedule. Everyone happily crowded onto the highway to watch the rumble of traffic that had been besieged for so many days. Every eastbound car that passed the Nuba section honked to greet the officers and soldiers of the armed police. There was a continuous ring of car horns that echoed through the snow-capped mountains for a long time.

After lying in bed for five days, Feng Xiaoli couldn't sit still any more. Asking An Ning to support her, they went to the highway with Guo Hong, Xiulan, and Xiaoxue. The county magistrate and district commissioner, along with several lamas in red cassocks, brought highland barley and hadas as an expression of gratitude to the troops. Among the crowd, An Ning saw the Living Buddha the women had met on their travels.

The Tibetan people from neighboring areas formed a circle on the grass beside the road. Joining hands, they danced joyously. The general and the local leaders wore hadas and danced with everyone else. The herdsman sang and danced. The songs were all in Tibetan, so An Ning couldn't understand a word. Feng Xiaoli translated for them:

> The song sung standing on the mountain
> Is the loudest song of all
> Lower your head before the snowy mountain range
> May our song fly to Chairman Mao's side

Feng Xiaoli explained in a low voice, "This is a song from the 1950s. It has been circulated in this area ever since. The herdsmen never get tired of singing it. In the minds of the Tibetan people, Beijing is the motherland,

and Chairman Mao is the Party. They still hang portraits of him in their tents."

When the herdsmen had finished that song, they sang another.
The door to song and dance opens from the snowy mountain
White lion atop the mountain's peak
Please lead us to dance among the galsang!
The door to song and dance opens from the cliffs
White-breasted eagle atop the cliffs
Please lead us to dance among the galsang!
The door to song and dance opens from the prairie
Golden deer on the prairie
Please lead us to dance among the galsang!
Let's go! Let's dance together!
An auspicious golden bridge, built just for us
Let's dance! Let's dance together!
The fields of galsang sing and dance with us

An Ning was moved by the scene and couldn't help but join the crowd's dancing. The joyful song and dance continued throughout the afternoon, when the crowd finally dispersed. The battalion leader and Deng Gang went to see the general and colonel off when they left.

On the way back to the barracks, An Ning noticed that Guo Hong was a little subdued. Though her friend sometimes joked and laughed, An Ning sensed a trace of anxiety and unease in it. She knew what Guo Hong was thinking. Traffic was open now, so there was no reason for things to drag on between Guo Hong and Deng Gang. It was time to resolve the issue. But so much had happened recently, and that made Guo Hong hesitate. She was uncertain, not quite sure what to do. An Ning and Xiulan had discussed matters earlier, and they planned to leave that afternoon, continuing their journey. Deng Gang had arranged a jeep for them. Now, seeing Guo Hong like this, An Ning changed her mind. She wanted to stay and talk to Guo Hong again, see if she could be of some help to the couple, then move on tomorrow. At any rate, it had already been such a long delay. What was another half day or so?

An Ning and Guo Hong had talked quite a bit over the past couple of days. Guo Hong had been evasive at first, but she later told An Ning what was on her mind. She wanted a divorce, but she was reluctant too. After all, they had been married for six years, and she had misunderstood Deng Gang's relationship with Feng Xiaoli. They could stay together, but she felt that Deng Gang didn't love her anymore. Although Deng Gang had not said anything, Guo Hong was sure it was only because he did not want to upset the troops.

An Ning did not believe that. She said, "I think he still loves you very much. You have nothing to worry about."

Guo Hong shook her head, resigned. She sighed and said, "Only the wearer can tell where the shoe pinches. To tell you the truth, even though we've been staying together, we've been sleeping on separate beds."

An Ning was shocked. "How can that be?"

Guo Hong said, "I'm telling you the truth. At first, he intended to do that, and he crawled into my bed twice late at night, but I pushed him out. He hasn't had any interest in me for the past two years. We only did it a couple of times during his forty days off for home leave each year, and he was always so reluctant every single time, like he was suffering. Now that I want a divorce, he's suddenly being good to me. I find it disgusting, like he's just doing it to get his own way. Later, after discussing the matter between him and Xiaoli, I found out that I'd misjudged him. I wanted to make allowances, and I hoped he would come to me at night, but he never did. Maybe I hurt him too badly. On top of that, he's always busy at the construction site. He rarely comes back, and when he does, he falls asleep as soon as his head touches the pillow."

When they had been dancing on the grass earlier, An Ning had taken Deng Gang's hand. She could tell that he was unhappy; the smile on his face couldn't hide his inner turmoil. An Ning thought he and Guo Hong must both be thinking the same thing, worrying that their marriage would end as soon as the rescue mission was completed. Now the rescue mission was completed. The road was open. There was no reason to drag on. He had to face Guo Hong; there was no escaping it.

But when An Ning asked him what was bothering him, he gave a different reason. "If you had ever led soldiers, you would know what's bothering me. As a commander, when the situation is at its worst, when your soldiers are down, you have to be confident and use your own positive mindset to keep your soldiers' spirits up. When your soldiers are celebrating a great victory, you have to stay calm and be prepared for danger. You have to always be vigilant and not give in to extremeness of either joy or sorrow."

Deng Gang's words surprised her. She wasn't surprised by how philosophical he was, but that he didn't seem to be the least bit worried about his marriage. She didn't know whether he really didn't harbor such worries, or if he just put on a show of unconcern in front of An Ning for the sake of his male ego. Either way, she really admired men like Deng Gang. If the couple did divorce, it would only be Guo Hong's loss.

Deng Gang said, "I'm always worried that something bad will happen."

An Ning smiled and said, "The road is open. What could happen now? You shouldn't wear yourself out. Relax a little."

When An Ning and Guo Hong reached the barracks, they were greeted by the Living Buddha, walking out of the barracks. He folded his hands together and greeted them with a tranquil smile, then walked away alone. Guo Hong recalled that the last time they had seen the Living Buddha, he had said he and Deng Gang were friends, but Deng Gang had gone to see the general off and was not in camp now. What was the Living Buddha doing here?

Not long after Guo Hong went into the house, Hou Qing came over, carrying a sheepskin bag in his arms.

Guo Hong asked, "What's this?"

"Tibetan medicine. The Living Buddha brought it over just now," Hou Qing said. "It's the last dose. He said that within two weeks, the captain's ailment should be cured."

"What's wrong with him?"

"This ailment ... it's been almost two years. You don't know?"

Even more surprised, Guo Hong said, "He never told me! What's wrong?"

Seeing Guo Hong so upset, Hou Qing became more alert, realizing that Deng Gang had hidden it from Guo Hong. No man would want to let a woman know about such an ailment. Hou Qing regretted that he had been foolish enough to overlook that point. He quickly changed tack. "Oh, it's nothing! If that's all, ma'am, I'll be going now."

He was about to leave, sheepskin still in hand, but Guo Hong stopped him. "What's going on? You have to tell me!"

There was nothing else to do, so Hou Qing told her the truth. Two years earlier, Deng Gang had fallen from the retaining wall while directing the construction works. He landed hard on his groin on the rocks, and he almost passed out from the pain. The comrades nearby helped him up, and seeing that there was no obvious injury, they went on about their work without bothering about it any further. Deng Gang was in so much pain he could barely stand, but because Feng Xiaoli was present, he couldn't tell the others what had happened. In the evening, he found Hou Qing and quietly told him what happened. With his background in Chinese medicine, Hou Qing started treating him secretly, giving him acupuncture for two weeks, until the pain finally subsided. But he was still not feeling well, and it was painful when he urinated. By then, it was winter, and the troops would descend soon. Hou Qing couldn't do more, and he suggested Deng Gang have it checked at the hospital in Chengdu while he was on home leave, to prevent potential long term issues.

During his time at home, without telling Guo Hong, Deng Gang had visited many hospitals, but had not received good news from any of them. What embarrassed him was that when he finally reunited with his wife, he couldn't perform. It wasn't that it was impossible, but that the entire process left him in unbearable pain. It hurt every time, making him sweat profusely and almost making him pass out. He didn't want to tell Guo Hong the real reason, fearing that she would be disappointed in him, so he made himself go through with it each time. The next year when he was back on home leave, he had continued to seek medical treatment, trying everything he could think of, but the condition still did not improve. One day at the beginning of this year, the Living Buddha came to the camp. Hearing that the Living Buddha was very knowledgeable and skilled in traditional Tibetan medicine, Deng Gang shared his secret with their guest. The Living Buddha had been treating him with Tibetan remedies for the past six months.

Hou Qing opened the sheepskin bag and showed the contents to Guo Hong. "See, this is the Tibetan medicine."

There were many black pills inside, each the size of a bean. Guo Hong's vision blurred and her nose burned. Tears flowed down her cheeks.

So he had been sick all this time! Why hadn't he told her?

Hou Qing said, "The Living Buddha said this type of ailment is very painful. It will flare up when the weather changes, and it will hurt every time you urinate. He said the captain has great endurance and is really an amazing guy. It's difficult for anyone, and he's been enduring it for two years."

The tears rushed wildly down Guo Hong's face.

Hou Qing said, "Actually, I knew you came here to divorce the captain. Bai and I both heard you two quarreling at night. Ma'am, the captain really is a good person. You can't leave him. Anyway, the Living Buddha said that after he takes the last of this medicine, he'll be completely cured."

As Hou Qing went on, tears streamed down his face too. "Ma'am, I'm just a soldier, and I know there are some things I shouldn't say. But I'm also an old veteran, and I have my own wife and children. I won't be happy if I don't tell you this. Do you have any idea how hurt the captain was when he realized you had come all the way here to divorce him? But he didn't want to affect the morale of the troops, so he quietly swallowed his own bitterness. A man is only human, and he needs understanding, support, and comfort. Ma'am, you know, the captain loves you very much. Yesterday, when I went to the construction site to deliver the meal, as he squatted by the road to eat, he asked about you. He said you'd never been to the plateau and might have altitude sickness. He told me to take good care of you. I asked him quietly, 'Is she really going to divorce you?' He glared at me and told me to keep quiet. He said that if word got out, he would deal with me. Then he sighed and said, 'I don't want to divorce, but my wife has made up her mind. I have no choice. I can't drag her through all this suffering with me.' He said he had wronged you by marrying you, and that he felt really sorry for you. He said he didn't see you all year, and he couldn't give you a good life, and he felt very guilty about that."

Guo Hong covered her face and wept. "Stop, I need to be alone for a while."

Hou Qing wiped his own tears on his sleeve and left.

Guo Hong was still crying when An Ning came in. An Ning was scheduled to leave the next day, and she wanted to urge Guo Hong one more time before leaving. Seeing Guo Hong lying on the bed crying, she didn't know what had happened. She walked over and asked, "You were fine just now. What happened?"

Guo Hong wept, her whole body shaking. An Ning stroked her back and asked anxiously, "What's wrong?"

Guo Hong stood up and threw her arms around An Ning. "I wronged him!" And, in starts and stops, she told An Ning the whole story.

Later, An Ning recorded the story in a column she entitled "The Secret is in the Sheepskin." But because the matter involved someone's personal privacy, she decided not to publish it.

Hearing Guo Hong's story, An Ning laughed. "This is good! The misunderstanding is resolved. You should be happy."

Guo Hong wiped her tears and said, "I feel awful. I feel so sorry for him. Look at how thin he's become!"

Xiulan walked in while they were talking. After listening to An Ning's recap of the matter, she said happily, "That's great! I'll just say, the captain seems like a good person."

The other two women comforted Guo Hong until she finally stopped crying. They continued talking for a while, and Guo Hong gradually started to smile. An Ning thought of now she was going to leave Guo Hong, and she couldn't help but share her own plans to marry Li Qingge. Guo Hong and Xiulan were very happy when they heard the news, but then Guo Hong pretended to be angry. "I've treated you like a sister. I told you everything! You have this huge happy news, and you kept it to yourself all this time."

An Ning said, "I'm sorry, but I was afraid if others knew about my plans, it would lose the romance."

Guo Hong said, "I'm jealous—such a romantic wedding!"

An Ning said, "Keep this secret between the three of us. Don't tell anyone else for now."

It grew dark as they talked. Before going out, An Ning told Guo Hong, "Deng Gang will be back soon. You should get the ball rolling. Have good talk with him."

But they didn't come to an understanding that night. Deng Gang came back very late, and as soon as he came in, he immediately fell asleep on the bed. He was obviously exhausted. Looking at her skinny, exhausted husband, Guo Hong's nose burned, and her tears welled up. She thought to herself, *He's too tired. I won't disturb him. Let him rest, and I'll tell him what's on my mind tomorrow.*

28

That night, An Ning packed up her things and prepared to go to bed. Seeing that Xiaoxue was still folding the little paper cranes, she walked over and sat beside the bed, running her hand over Xiaoxue's hair, she asked, "You've been folding cranes throughout the entire journey. Still not finished?"

Xiaoxue continued to focus on her folding. Without looking up, she said, "Just nine more to go."

"How many do you want, all together?"

"One hundred," Xiaoxue said. "I should have done a thousand, but I don't have enough paper, so I'll just do a hundred."

There were five or six cranes on the bed that had just been folded. They were delicate and quite pretty. An Ning picked one up and admired it.

"They're beautiful! I'm sure your dad will be so happy to see them."

Xiaoxue did not answer.

An Ning asked, "You miss your dad, don't you?"

Xiaoxue still did not answer. Xiulan was on one side, folding clothes. Seeing that her daughter didn't answer, she said awkwardly to An Ning, "She never has been very talkative, even when she was little."

She then said to Xiaoxue, "Put them away now. Time for bed. We'll be on the road again tomorrow."

Xiaoxue's head was so low her chin nearly touched her chest. Her voice was low, but firm. "I'm not going to bed. I want to finish them tonight."

An Ning said, "Xiaoxue is right. If she doesn't finish them today, how can she give them to her father tomorrow? Here, let me help."

An Ning picked up a piece of paper and was about to fold it, but Xiaoxue stopped her. "No, I want to do it myself."

A little embarrassed, An Ning stood up and said, "I understand. You want to fold it for your dad. I won't bother you. You're doing very well."

"Ignore her. She's stubborn," Xiulan said.

An Ning smiled and said, "She's got spunk. I like it. When she grows up, she'll be very assertive. She has a bright future."

It was still early; the signal for lights out had not even sounded yet. An Ning went out by herself, wanting to see Feng Xiaoli to say goodbye. But when she walked into Xiaoli's room, she realized that her timing was bad. There was a man in the room, a captain. The two were talking quietly. An Ning hesitated, feeling that the face was familiar, but she couldn't remember where she had seen it before. She could see that it was Xiaoli's boyfriend. He looked a lot like the general who had come to the camp.

Seeing An Ning come into the room, Xiaoli quickly stood up and introduced them. "This is the reporter from the *Rongcheng Daily*, An Ning. And this is—"

"No need for introductions," An Ning said. "You must be Gao Hu."

Gao Hu smiled awkwardly and scratched his head awkwardly. He said, "You must be an investigative reporter. That's impressive!"

Xiaoli said to Gao Hu, "She's Li Qingge's girlfriend." An Ning had told Xiaoli why she had come to the plateau.

Gao Hu and Li Qingge had been classmates in the military academy, but he didn't know Li had a girlfriend. His eyes widened in surprise, and he said, "Really?"

Xiaoli said, "She came up here to marry him."

Gao Hu was shocked. "Why didn't that rascal tell me?"

Xiaoli said, "Do you think everyone's like you, wanting to publicize their business to the whole world as if they're afraid people won't know?"

Gao Hu laughed and said, "I'm just afraid you'll back out. If I announce it everywhere first, it will be too late for you to back out. But Li Qingge, that kid's lips are sealed tight. No secret will slip out."

An Ning said, "I didn't tell him I was coming."

Xiaoli and Gao Hu both looked at her in surprise.

"I wanted to surprise him," she said.

The couple looked at each other, understanding.

Xiaoli said, "You came up here to get married, but Li Qingge doesn't even know. That's so romantic."

Gao Hu joked, "So let's all be romantic together. Let's call Li Qingge over here, and we'll have a double wedding."

An Ning said, "Don't tease! Seriously, when do you two plan to get married?"

Xiaoli said, "We're planning for August 1. What about you?"

"When I see Li Qingge, we'll get married," An Ning said. Then she told Gao Hu, "Don't tell him."

Gao Hu said, "Don't worry. I'll let you see your romantic plan through to the end." Then he added, "Li Qingge is in Dongjiu, about a day and a half out of Lhasa. Why did you need to travel so far?"

Before An Ning could answer, Xiaoli said, "It's romance! It's not about the outcome, but about the process. She chose a long journey so she could prolong the process."

An Ning was saved from any further embarrassment by the signal for lights out. She says, "I'll leave you two to your romance. I won't disturb you anymore." And she turned and walked out.

Back in her own room, she found that Xiaoxue had finished folding the paper cranes and was now counting them.

Xiulan said, "That's enough, Xiaoxue. You've counted them three times."

As if she had not heard at all, Xiaoxue concentrated on counting the cranes. When she was done, she put them into the bag and went to bed.

At night, An Ning heard Xiulan tossing and turning, but she did not fall asleep. She was going to see her husband the following day, so of course it was hard to sleep. Perhaps she was too excited, or maybe it was something else. An Ning couldn't be sure. When they arrived at Bomi the next day and met Xiulan's husband, maybe everything would be clearer.

With that in mind, she stopped bothering about Xiulan's affairs. She thought of Li Qingge. When she had seen Feng Xiaoli and Gao Hu's affectionate demeanor, she had started thinking of him. It would be so good if he was with her now, but he was somewhere a hundred kilometers away. Was he thinking of her, like she was thinking of him? Maybe he was already asleep. He did not know she was on her way to see him, so of course he was not excited, not losing sleep over it.

Tomorrow they would reach Bomi, and the day after that, Dongjiu. And when they arrived at Dongjiu, she would see Li Qingge. As she came closer to Li Qingge, she grew more and more excited, even a little nervous. She wondered what his expression would be like when she suddenly appeared in front of him.

29

The first time she saw Li Qingge, An Ning felt that he was shy. His smile left a deep impression on her. She suspected it may have been his smile that made her fall in love with him.

It had been winter vacation three years earlier, when An Ning was preparing her graduation thesis. She had been living in the student dorms since she moved out from home. Even though it was the winter vacation, many of the students had not gone home, but were staying in the dorms instead. Some used the vacation to take supplementary courses or to write their graduation thesis. Others spent the vacation traveling around the city to try to find a job that would allow them to stay in Chengdu after graduation. Some tutored or worked, busily earning the next term's school fees.

An Ning was looking for materials in the library when her phone rang. She glanced and saw it was her sister. An Jing told her that Li Qingge had come back from Xizang, and they all getting together for dinner that evening.

When she heard that Li Qingge was back, for some inexplicable reason, An Ning was very excited. Though she had not met him before, her sister had mentioned him frequently since returning from Xizang.

An Ning knew nearly everything that had happened along the way when An Jing's troupe had toured Xizang, so in An Ning's mind, Li Qingge was already a familiar friend. But she said on the phone, "I don't know him. What's it got to do with me? I'm not going."

An Jing said, "You've always been ready for a good meal. Don't you want to go to Douhua?"

An Ning loved to eat at Douhua. It was her favorite restaurant. Sometimes, she would get a craving for it, and she would drag An Jing there for a meal.

Not giving An Ning time to answer, An Jing said in her most domineering manner, "Come out now. I'll be waiting for you at the school gate."

An Jing was at the gate, just as she had said she would be. But she was not alone. There were two other girls with her. One was tall and thin, with a sunny face, and she wore a denim jacket. The other looked a few years older. She was not as tall, but she had a fuller figure. They were all from the same school, and they looked familiar, but An Ning didn't know them.

An Jing introduced the plumper girl first. "This is Lu Wei, the teacher with the Youth League Committee."

No wonder she looked so familiar! But An Ning was still surprised. She looked more like a student than a teacher.

As if she had read An Ning's mind, Lu Wei said, "I just graduated last year. Please don't call me Miss Lu. Just call me Lu Wei."

An Ning said, "Hi, Lu Wei."

An Jing introduced the tall girl. "This is Chang Na. She's a sophomore in the art department."

Chang Na said sweetly, "Hello."

Douhua was not far from the school, about three bus stops away. The four girls laughed and chatted all the way there. An Jing said she had wanted to get all the students who had gone to Xizang to join them for a night out, but all except Lu Wei and Chang Na had gone home. Lu Wei didn't have time off during the winter vacation, and Chang Na lived in Chengdu.

An Jing said, "This might just kill Li Qingge. Four beauties accompanying him for dinner."

Lu Wei said, "Yes, just nice. Four beauties." They all agreed.

Chang Na asked, "Then, who is who?"

An Jing said, "You're so thin. You must be Xishi. Lu Wei is the fuller figured, well endowed beauty from the Tang Dynasty, Concubine Yang."

Half annoyed, Lu Wei joked, "Are you complimenting me or insulting me?"

An Jing said, "Of course I'm complimenting you. Concubine Yang is the most attractive of the four beauties, the sexiest, the one men take notice of. Which man doesn't like a well endowed woman?"

Chang Na said, "Don't you have bigger boobs than Lu Wei? Why aren't you Concubine Yang?"

An Jing said, "I'm not as big a tease as Lu Wei is."

Lu Wei swatted at An Jing. An Jing laughed and dodged. When they finished messing about, Chang Na asked, "Then which one are you?"

Seizing the opportunity to get her revenge, Lu Wei said, "She must be Diaochan.

Diaochan had that long scheme to kill Dong Zhuo with the help of Lü Bu. Of the four of us, An Jing is by far the most cunning. She must be Diaochan."

An Jing said, "Okay, teacher knows best. I won't object. We're even now."

Chang Na said to An Ning, "So you're Wang Zhaojun?"

An Ning said, "Talk softer. Everyone is looking at us. Kind of embarrassing, calling ourselves four beauties!"

The four girls chatted and laughed, and before long, they arrived at Douhua. They asked for a private room, and no sooner than they were seated, Li Qingge came in. The three girls who had traveled through Xizang with Li Qingge were very affectionate with him, practically smothering him in a group hug. But Li Qingge did not know An Ning. When An Jing introduced her, he realized that she was An Jing's younger sister. Li Qingge looked at her for a moment, as if he didn't believe it.

An Jing asked, "What are you looking at? Doesn't she look like my sister?"

"She does. I just thought she was your older sister."

An Ning said, "You mean, I look old?"

Realizing he had said the wrong thing, Li Qingge hurried to explain, "I didn't mean that! I mean, you look quieter and steadier than your sister."

An Jing said anxiously, "So I'm flighty?"

Just two sentences, and he had offended both of them! He blushed, suddenly at a loss for words.

Lu Wei came to the rescue. "Stop bullying the poor fellow. You're making him sweat!"

The four girls continued their banter as they placed their order. Li Qingge sat there, very restrained and seldom speaking. Whey they asked him a question, he smiled shyly and answered. An Ning didn't talk much either. She just sat watching Li Qingge. An Jing had said he was so good, so pure, and An Ning wanted to see if it was true. She had a good feeling about him from the moment they met, not because of anything else, just his smile. When he wasn't smiling, he looked very ordinary. Aside from his military bearing, he wasn't much different from any other man. But the moment he smiled, An Ning's eyes lit up. When she later described it, she said his smile was contagious, touching her, making her tremble, making her feel bathed in light. There was an innocence and simplicity about it, like the smile of a newborn baby. A smile like that couldn't be found on the face of an urban man anymore. When she saw Li Qingge's face, she suddenly recalled the line, *His smile is untarnished.*

They were all happy at the restaurant that night. They ordered red wine, Great Wall Dry Red. They were rowdy, drinking and singing until late.

Later, An Jing mentioned how they had compared themselves to the four beauties on the way there. Staring at Li Qingge, she asked, "You know the four beauties?"

Li Qingge recited, "Isn't that, *Outshining the moon, and putting the flowers to shame, a beauty beyond compare.*"

An Jing said, "Correct answer! That's ten points. Now, can you guess which of us is which of the four beauties from ancient times?"

Looking at the four girls, Li Qingge shook his head.

An Jing said, "If you guess one of us right, that person drinks. If you guess wrong, you drink."

Li Qingge laughed and said, "Let's not drink."

An Jing said, "No, you must guess."

Pretending to be embarrassed, he said, "Even the strongest fellow couldn't pass this obstacle."

"Are you going to guess or not?"

An Jing picked up a glass of wine and forced Li Qingge to drink. Li Qinggge pushed the glass away with his hand and said, "Okay, okay, I'll guess."

An Jing pointed at Chang Na and said, "Her first."

Li Qingge said, "Everyone talks about how skinny Xishi was. Chang Na must be Xishi."

Chang Na said "I'm not skinny," but she drank quite happily, all the same.

An Jing pointed to Lu Wei and asked which of the four beauties she was.

Li Qingge said, "Are you from Shaanxi?"

The girls hesitated, uncertain what he was getting at.

An Ning said, "He guessed it. Lu Wei drinks."

"What did he say to make me drink?"

An Ning said, "Concubine Yang was from Shaanxi."

Everyone suddenly realized that he was right. Lu Wei drank, and An Jing pointed at An Ning.

"How about her?"

Not even looking at An Ning, Li Qingge pointed to the sky. Without saying anything, An Ning picked up her glass and drank. Everyone thought for a moment, and they all understood. In pointing to the sky, Li Qingge was referencing Luoyan and Wang Zhaojun.

Lu Wei said, "Wow, you're good!"

An Jing said, "What made you say she was Wang Zhaojun?"

He said, "She was neither humble nor arrogant, but was always very savvy.

She refused to bribe the painter, so he deliberately made her look bad in his work. When the emperor gave it to Chanyu by mistake, she was sent to Xiongnu to be married off."

An Ning said, "So I have the worst fortune. I'll only be able to get married to someone far away."

Lu Wei teased, "Li Qingge gave you the highest evaluation. You're still not satisfied? I saw it right away. The two of you have good chemistry. With the slightest gesture from Qingge, you know exactly what he means."

Li Qingge's face turned very red. An Ning was embarrassed too. She peeked at An Jing, but An Jing seemed unperturbed. She continued to tease Li Qingge.

"Li Qingge is the happiest person in the world today. Four beauties from four different dynasties all coming out for dinner with him. He's happier than the emperor of any single dynasty, that's for sure!"

Li Qingge looked at An Jing. "Do I still have to guess who you are?"

An Jing said, "What's to guess? Diaochan is the only one left. I'll drink."

Saying that, she suddenly came to her senses. "So, actually, you already knew. You were pretending, acting like you couldn't figure it out, but you just wanted to make us drink. Girls, we've been taken in by his honest looks. Li Qingge, you're not getting off so easy. You have to drink too!"

The girls were quite rowdy, forcing Li Qingge to drink.

An Ning had promised to pay the bill, but when the time came, the waiter said the gentleman had already settled it. No one had seen him go to pay. An Jing was quite unhappy, saying she meant to host him, but he hadn't given her face, as if he was afraid she couldn't afford it. Li Qingge just laughed and didn't say anything else.

An Jing said, "Well, if you won't let me buy dinner, let's go for karaoke."

They went to the karaoke club together. When they got into the taxi, they still had not decided which one to go to. As they bickered over it, An Jing's phone rang. She glanced at the screen then, putting her finger over her lips, she sniffed and answered the call. The sound was very loud, and An Ning could hear everything, sitting next to An Jing as she was.

The call was from Chen Kai. When he asked where she was, she said she was having dinner with her classmates. When he asked when she would be done, she said they had just started and the night was still young. She signalled to An Ning and the others to say something loudly so that Chen Kai would hear.

After the call, they continued squabbling over which karaoke club to go to. An Jing suggested Shambhala, because the private rooms were more distinctive and had a Tibetan feel, so they went there.

They had a wild, fun night at Shambhala. They drank a lot of beer, and they sang many songs. Everyone sang. Even Li Qingge, who was a terrible singer, got the fever and learnt to sing one of Ya Dong's songs entitled, "Longing for the Condor." The highlight of the night, though, was when An Jing sang "Galsang Blooms in a Snowy Land."

> Back to Shambhala
> Seeking again the galsang in bloom
> My Shambhala
> My galsang flower
> That day I saw the kelp flying over the sea
> And at night I dreamed of the grassland's waves of flowers
> Some places in this world make us yearn
> The feelings for the grassland can't be shaken
> A yearning, like a snow lotus
> Blooming in the sunlight
> A heavy pack, like a condor
> Flying back home to the snowy land

As she sang, An Jing started to cry. Lu Wei and Chang Na burst into tears too. They went and threw their arms around An Jing, and the three of them finished the song together. An Ning was moved as she watched, catching a glimpse of the place their experiences in Xizang held in their hearts. In that moment, An Ning was struck with an impulse: she wanted to go to Xizang.

When An Ning went to the restroom, she saw Chen Kai sitting alone on a sofa in the main karaoke hall. It was very late, past midnight. She ran back into the private room and pulled An Jing aside, whispering that Chen Kai was outside. An Jing told the others she had something to attend to, and she left. An Ning purposely dragged on with Lu Wei, Chang Na, and Li Qingge, saying she wanted to sing a little longer, hoping this would prevent them from finding out about An Jing's relationship with Chen Kai.

An Jing and Chen Kai had their first quarrel that night. An Jing said she hadn't done anything wrong, and she demanded to know why he had followed her. Chen Kai said that if she hadn't done anything wrong, she wouldn't have needed to lie to him. As it turned out, when she had answered Chen Kai's call in the taxi, An Jing failed to hang up the phone, and Chen Kai heard what they had said. It was the first time she had lied to him. He grew suspicious, so he went to Shambhala. He was very cool-headed and did not just barge into their room, but sat there waiting all that time. He had been waiting for a full four hours.

For the next six months after that, Chen Kai and An Jing argued often. An Ning said that Chen Kai should not have made such a fuss over An Jing going out to the karaoke bar just that one time—and anyway, it wasn't like she and Li Qingge had been alone. She wondered whether Chen Kai had discovered the nude photo. An Jing said that Chen Kai was very open about such things. As soon as she had come back from Xizang, she had enlarged the photo, put it in a beautiful frame, and hung it on the wall in their bedroom. Chen Kai said it was beautiful, and even added that it was the most beautiful photo of her. She told him a man had taken it, but he was not jealous. He said, "You are telling me about it so openly and are bold enough to hang it up. That shows that you're open minded, and it has nothing to do with that man."

What Chen Kai could not figure out was why she lied to him the night she went to the Shambhala. Actually, he felt that she had changed since she came back from Xizang, that she was somehow different from before, but he couldn't tell what it was that was different.

The Shambhala incident was the event that triggered the breakdown of their relationship. An Jing told An Ning that she realized after she returned from Xizang that she did not love Chen Kai. Her feelings for him grew out of her reliance on him when she was helpless, a sort of filling of her emptiness. But that wasn't real love.

She said she had not fallen in love with Li Qingge either. Some time after she returned from the plateau, she realized that what she had fallen in love with was not Li Qingge, but all the soldiers she had met there. She loved their simplicity, their selflessness, their unassuming smiles, and their optimistic spirit. Every day on the plateau, she was both moved and infected by them, and her soul was purified, made clean. In that sort of environment, it was impossible not to have a purer, broader love surge through one's breast.

An Jing said that, upon returning from Xizang, her life was empty, flavorless, and even dirty. What she had before called her love was thin and pale, like a weak little flower growing in the ruins. She was not willing to go on like this. She wanted to find a life that was truly hers, and a love that was truly hers.

An Jing had a lot to say to An Ning during that period. Some of it was beyond An Ning's understanding, and some were things she didn't understand at the time, but gradually came to understand later. She felt that perhaps An Jing was right to do as she had done.

30

After she met Li Qingge, as An Ning sat alone at KFC at noon one day, eating a Mexican wrap and drinking black tea, she saw Li Qingge walking on the street outside the window. She ran out and caught up to him. Li Qingge was very pleased to see her.

An Ning asked, "What are you doing?"

Li Qingge said, "I'm going to Chunxi Road to develop photos."

An Ning said, "I have a bit of free time now. I'll go with you."

In the photo studio, Li Qingge handed several rolls of film to the salesperson. An Ning said, "The photos you took of my sister are amazing. I really like them."

Li Qingge said modestly, "That's because Xizang is so beautiful."

An Ning said, "Can you give me a few photos?"

Li Qingge said, "Sure, what kind do you want?"

"Anything from Xizang is fine—figures, scenery, whatever." Before Li Qingge could answer, she added, "Just make two sets of the ones you're developing now. One for you and one for me."

Li Qingge smiled, but didn't say anything.

"What? You feel the pinch?"

"I'm not that stingy," he said. "If you'd like, you can choose whatever you want when they are developed."

An Ning went so far as to say, "You can't back out! I'm not only choosing from the ones you developed today. I want to see everything you've taken and take whatever I want."

Li Qingge said, "You seem very quiet, but you're actually even more domineering than your sister."

When they parted, they made an appointment to meet the next day at a teahouse by the Funan River so that An Ning could choose the photos she wanted from Li Qingge's collection.

Li Qingge was a man of his word. The next day, he not only brought the photos he'd had developed the day before, but also brought many of his previous works. There were many shots of local customs in Xizang and of snowy scenes, along with many close ups of military construction scenes and the soldiers there.

Li Qingge said, "I have the negatives. Choose whatever you want."

An Ning chose a dozen pictures. Li Qingge was happy to see that she liked his work so much. He said, "If you'd like, I can bring you a few new ones each time I come back in the future."

An Ning said, "It would be best if you could write an explanatory note on each one."

When she said it, she didn't think Li Qingge would actually do it. But every time he gave her photos, whether when he came back for vacation or when he sent them directly from Xizang, there was always an explanatory note on the back of each photo. What surprised her was that he was not only an excellent photographer, but also an excellent writer.

For instance, on the back of a picture of a desolate mountain, Li Qingge might write, *The folds of the mountain are the footprints of the wind.* Or on the back of a photo of a pilgrim on a highland road, he would write, *Only the saint knows how long the pilgrimage is.* And on the back of a photo with a group of Mongolian gazelles running in the Gobi Desert, she might find the words, *A gazelle can keep calm and think independently, but a herd of gazelle will grow restless and run around blindly.*

In one photo, there was a bird on a cliff. On the back of it was written, *A bird stood on the mountain's head and said, "I'm taller than you." The mountain remained silent. A gust of wind came, and no one knew where the bird went to, but the mountain remained unchanged.*

In another, a foreigner with a backpack hiked up a mountain road to where the clouds and sky met the road. On the back, he wrote, *When you walk on the plateau, you enter the mystery, and when you leave the plateau, you enter the loneliness.*

Before she knew it, three years had passed, and she had two hundred photos by Li Qingge. At first, she didn't think of publishing a photo book for him, but one night in the fall of the following year, on that isolated island, the idea suddenly came to her.

When Li Qingge's vacation was coming to an end, they got together again, but this time, Lu Wei and Chang Na could not join them, leaving only An Jing, An Ning, and Li Qingge. They did not go for a meal, going to a bar instead. Perhaps An Jing thought she might get drunk that night—or perhaps that was her aim, and that was why she made these arrangements.

An Jing drank a lot that night. There was no stopping her. Anyone who tried to stop her would just make her agitated. Before long, she was drunk. Aside from her birthday years earlier, she had never been drunk before. It felt so damn good to be drunk! The drunk An Jing was no longer An Jing. She slid down from the stool and sat on the ground, talking and laughing, and she attracted many eyes. An Ning tried to help her up, but she just sat down again, then pulled An Ning to sit on the ground beside her. She said nothing as she sat on the ground, until she asked for a cigarette. An Ning had never seen An Jing smoke before, but she was afraid anything she said to interfere would provoke her sister to make more trouble, becoming even more violent, so she simply let it be.

Smoking a cigarette, An Jing said, "I'm really happy tonight. I'm here with my closest relative and with the man who makes me feel most secure."

Holding the cigarette, she laughed bitterly and said, "It's so damn easy to be a bad woman."

She cried quietly. It wasn't a raucous crying, but crying with a smile and tears on her face at the same time. It was possible she didn't even realize she was crying.

She leaned on An Ning and said, "No one in the world loves me. My father doesn't love me. My mother doesn't love me. No one really loves me. Men love me because they want to marry me or sleep with me. None of them are any good. Li Qingge, I'm not referring to you. You are a good man. I like you. But liking isn't love, you know? I used to think I loved Chen Kai, but I didn't. He was very nice to me, though. But he doesn't really know me. He only knows how to give me money, or sleep with me. He doesn't know what I really want. He can't help me. No one can help me."

Embarrassed, An Ning tried several times to stop An Jing, but it was no use. Listening to An Jing cry, Li Qingge was shocked. He didn't know that the beautiful, kind An Jing's life was like that. He sat there, saying nothing. An Ning hugged An Jing as she cried.

"Jing, don't do this."

Later, Chen Kai came and picked An Jing up and took her home. It seemed Chen Kai always showed up at the wrong time.

Standing at the door of the bar as An Jing sat in Chen Kai's car and disappeared down the street, An Ning said to Li Qingge, "I want to go to Tianfu Square. Can you go with me?"

They went to Tianfu Square and sat on the steps beneath the statue of Chairman Mao. They sat for a long time, but neither of them spoke. With Li Qingge by her side, An Ning did not feel lonely. Though they had both had a lot to drink, and though An Ning longed for him to embrace her, Li Qingge did nothing. He just quietly kept her company.

Perhaps it was because he did nothing that night that An Ning fell in love with him.

The next summer, after An Ning graduated from university, she became a trainee reporter for the *Rongcheng Daily*. An Jing finished graduate school at the same time, and she left Chengdu. An Ning suspected she might go to Xizang, but instead, she went to England. An Ning knew of her plans just before she left and was quite surprised. She thought perhaps An Jing was going to study overseas, but her guess was wrong again. An Jing was not going overseas to study, but to work part time. On the eve of her graduation from grad school, An Jing had seen online that a British music company was recruiting people who understood Tibetan music. She took the initiative to contact them.

An Jing did not tell Chen Kai she was going overseas. At the airport, she gave An Ning a letter and a key, and she asked An Ning to give them to Chen Kai. She also urged An Ning, "Don't tell Chen Kai where I'm going."

31

A few months after An Jing's departure, in early autumn, Li Qingge returned to Chengdu to attend to some work matters. An Ning told Li Qingge all about her sister's situation. He was surprised, but after a moment of silent thought, he said, "Maybe she's right."

The newspaper sent An Ning to Wenjiang for an interview. An Ning asked Li Qingge to go with her, saying it was a simple interview and would not take long. She wanted to go to Baita Lake when the interview was finished, partly because he could take photos of her, but also because she wanted him to teach her how to shoot photos of her own. He happened to have the day off that day, so he went with her.

The interview really was a very simple matter. A woman who had been laid off from work had set up a vegetable stall, and one day, a customer had given her a torn five-yuan note. When she objected, the customer said she could go to the bank and exchange it. He added that the government had issued new regulations—it had been broadcast on TV—saying that notes that had been defaced on less than one third of the surface area could be exchanged for full value. Anything that had more than one third of the surface area defaced could still be exchanged for half its value.

When the stall keeper saw that the damage to the note affected less than a third of its surface area, she happily accepted it and took it to the nearby Agricultural Bank to exchange it. The teller there said it could only be exchanged for half its face value. When the woman objected, insisting that it could be exchanged for full value, the bank staff told her they had not seen any news of the regulation she mentioned, but she could take it to another bank and try there. She left and went to ICBC, with the same results. She went to several more banks, only to be told she could not exchange it for the full amount.

The woman was so angry that she called the newspaper. The newspaper sent An Ning to interview her. When An Ning found the stall keeper whom she was supposed to interview, she took the five-yuan note and a newspaper report detailing the new regulations to several banks as an ordinary walk-in customer, but none of them would exchange the note. An Ning gave the stall keeper a new five-yuan note and kept the damaged one, ready to take it back and report the matter in the newspaper.

And that was it. She had finished the interview very quickly.

Surprised, Li Qingge asked, "That's it?"

An Ning said, "Yes, that's it."

"But the matter hasn't been resolved."

An Ning said, "The newspaper only reports the facts, and that can play the role of directing public opinion. It is not necessarily the newspaper's job to solve problems. When the matter appears in the newspapers, it is only natural that the relevant departments will come forward and resolve it. This is not a problem with the bank notes, but with the implementation of policy throughout the banking industry. It's an issue of regulation and professional ethics."

Li Qingge understood, and he said nothing more. They took a bus from Wenjiang to Baita Lake, named for an island in the lake that had a white pagoda on it. It was not a holiday, so there were few tourists, just a few cruise ships floating on the lake. Li Qingge liked this sort of situation, saying it was ideal for shooting photos. They hired a boat and took pictures on the lake. The scenery among the hills and lakes was quite stunning, and Li Qingge became very focused, shooting numerous photos that he was sure would turn out very good.

Later, they abandoned the boat and landed on the island. It was even less crowded there, with winding bluestone paths leading to secluded spots, where wooden houses were vaguely discernible deep in the woods.

"This place is so beautiful! It's paradise," An Ning said enthusiastically.

Li Qingge could not be bothered to say anything. He ran back and forth, raising his camera to take photos of An Ning.

An Ning said, "You don't need to take photos of me. Teach me to take photos."

Li Qingge snapped a photo, explaining to An Ning why he framed it the way he did, how it could be composed in a fresh way, what the aperture should be at this time, and what the shutter speed should be. An Ning had gone through some photography training after she had joined the newspaper, so she had some basic knowledge, but she pretended not to know anything. She liked Li Qingge's serious expression as he explained things.

Tired, they sat under a gingko tree to rest. An Ning wondered if Li Qingge had been so serious when An Jing had been in Xizang. An indescribable feeling came over her. Suddenly thinking of the nude photo of An Jing, she asked Li Qingge, "Are you the one who took the photo of my sister?"

An Jing had actually told her long ago that it was Li Qingge who had taken the photo, but for some reason, she wanted to hear it straight from him.

He wasn't sure what she meant. "Which photo?"

"The ... nude photo."

Li Qingge blushed. "I did. But, at the time—"

An Ning said, "I'm not implying anything else. Don't get me wrong. It's a beautiful photo."

Embarrassed, Li Qingge said, "That's because your sister is beautiful. It's the most satisfying work I photographed."

"It's obvious that the photographer was full of passion when he shot it." An Ning pondered what he had said. "Actually, that's not what I wanted to say. What I meant to say was, are you in love with my sister?"

Li Qingge lowered his head, unsure how to answer.

"Do you love her?"

He thought about it, then said, "To be honest, your sister is beautiful, smart, passionate, and energetic. Anyone who sees her will like her, but she is not right for me. She's too romantic, too idealistic. Xizang had a great impact on her life, breaking through her quiet life. Xizang was a mirror, showing her some flaws in her life and letting her see clearly what she really needed, which was to live a truly independent life, a life of innovation—constant innovation. Only this type of life can bring her real romance, so she left. She's a restless girl. If she didn't go to England, she would have gone somewhere else. What she liked was not me, and it wasn't Xizang. She liked the novel feeling of Xizang, and the ideals and beliefs that we soldiers in Xizang hold to so firmly. These things are hard to find in modern cities, so Xizang moved her, and we moved her. In her eyes, Xizang and the interior regions are two different worlds. She likes such differences. She regards hardship as a sort of romance, but such hardship is something she can only take for a short time, not for too long. If you asked her to live in such an environment, it would not be long before she would regret it. So she's not right for me, not suited to be a military man's wife. I've known this for a long time, but I liked her calmness and her courage to change herself and her life."

An Ning had not expected Li Qingge, who was not usually good with words, to have so much to say about An Jing, nor for it to be so accurate and incisive. He was right. That was exactly the sort of person An Jing was.

An Ning said, "So all the understanding and warmth between you and my sister, it's just ordinary friendship, not love?"

Li Qingge said, "You could say that."

An Ning smiled and said, "Have you ever been in love with someone else?"

Li Qingge laughed shyly.

An Ning said, "Don't tell me you've never been in love. You're twenty-six. There must have been someone."

Li Qingge said, "To tell you the truth, I've never been in a relationship. I was in the military academy, and it was all men just like me. Those weren't conditions conducive to falling in love. We almost never saw women. Who was there to fall in love with?"

"I don't believe it. You mean, you've never even had a crush on someone?"

Li Qingge glanced at An Ning, then lowered his head again.

An Ning said half jokingly, "You don't mean it's me, do you?"

Turning his head away, he said, "You're right. It's you."

An Ning did not say anything. Her heart was pounding, threatening to burst through her chest.

Once it was out, Li Qingge grew calmer and just went on to finish what he wanted to say. "I know it's a cliché, always something you see in books and movies, but I still want to say it again. It was love at first sight. I felt that we would get each other, that you would understand many things. Did you feel the same?"

An Ning said, "Yes. Actually, I liked you too, but I thought you liked my sister. Now, I don't have to worry. You don't know how charming your smile is! You gave me such a solid, fresh, pure feeling. No guy has ever made me feel that way before."

An Ning thought that when she said this, Li Qingge would embrace her passionately and kiss her, but he did nothing. He just sat calmly, not ever looking at An Ning.

Head lowered, Li Qingge said, "I'm very grateful to you. No girl has ever said such things to me. I like you, but I know it's impossible. It's not that I have an inferiority complex. it's just that I do like you so much, so I don't dare to have you. I'm a soldier's son, and I saw in my mother how difficult it is to be a soldier's wife. In all my childhood memory, I only have images of my mother, none of my father. Even when he appears in a memory, he is very vague. To me, father is just a word you call someone. The clearest impression I have of my father is from when I was in third grade. My mother suddenly fell ill in the middle of the night. She had a high fever and was trembling all over and sweating profusely. I carried her on my back to the hospital in the middle of the night. Afraid she would crush me, my mother broke free and insisted on walking by herself. I couldn't stop her, so I supported her as she walked. She was very ill, and she had to stop and catch her breath after just a few steps. We went like that, in starts and stops, all the way to the hospital. It took all night, and as soon as we got into the hospital, my mother collapsed.

"Not long after my mother was hospitalized, the Mid-Autumn Festival came around. I went to visit her after school. The husband and daughter of a woman in the same ward brought her food, two bowls of dumplings. Their family was very affectionate, laughing and chatting together. And here we were, mother and son, desolate. Neither of us had even eaten. I said, 'Ma, you lie here, and I'll go buy something to eat.' I spoke very softly, but the woman heard me, and she told her husband to put some dumplings in another bowl and give it to us. My mother couldn't reject it, so she ate with me. I heard the woman whisper to her husband that my father was a soldier in Xizang, so my mother and I were to be pitied. My mother heard, and it made her cry.

"When my parents had been married for more than thirty years, my mother calculated and found that the time they had spent together was less than three years total. When my father finally reached retirement age and was able to come back to be with my mother, his health was no good. He had gotten used to the climate on the plateau, and he could not adapt to the conditions at lower altitudes. As soon as he returned, he was dizzy, nauseated, and exhausted. He was only well when he went back to the plateau, so he had to stay there all the time. As a result, the three of us were scattered in three places. My mother was in Chengdu, my father lived in Golmud, at the foot of the Kunlun Mountains, and I was on the Sichuan-Xizang Line. My father retired. He shouldn't have kept staying on the plateau like that. He loved my mother and always said she had had such a hard life. It was time for him to come back and be with her. So he did take the risk to come back to be with her in Chengdu, but after less than six months, his lungs became so swollen that he died. I was on a rescue mission on the Sichuan-Xizang Line at the time and couldn't even come back for the mourning."

As An Ning listened, she started to cry. Li Qingge did not cry. He just said, "I don't want you to suffer all your life like my mother has."

An Ning wiped her tears and said, "But you can't be single all your life. I love you, and I want to marry you."

Li Qingge stood up and said, "It's getting late. We should head back."

It was already late. The surrounding trees had become a blur. When the two of them reached the ferry point, there were no boats in site. They looked around and found a wooden house. A woman inside told them the last ferry had left. She said, "I have food and shelter here. You can stay with me. A chicken can be cooked in three different ways, and it's very cheap."

Dumbfounded, Li Qingge looked at An Ning. "What should we do? This is my fault. I wasn't watching the time."

An Ning was quite happy to spend a night on the deserted little island. "It's no big deal. Let's just spend the night here."

The woman said, "It's very safe here. You have nothing to worry about."

Seeing that the woman had misunderstood their intentions, Li Qingge started to explain, but An Ning said, "Ma'am, we'll stay with you here tonight. Please prepare the meal for us. One chicken cooked in three ways, and please cook two vegetables to go with it."

The food came to the table quickly, and An Ning asked for a bottle of red wine. The moon had just come out, shining on the wooden house and bamboo tables and chairs. The breeze was gentle, and the mood was light. As they ate and drank, An Ning asked Li Qingge, "What is your greatest wish?"

Li Qingge said, "I'd like to publish a photo book of my own some day."

An Ning tucked this answer away in her memory. She was a little dizzy, but she was not at all fuzzy about what she wanted to say now. "You know what my greatest wish is?"

"What?"

"To be your bride."

Later, she got drunk and fell into his arms. But perhaps it was not the wine that was intoxicating; it was him.

"It feels good to be drunk. No wonder my sister likes drinking. Are you Li Qingge? Li Qingge, let me tell you, I want to be your bride. I love you, Li Qingge. Marry me."

She wasn't sure how he got her into the guest room that night. She thought of what he would do to her—what she hoped he would do to her—but when she woke the next morning, she was still fully dressed. She lay in bed, and everything was fine, as if nothing had happened. Li Qingge sat beside her, looking at her affectionately. He had watched her all night.

She sat up and put her arms around his neck. They kissed for the first time.

From that day on, An Ning began to secretly prepare to publish a photo book for Li Qingge. She went to the publishing house and found that it would cost fifty thousand yuan to produce such a book. She tried desperately to pull the money together, but after a year, she could still only come up with ten thousand. She could have gone to her father for the money, but she didn't want to do that. She wanted to publish the book for Li Qingge with her own money.

Before Li Qingge even knew about her plan, she found a designer to create a sample book titled *One Man's Plateau*. She wanted to give it to Li Qingge at the wedding, and then publish it with his consent.

32

When she woke in the morning, An Ning had a bit of a headache. She had fallen asleep late the previous night, thinking of Li Qingge. When Yu Xiulan woke her, it was already bright outside. The soldiers had eaten breakfast and were at the construction site.

Xiulan said, "Time to get up. The car is waiting. Let's have something to eat, then go." She added, "You didn't sleep well last night? I heard you tossing and turning for a long time. When you finally fell asleep, you talked in your sleep."

An Ning was surprised. She never talked in her sleep. Why had she suddenly done so now?

As she got dressed, she asked Xiulan, "What did I say?"

Xiulan smiled. An Ning rarely saw her smile. She looked good when she smiled, much younger.

Still smiling, Xiulan said, "I didn't hear it very clearly. All I could make out was, 'I want to marry you.'"

An Ning blushed, feeling very embarrassed.

They ate quickly and were about to leave when there was an accident among the troops. It was a big accident.

When it happened, Feng Xiaoli, Guo Hong, and the messenger, Bai, were helping the women load their bags into a Mitsubishi jeep. Xiaoli's ankle was much better, and she was able to walk now. She told the driver to take it slowly and drive safely.

Two soldiers ran in, their faces pale. When they saw Bai, they shouted, "Hurry and get the safety rope! There's been an accident at the construction site."

They were all shocked. Xiaoli asked, "What happened?"

The two soldiers had already run into the warehouse with Bai, and they did not hear. They soon ran out again, each carrying a roll of safety ropes.

Feng Xiaoli ran after them, asking, "What happened?"

"Someone fell down the cliff."

Stunned, Guo Hong asked in a trembling voice, "Who?"

As the soldiers ran out, they said, "We don't know yet."

Looking panicked, Feng Xiaoli said to An Ning, "I need to go. Wait here."

Feng Xiaoli got into the truck and told the two soldiers to get in too, then told the driver to hurry to the construction site. As soon as the car left the camp gate, Guo Hong's body went limp, and she almost fell to the ground. An Ning caught hold of her.

Guo Hong said, "When I woke up this morning, my head was pounding and my heart skipped a beat. Do you think Deng Gang is alright?" Tears welled up in her eyes as she spoke. "I'm sorry, Deng Gang. I'm so sorry."

An Ning comforted, "We don't know anything yet. Deng Gang will be fine."

Too restless to sit in the house, the women rushed to the gate and looked out in the direction of the construction site. Several times, Guo Hong wanted to run to the site, but An Ning stopped her. They anxiously waited for news.

After some time, a jeep finally appeared. Behind it was another Mitsubishi jeep. When the cars entered the courtyard, Deng Gang leapt out. Guo Hong ran over anxiously, wanting to ask something, but Deng Gang didn't even look at her. His expression was very serious.

Two more officers got out of the car, and together, they carried another person from the vehicle. He was covered in blood. They carried him into the house. The battalion leader, Feng Xiaoli, and two other officers got out of the second car and followed them into the house. More than a dozen soldiers ran over and gathered around the door. Someone started to cry softly.

The person they had carried back was Zhou Ming, deputy instructor of Squadron 2. His life had been sacrificed.

Feng Xiaoli told the women that there had been another small landslide that night, a common occurrence on the Sichuan-Xizang Line. After a large landslide, there were usually a series of small landslides, like aftershocks following an earthquake. This one had not blocked the road, and the east-west traffic moved as it normally did. The soldiers had gone up to the construction site early in the morning to clear the sand and stones that had fallen on the road. Zhou Ming, deputy instructor of Squadron 2, was commanding the troops from the roadside. They did not realize that the roadbed had been hollowed out by the surging waters when the Nujiang had been diverted a few days earlier, causing the water level to rise.

When the news reached Deng Gang, he dispatched the leader of the detachment, who was organizing the work ahead, telling him to rush to the scene and organize an emergency rescue team. Deng Gang tied a safety rope to the tire of the car and lowered the rope to the bottom of the cliff. Halfway down, he found something like a pile of white flowers on a protruding rock. Everything went dark for him. He knew Zhou Ming had already lost his life.

An Ning and Yu Xiulan did not leave that day. They worked all day with Feng Xiaoli and Guo Hong, folding paper flowers for Zhou Ming.

Xiaoli said, "I saw him yesterday. He was so happy. He told me he was going to be a father. But now ... He just got married when he went back for the Spring Festival. His wife is six months pregnant."

Xiaoli burst into tears as she spoke, and the other women followed suit. Xiulan was the saddest. She kept crying, not saying anything.

It started to rain the next morning, but even a light rain was enough to turn the road muddy, stopping them in their footsteps. People walked up the hill behind the camp in clusters. The officers and soldiers were there, the leaders of the county party committee and county government were there, and so were Tibetan people from the surrounding area. A teacher brought a group of elementary school students. Tenzin Rinpoche came with a group of a dozen lamas. They sat on the hillside, sending off the soul who had just passed on.

It was the same hillside An Ning and Guo Hong had climbed a week earlier. Now, it was the site of a funeral for a soldier who had lived on the road for twelve years, for a husband who had been married for just seven months, for a father who had never seen his child, for the after-school tutor of sixteen Tibetan children, for the patron supporting three Tibetan children through school. It was a simple, solemn funeral.

The officers and soldiers took off their hats and saluted. The Tibetan people sprinkled mellow barley wine on the newly raised tomb, offered white hadas, and inserted five-colored prayer flags. Sixteen children presented newly picked galsang flowers. Three children knelt, their tears flowing in the rain.

An Ning later learned that the village nearby was called Longya Village—Deaf and Mute Village. Later, she realized that the characters were written differently than she had first thought when she heard the name, and that the name Longya actually meant something like *the song of the dragon*. It was a small village of just twenty or so households. It was far from the road, nearly completely isolated from the world, and traffic and information were basically cut off. There had not been a scholar in the village for generations, and there was no television or radio.

The people in the area often called it Deaf and Mute Village for this reason. The squadron had built a road to the village four years earlier. With the labor of the officers and soldiers, a way had been broken that allowed the villagers to leave the snow-capped mountains if they chose to. The road allowed Tibetan medicines and timber to be transported out of the village as well, and the village prospered from it. Two families in the village had already purchased vehicles for transportation. Zhou Ming had mobilized the soldiers to make voluntary donations to buy a satellite receiver and television set for the village, allowing the villagers to watch TV for the first time, getting their first glimpse of Tiananmen Square in Beijing. Zhou Ming led the officers and soldiers to build a wooden structure in the village, building the first primary school in the village's history, which allowed sixteen school children of different ages to go to the bright classroom. Zhou Ming and the other educated officers in the squadron took turns to teach the village children. When county officials later learned about this, they were very moved. They sent a teacher to the village and officially named the school Yushui Primary School. Zhou Ming then became an after-school tutor. The officers and party members in the squadron took up the responsibility of paying the tuition and miscellaneous expenses for the sixteen children, and Zhou Ming had personally been responsible for three of them until the day he died.

On the night of Zhou Ming's burial, Xiaoli was talking with An Ning and Xiulan in the room when they suddenly heard Deng Gang shout loudly in the room next door, "Don't you just want a divorce? Fine, I'll give you one."

Then they heard Deng Gang go out.

They looked at each other in dismay, but then immediately understood. They ran out to see that Deng Gang had already gone out the front door. Bai tried to stop him, but Deng Gang shook him off. Bai came back in despair.

Xiaoli asked Bai, "What happened? Where is he going?"

Bai said, "The captain is very angry with his wife and is going to stay in a tent at the construction site."

An Ning urged Xiaoli, "Go and persuade him to come back. Now!"

"It's no use. I know how bad his temper is. No one can persuade him," Xiaoli said. "Let's go and see Mrs. Deng instead."

They walked into the room and found Guo Hong, covering her face as she cried. After much urging, she finally stopped crying. She said she had tried to talk to Deng Gang, but he assumed she still wanted to talk about divorce, and he had suddenly lost his temper. He accused her of bringing bad luck, saying she had brought the ill fortune that led to Zhou Ming's death. Without letting her explain, he took the divorce papers from the desk drawer, signed them, dropped the pen, and stalked out.

An Ning said, "This wasn't the right time to bring it up."

Aggrieved, Guo Hong said, "I was trying to apologize. I wanted to tell him I had misjudged him and didn't want a divorce. But as soon as I said a word, he got angry."

Xiaoli comforted her, saying, "Zhou Ming just lost his life. Deng Gang is just sad and stressed. Don't worry, sis. You can talk to him again when he calms down."

Guo Hong's tears welled up again, "Who knows whether he will forgive me."

Early the next morning, An Ning and Xiulan left Baima and took a Mitsubishi jeep to Bomi.

33

The trip was very smooth. They traveled more than two hundred kilometers and arrived at their destination before noon.

As they sped into Bomi County, the driver asked Xiulan, "Is your husband in the battalion or the security squadron."

She replied, "Not in the battalion."

The driver said, "The security squadron, then. Bomi only has these two units."

Xiulan did not say anything.

The driver took them directly to the security squadron, then returned to Baima.

When they walked into the squadron headquarters, they saw a soldier pasting a small red flag onto a chart on the wall. When he saw them, he jumped off the stool and asked, "Who are you looking for?"

Xiulan said, "The person in charge."

An Ning was surprised that Xiulan did not ask for her husband, Wang Li, but looked for the person in charge instead. Hadn't she said her husband was a soldier? Or had he somehow become squadron commander, just like that?

The soldier asked, "What business brings you here?"

Xiulan said blankly, "I want to see the person in charge."

The soldier looked at Xiulan, then he looked at An Ning and Xiaoxue. Unable to figure out what they were doing here, he walked out in confusion, not saying anything more. After a while, a lieutenant was called. He had a scar on his forehead. As he entered, he asked, "Who is looking for the person in charge?"

When he saw that the three visitors did not know who the officer was, the soldier introduced him. "This is our squadron leader."

Xiulan asked the squadron leader, "Did you know the soldier named Wang Li who used to be here?"

The squadron leader took a step back in surprise. "You're ..."

"I'm his wife," Xiulan said.

The squadron leader froze where he was and looked at her in surprise. The corners of his mouth started to tremble. He quickly took a step forward and clasped Xiulan's hand.

"Ma'am! Why did you come all the way here?" As he spoke, the rims of his eyes turned red, and tears dropped from his eyes.

"I came here to see him."

Xiulan's tears started to flow as well. Seeing her mother cry, Xiaoxue hugged Xiulan and cried too. Not knowing why they were crying, An Ning and the soldier stood to one side.

The squadron leader wiped his tears. Stroking Xiaoxue's head, he said, "Is this Xiaoxue? It's been ten years. She's so grown up! Ma'am, you don't know me, but I know you, and I know Xiaoxue. I used to go out in the field with Wang Li, and he often talked about you. My name is Han Yi. I was Wang's apprentice. When I went back to visit my family, I tried to find you, but the villagers said you took your child and went to the city to work. Ma'am, why didn't you let us know you planned to come up?"

"I didn't want to trouble the troops."

Han Yi hurriedly poured water and tea. He sent the soldier to instruct the cooking crew to prepare a meal.

Xiulan said, "Don't go to any trouble. We had lunch on the way here." Then she added, "Just take me to him."

Han Yi said, "You've had a long journey, and the road is a hard one. Rest today. You can go tomorrow."

Xiulan said, "I've waited for this day for ten years. You can take me and my daughter there now."

Han Yi said, "Alright. Let's go."

Han Yi went out to arrange for a vehicle. An Ning was still in the dark about what had happened to Xiulan's husband. Seeing what had just happened, she recalled Xiulan's taciturn, secretive ways as they had traveled, and she was almost certain she knew the truth. When she saw they were ready to go, she said to Xiulan, "Sis, let me go with you."

Xiulan said, "Sis, I'm sorry I've kept it from you while we were traveling. I didn't want to talk about it. I was afraid I would be too sad as we traveled, and I wouldn't have the strength to come all the way here. I didn't want anyone to know. I didn't want anyone to feel sorry for me."

Her eyes reddened again as she spoke.

An Ning said, "Don't cry. If you do, Xiaoxue will cry too."

In a weepy voice, Xiaoxue said, "Ma, don't cry."

Xiulan said, "I'm not going to cry."

But the tears of both mother and daughter flowed more than ever.

Han Yi came back and said to Xiulan, "Ma'am, the car is coming. Let's go."

The little group got into the jeep and went out of the gate of the compound. Turning right, they got back onto the Sichuan-Xizang Highway. Han Yi sat in the front, while An Ning, Xiulan, and Xiaoxue sat in the back. After a journey of about an hour and a half, Han Yi told the driver to stop. He got out of the car, opened the back door, and helped Xiulan from the car.

"Ma'am, this is where the accident happened. Come and have a look."

When she got out of the vehicle, An Ning saw that they were on a sharp curve, and the road was so narrow it almost seemed to be suspended in air. It had obviously been a challenge to carve this road from the cliff. More than ten meters below them ran a turbulent river.

Pointing to the cliff below them, Han Yi said, "The car rolled over from here."

Xiulan swayed and almost fell. An Ning quickly supported her.

Han Yi said, "It was raining lightly. Wang and I went to the tree farm up ahead to haul timber back. He had just returned from a long haul the night before, and he should have stayed in camp to rest, but he was afraid the road would be too slippery after the rain. I was worried about him, so I went with him. I was driving, and he sat beside me. When we got here, a stone suddenly rolled down the cliff onto the road in front of me. I panicked and slammed on the brakes. The truck slid and dropped. I was thrown from the vehicle and ended up hanging onto a tree on the cliff. Wang was in the truck when it fell into the river."

When the time came to cry, Xiulan did not shed a tear. She slumped in An Ning's arms, staring blankly at the turbulent waters below.

Han Yi took out a cigarette, lit one, and placed it respectfully on a rock on the edge of the cliff. Facing the waters, he said, "Wang, sir, your wife and Xiaoxue have come to see you."

Xiulan burst into tears then, and Xiaoxue followed suit. An Ning cried too, one arm around Xiulan, and the other clasping Xiaoxue to her bosom.

Han Yi said, "Wang was a big smoker, a pack a day. Every time I pass by here, I light a cigarette for him and sit with him for a while. Back then, he didn't know what to do. He always bugged me, talking about you constantly. He felt sorry for you and Xiaoxue, always talking about how he didn't go back to take care of you when she was born. He said that when he and the troops were supposed to come up the mountain, you visited and he got to hold his newborn little girl, Xiaoxue, but he only let you stay for three days, then made you go home. Even before you and the little one left, he was on his way up here with the troops. When you two parted, you grabbed his backpack and begged him not to leave, but he pushed you to the ground. When you cried, the baby cried too, but he didn't even turn back to look as he walked out. What you didn't know is that he was crying too. He said he regretted pushing you when the two of you parted."

Tears flowed down Xiulan's face. Xiaoxue took out a handkerchief and wiped her mother's face over and over. Xiulan took an empty mineral water bottle from her bag and walked to the edge of the cliff and looked down, as if searching for something. An Ning wondered what she was looking for.

Han Yi asked, "Ma'am, what are you looking for?"

"I want to go down and get a bottle of water."

An Ning understood. Xiulan wanted to carry home with her a bottle of water from the river where Wang Li had disappeared.

Han Yi understood too. He cried, "Ma'am, you can't go down there. I'll go."

He took a safety rope from the jeep, secured one end to the bumper, and tied the other end around his waist. Taking the bottle from Xiulan, he started descending the cliff.

After a while, Han Yi came back to the top of the cliff. He handed Xiulan a bottle full of water.

"Let's go, Ma'am."

The jeep continued on for several kilometers before reaching the Martyrs Cemetery on the side of the road. There were several tombs of various sizes. It was almost evening, and the setting sun cast a blood red glow, staining the snow-capped mountains that faced them.

Han Yi walked to two graves that stood side by side and said to Xiulan, "Right here, ma'am."

An Ning was stunned. The tombstones at the head of both tombs bore the same words: *Tomb of the Martyr Wang Li*. How could one person have two graves?

Xiulan was not surprised at all. It seemed she had known along that this would be the case. She pulled Xiulan to plop to the ground, kneeling in front of the graves. Crying, she said, "Li, Xiaoxue and I have come to see you."

The cries of both mother and daughter echoed across the foot of the snowy mountain for a long time. An Ning and Han Yi stood behind them, crying silently.

It got cold in the evening on the plateau. The weeping of the woman and her daughter made An Ning feel even more distressed.

When they had wept for some time, An Ning pulled Xiulan up. "Sis, get up now. Don't overdo it."

Xiulan stood up, but she had no intention of leaving. She had been waiting for ten years. How could she bear to go away so quickly? Tearfully, she walked around the two tombs, first one, then the other. Perhaps she was uncertain which tomb her husband was in.

Xiaoxue took the little paper cranes from her schoolbag and tossed them, one by one, onto the graves. The paper cranes fell silently, like snowflakes.

Choked up, Xiaoxue said, "Pa, when you miss Ma and me, come back on the paper crane."

An Ning now understood why Xiaoxue had always quietly folded paper cranes on their journey. Paper cranes, even one hundred of them, could they bring her father back? Poor child!

Xiulan said, "I'd like a little time here alone."

An Ning and Han Yi led Xiaoxue from the cemetery and walked to the roadside to wait for Xiulan. An Ning looked at the scar on Han Yi's forehead and asked, "Is that from the accident ten years ago?"

Han Yi said, "Yes, I was injured by a branch."

An Ning asked curiously, "How come her husband has two tombs?"

Han Yi said, "After the accident, we never found Wang. We search along the river for more than ten days before we found half a body downstream. Thinking it was Wang, we buried him. The following spring, a Tibetan herdsman found a mutilated body in the lower reaches, thirty miles away, and he reported it to the country public security bureau. The staff there noticed that the body was wearing a belt with the armed police logo on it, so they notified our battalion. When the battalion leader went to take a look, he found nothing but a pile of bones. It was impossible to confirm whether it was Wang, so he called me to see if I could identify the body. When I got there, I saw a scrap of a sweater wrapped around the body, and I knew it was him. I recognized the sweater. It was one his wife had knitted for him, with yellow and blue yarn. He was wearing it the day of the accident. So he was buried again, and now he has two tombs."

Han Yi said, "Actually, before the accident, Wang encountered two disasters, but he survived both. The first was on the Qinghai-Xizang Line. We still hadn't moved to the Sichuan-Xizang Line then. We were rebuilding the Qinghai-Xizang Highway. One day, Wang came back from the construction site in the middle of the night. There was no one in the barracks. They were all at the construction site. It was very cold then, so he lit the stove and went to sleep. When his fellow soldiers came back from the construction site the next morning and knocked, there was no response. There was a strong smell of gas. They knew something was wrong, so they kicked in the door and rushed in. Wang had passed out from the gas. They rushed him to the 22nd Hospital, where the staff spent three days and three nights trying to revive him before he finally pulled through.

"The next incident was on the Sichuan-Xizang-Line. On his way back to Chengdu when he was transporting construction materials, he was trapped by heavy snow on Mount Anjiura. He didn't have anything to eat or drink for five days and five nights. When he was hungry, he ate the grass roots that he dug out from under the snow, and when he was thirsty, he put a handful of snow in his mouth. It wreaked havoc on his stomach. When he was rescued, he was freezing in the cab. He was confined to bed for two weeks under the care of the medical team before he finally recovered."

Han Yi said, "Who would've guessed he wouldn't survive the third time?"

Night fell, and Xiulan came out of the cemetery. When they got into the car, An Ning saw that Xiulan carried a handful of soil. She did not need to ask. She knew it was soil from Wang Li's grave. Xiulan wanted to take it home, like the bottle of water from the river. An Ning found a half page of newsprint and helped Xiulan wrap up the soil in it.

That evening, many people from the squadron and battalion organization came to visit Yu Xiulan. The battalion leader had returned from the office in Baima. When he heard that Yu Xiulan was there, he brought other battalion leaders to meet her too. He asked Xiulan if there were any difficulties she needed help with, but she said no. He asked several times, and each time, she said no.

Xiulan did not cry in front of the battalion leader. Perhaps her tears had been dried up that afternoon—or, more accurately, over the past ten years.

Seeing Xiulan regain her peace on this journey, An Ning admired her. A woman who had been through ten years of hardships could only be admired.

That night, An Ning and Xiulan shared a room, and they talked most of the night. It was Xiulan who did most of the talking, and it was more like she was talking to herself than to An Ning. As An Ning listened to her, the title of an article came to mind: "Forever a Military Wife."

34

Xiulan said, "He was very good tempered. He never raised his voice to me. But the morning we parted, he got angry and pushed me to the ground. He didn't care that I sat on the ground crying. He walked out the door without looking back.

"Actually, I knew there was nothing he could do about it. He was a soldier and couldn't disobey orders. It was my fault for coming to camp with the baby without telling him in advance. Three days after I arrived, they were scheduled to go to the Sichuan-Xizang Line. I said, 'The baby and I just got here. Can't you stay with us for a few more days and go up with the last group?'

"He said, 'No, the squadron has been set. I have to be in the first group. I'm an experienced soldier. I have to lead the team.'

"He bought my return ticket without discussing it with me. He wanted to see me onto the train, but I was determined not to go. Seeing how stubborn I was, he sighed and said, 'I'll go talk to the leader,' and with a long face, he went out. I knew he wouldn't go. I knew him too well, and I knew not to trust such a promise from him. I followed him out, watching from a distance as he walked around the courtyard a few times, then came back.

"I went back into the room before him, to see what he would say when he came back. Who knew he was such a good actor? When he came in, he told me very seriously that the leader didn't agree. I was so angry. I said, 'You're lying! I'll go see your leader myself!'"

I rushed out the door like a madwoman. He stopped me, closing the door behind him. I hit him desperately, pulled the door, and yelled at him. He raised his hand and slapped me. We were both stunned. Neither of us had ever imagined he could hit me. I stopped crying and looked at him, dumbfounded. He looked at his trembling hand, just as dumbfounded as I was. He suddenly pulled me into his arms and said tearfully, 'I'm sorry! I'm so sorry. I wasn't in my right mind. I was stupid!' He slammed his hand into the wall hard, so hard it started bleeding.

"I pulled his hand to me, hugging it tightly. Crying, I said, 'Don't do that! Your hand is injured. How will you drive up the mountain tomorrow?'"

Xiulan went on, "It was the first time we ever argued. Who knew he would never come back after he left the next day? I always regretted that. I regretted that I was so unreasonable and argued with him. Now, I can't argue with him, even if I want to. Even if I wanted him to slap me again, he can't."

She said, "I knew he was gone, but I couldn't let go. Ten years ago, the soldiers handed me his martyr's certificate and showed me photos of his burial, but I just couldn't believe it.

"How could he leave? How could he go away without his wife and daughter. Xiaoxue was less than half a year old when he died. She didn't even know how to call him Pa. How could he leave without hearing his daughter call him Pa?

"I didn't want to believe he was really gone. Maybe they had made a mistake. Maybe the mutilated corpse they found wasn't him. Maybe the river had swept him to some deserted place and he had lost his way back. He was stuck somewhere in the mountains. Or maybe he had been rescued by some kind person and was still living there. Maybe he had injured his brain in the fall and forgotten his way home.

"I thought about it for ten years, dreaming up all sorts of possibilities. I thought one day he would come back to us, his wife and daughter. Every time I closed my eyes, I could imagine what he looked like when he was alive. At night, I often dreamed that he came home. I was happy and ran to meet him. But when I woke, there was nothing. Still, I always believed he would come back.

"I've counted carefully. We were married for three years, and we only had sixty-six days together. For ten years, I've thought about those sixty-six days over and over, thinking about him every day. Each word, each action, each expression. When I think about it, I take out the album and look at his photos. I recall each scene from each photo of us together, what he said, how we took the photo. I think about each one for a long time, recalling many details. I've survived the past ten years because of these memories.

"I've worked in two different places, and no one in either place knew that my husband was a soldier or that he had passed away. I don't want to tell anyone. I don't want to see the pity in their eyes. When my daughter was young, she asked about her father. I just said he was a soldier. When she asked why he never came home, I lied and told her he was on a special mission in Xizang and couldn't come back. Later, when she grew up and went to school, she guessed that I was lying, and she asked if he was dead. I insisted, 'Your father is not dead. He'll come back.'

"Once, when I was at work, she found his martyrs card at home. When I saw that she already knew, I told her the truth. We hugged each other and cried all night.

"Ten years ago, I wanted to come to Xizang to see him, but my daughter was too small to make the trip, and I couldn't leave her at home. When she grew up, I didn't dare to make the trip. I was afraid that my illusion would be shattered the moment I saw the tomb. How could I live without my illusion?

"For years, I've been living in my own fantasy. For so many years, I've been raising my daughter alone, and it's my illusion that keeps me going. I don't know what's wrong with me. There must be something wrong with my brain. Don't I know he's gone? Even now, I'm still waiting for him. Sometimes I see someone in a military uniform on the street, and my heart skips a beat, thinking its him, coming back home. I approach the person to get a closer look, sometimes following them for some time.

"Am I sick?

"It wasn't until his younger brother, Wang Bo, said to me one day, 'Let's live together,' that I woke from my fantasy. He was right. My husband has been gone for ten years. I shouldn't keep living in a fantasy. If not for myself, then for my daughter."

"Wang Bo is very kind to me and my daughter. When he was working in Guangzhou, he sent us money every month. After he came home, he was even better to us. I had never thought of him in that way before. If his situation had not gone the way it did, it would have never crossed my mind. He regarded me as his sister-in-law, and I regarded him as my own brother. How could I think of him like that?

"After he said that to me, I didn't sleep all night. Later, I asked Xiaoxue if she would like for her uncle to be her father. She jumped up and down and shouted, 'Yes! Yes! Yes! Uncle Bo loves me more than anyone, and I like him more than anyone too! Please let him by my father!'

"She has no impression at all of her father. She wasn't even six months old when he passed away. If she ever received any fatherly love, it was from Wang Bo. I later decided—not to take up Wang Bo's offer, but to come to Xizang. I told Wang Bo, 'I have to go to Xizang. I need to see your brother and tell him about this. We can talk about it when I come back from Xizang.'"

35

The next afternoon, An Ning and Yu Xiulan arrived at Dongjiu, the end point of the eight hundred kilometer section of road maintained by the military. Li Qingge's squadron was in Dongjiu, but Li himself had left the previous day. He had gone to Chengdu for a training class for grassroots leaders and officers that was to be conducted by the team. It would be forty days before he would return to Dongjiu.

36

On July 25, An Ning and Xiulan parted at Lhasa Gonggar Airport. The same afternoon that she returned from Xizang to Chengdu, An Ning went to the training class to find Li Qingge. The couple agreed to have their wedding in Chengdu when Li Qingge's training class ended.

As soon as she went back to work, her editorial director, Yuan Ye, told An Ning that her sister An Jing had called several times to see if she was back. An Jing had said she wanted to come back, but An Ning had not expected her to return so soon. She was very excited to hear that her sister was home. They had not seen each other for several years.

An Ning briefly told Yuan Ye about the interviews she had conducted on her journey, and she promised she would get the articles together soon so that the column *A Bride in Xizang* could get into readers' hands as quickly as possible. Then, she hurried to see An Jing.

An Jing was staying at the Minshan Hotel. When An Ning walked into the room, An Jing was discussing something with a foreign man.

An Jing said, "This is David, my colleague."

David was tall and stood very straight, with a gentlemanly bearing. When An Ning came in, he politely excused himself as soon as he had greeted her.

The sisters looked at one another, then embraced tightly.

An Jing said, "I've missed you."

An Ning said, "I missed you too."

Both girls' eyes were wet.

Breaking the embrace, An Ning held An Jing at arm's length and said, "You've lost weight, but you're prettier than ever."

It was very sunny that morning, a rare day of good weather in Chengdu. The two sisters sat in the room, whispering as they drank coffee that An Jing had brought back from England. They had endless topics to whisper about. An Jing talked about her life in the UK, and An Ning talked about her recent experience in Xizang. Though they intentionally avoided talking about their parents at first, they didn't gloss over it later.

An Jing said, "I heard he and Wang Jue divorced."

An Ning knew who "he" was. Since their father had married Wang Jue, An Jing had stopped calling him Pa.

An Ning was surprised by the news. "Did he? Why didn't I know about this?"

"It was just after you left, when you were on your way to Xizang. One of my old classmates told me." An Jing was clearly gloating. "I knew this day could come. It couldn't have been love. That bitch was just eyeing his power, and later, she set her sights on his wallet. Now that her wings are strong, of course she's flown. When they divorced, she was awarded half the company assets. Then she started a new company of her own, and another one after that."

An Ning was depressed. "Pa was cheated. Poor guy."

An Jing said angrily, "It was his choice. He deserved it!"

They talked about their mother as well. An Jing asked, "Has she married that civil servant yet?"

An Ning said, "Not yet." Then, a thought struck her, and she added excitedly, "Oh, that's good then! Ma and Pa can remarry now."

An Jing said coldly, "Not possible."

An Ning asked, "Why?"

An Jing said, "Let's not talk about this anymore. Talk about something else. How's Li Qingge?"

Finally, she asked about Li Qingge. An Ning said she had seen him the day before, and they were going to get married as soon as his training ended.

An Jing asked, "When is that exactly?"

An Ning said, "September 9."

An Jing said, "When the time comes, I'll definitely be there." After thinking for a moment, she added, "I'll put on a concert that day. A wedding gift for the two of you."

An Ning was moved. She glanced at An Jing. "You aren't mad at me, are you?"

An Jing laughed and said, "Don't be silly. Li Qingge doesn't belong to me."

An Ning said, "I really do love him."

An Jing said, "I know. I wish all the best for both of you."

An Ning said, "How are your concert preparations coming along?"

An Jing said, "We're still getting it ready. The funds are in place. Our company raised a million yuan, and a cultural group in Chengdu invested two million. I didn't expect things to go so smoothly. The two million in investment was only settled after some negotiation. When I had discussions with the vice president, I heard that their president was very interested in this concert. They said it's important for supporting Tibetan culture, and the investment should be made without worrying about making money. Unfortunately, I haven't met such a high-minded patron before."

An Ning asked about her plans for the future. An Jing said, "I don't plan to go back to UK. If I want to study Tibetan music, I shouldn't leave the country. I'll be traveling to Xizang frequently in the future. Our company is going to open a branch in Chengdu, and David and I will be in charge of it. We've already signed a cooperation agreement with the Conservatory of Music and the Tibetan Music Association. The company will officially start operations as soon as the *Galsang Blossoms* tour ends."

Thinking of David, whom she had just met, An Ning smiled. "You and that David ..."

An Jing said, "Don't speculate. We're colleagues."

An Ning said, "I can see from the look in his eyes that he liked you very much."

An Jing said, "If he likes me, that's his problem. There are lots of people who like me. It's not like you don't know. When have I not been surrounded by admirers?"

Both sisters laughed. An Jing was as confident as ever. Seeing her like that put An Ning at ease.

Suddenly thinking of Chen Kai, An Ning asked, "Have you seen him since you got back?"

"Who?"

"Chen Kai!"

An Jing said quietly, "No."

An Ning said, "Don't you want to know how he's doing?"

An Jing said, "People have told me. Didn't you say he got together with another girl pretty quickly after I left? I heard they're married now. Men are like that, especially rich men. Few can hold on and love just one woman."

An Jing smiled, "Li Qingge is an exception."

Speaking of Li Qingge, An Ning thought of the photo book. She told An Jing, "I called before and told you I wanted to publish that photo book for Li Qingge, right? You agreed to let me use your photo on the cover. Well, the sample is ready now, but Li Qingge doesn't know yet. I'm planning to give it to him at the wedding. You haven't changed your mind, have you?"

An Jing smiled, "Of course not! That's my most beautiful photo. It's my favorite. Why shouldn't more people appreciate it? When the company opens, I'm going to hang a big copy of it in my office."

Then she added, "It's romantic, you giving him this wedding present. You're much more romantic than me. My romance is all on the outside. Yours is in your heart. You have love in your heart too, and romance with love is real romance. I envy you!"

It was noon when she left the Minshan Hotel. Seeing that it was still early, An Ning went to the long distance bus station and bought a ticket to Pengzhou for the following day.

37

An Ning was going to Pengzhou to see the wife of Zhou Ming, the deputy instructor of Squadron 2, who had recently died on the Sichuan-Xizang Line.

Pengzhou was not far from Chengdu. An Ning left in the morning, and she arrived before noon. She went straight to Zhou Ming's home on the farm. It was not far from the city, but part of the journey was on a dirt road on which cars could not pass, but only trishaws. It took another half hour to get to Zhou Ming's house. There were three thatched houses on the gentle slope, with an orange grove in front. Zhou Ming was the youngest in his family. His older sister was married, and his older brother had been married, but was now divorced, leaving only his elderly parents at home now. His parents were honest folk. When they saw someone from the provincial capital coming to see them, they thought the government had sent a representative to console them. In recent days, people from the army and the county civil affairs office had come often.

Shyly, the old man kneaded his hands and said, "Thank you, officer, for your concern."

His own son had been sacrificed, and he was thanking the government. An Ning was moved, and tears welled up in her eyes. She said, "Sir, ma'am, I'm not a government official. I'm the girlfriend of Zhou Ming's fellow soldier. I just wanted to come visit his parents."

When Zhou Ming's mother heard she was the girlfriend of a fellow soldier, tears gathered in her eyes. As if it were her own son in front of her now, she clasped An Ning's hand and looked at her eagerly with teary eyes. Zhou Ming's father sighed, squatted, and wrapped his hands around his head.

The three thatched houses were not big. One was the kitchen, one was the older couple's, and one had been reserved for Zhou Ming when he came back. The furniture in Zhou Ming's room remained untouched, and there were three certificates of meritorious service hanging on the walls. What seemed to be a new addition was Zhou Ming's photo on the table in the mourning hall.

An Ning asked about Zhou Ming's wife, Shen Ping. The old man said that she taught at the county primary school and was a very dutiful daughter-in-law. She had come back to see them very often before, but she was now six months pregnant.

As An Ning prepared to leave, Zhou Ming's father said, "When you see Shen Ping, urge her to get rid of the baby and marry someone else. We've tried to persuade her several times, but she won't listen. She's young. She's a very good girl."

When An Ning found Shen Ping, she was grading her students' homework. She was very good-looking, looking a bit like the CCTV broadcaster Wen Qing. When An Ning introduced herself, Shen Ping quickly stood up. She wanted to get An Ning a cup of water, even with the inconvenience of her pregnancy. An Ning stopped her, poured the water herself, and sat down. When they talked about Zhou Ming, Shen Ping cried a lot, just as her father-in-law had. An Ning grew very uncomfortable, and soon, she was crying too.

When she had finished crying, Shen Ping told An Ning that she and Zhou Ming had met in the spring of the previous year. Zhou Ming was home visiting his family. Shen Ping invited him to come speak to her national defense education class, and they got to know each other then. After corresponding for a year, they got married when Zhou Ming returned for the next Spring Festival.

Shen Ping said that even before she met Zhou Ming in person, she knew who he was and had even been to his house—not once, but three times, when Zhou Ming won each of his meritorious service awards. The news of the awards had been sent through the Civil Affairs Bureau, and the bureau had invited the school to arrange for some students to beat drums and gongs as part of the procession. Each time, Shen Ping took the students to the house. Later, when the school wanted to start national defense education, she thought of Zhou Ming. When she asked about him, she found out that he was on vacation, so she invited him to talk to her class.

Shen Ping said that he had given a good talk, speaking about the troops on the Sichuan-Xizang Line. It was very touching. Many teachers and students cried, and the principal did too. The principal later told Shen Ping that she wanted Zhou Ming to speak to the students each year when he was home on vacation. But now, he would not be coming anymore.

When they talked about the child, An Ning asked, "What are you going to do?"

Shen Ping said calmly, "I'm going to have the baby."

An Ning said, "Your in-laws told me to persuade you to abort it."

Shen Ping said, "I want this child. It's mine and Zhou Ming's, together. I have no right to decide that alone."

In awe of Shen Ping, An Ning inwardly agreed with this course of action, but she said, "Have you ever thought about whether it will bring you trouble in the future?"

Shen Ping said, "I have. My relatives and friends, including Zhou Ming's parents, have all spent the past few days persuading me to abort the child. I've fallen out with my parents over it. I know they're all looking out for me. That's fine. But I want this child. Zhou Ming didn't leave me anything else."

An Ning told her Yu Xiulan's story.

Shen Ping said, "I won't keep living in illusions or fantasies for ten years, like she did. After the child is born, I'll marry a man who loves me, and who loves the child even more. I want to live a good life. I love Zhou Ming. It's because I love him that I want to live a good life with my child. If Zhou Ming had a spirit in heaven now, he would want me to do that."

On the way back to Chengdu later that day, An Ning thought of a title for the story of Zhou Ming and Shen Ping's relationship: "I Want this Child."

After she returned from Pengzhou, An Ning's column *A Bride's Journey through Xizang began to appear in Rongcheng Daily*, and it gained an immediate positive response. Yuan Ye said that when all the articles had been run, he would suggest to the president of the newspaper that they should publish An Ning's book.

38

On September 9, there was a special wedding ceremony for An Ning and Li Qingge. It was not so much like a wedding as a press conference.

Yuan Ye was very good at logistics, and he invited reporters from all the major newspapers, radio stations, and television stations in Chengdu. He wanted to bring *A Bride's Journey through Xizang* to a successful conclusion at An Ning's wedding. Later, he told her, "This has been the most successful project in my twenty years of journalism!"

When An Ning opened the gift box and presented Li Qingge with the photo book *One Man's Plateau*, all the cameras and microphones were aimed at Li and the book in his hand. Li Qingge's face was flushed, and he was speechless.

Of the hundreds present, only three people knew that the beautiful naked form on the cover of the book was the bride's sister, An Jing. An Jing stood at the back of the crowd, smiling as she watched the scene unfold.

Guo Hong attended the wedding. When An Ning and Li Qingge came to her table for a toast, she told An Ning that she and Deng Gang had made up.

An Ning's parents were there too. They did not come together, but being her typical alert self, An Ning noticed that they looked at one another across the table from time to time.

The *Galsang Blossoms* concert that was a huge success. At the final curtain call, An Jing found that the investor who had given two million yuan to the project, and who now stood with her onstage, was her own father.

The next day, the *Rongcheng Daily* published two different articles about Xizang. One was the final installment of *A Bride's Journey through Xizang*, "Finally, a Bride," and the other was a report on the success of the *Galsang Blossoms* concert. Almost every news outlet in Chengdu reported on these two events, and An Ning, An Jing, and Li Qingge's photos appeared in many newspapers that day.

With the successful media plan, Li Qingge's photo book, *One Man's Plateau*, was picked up by a publisher and hit the shelves not long after. Three months later, a book entitled *A Bride's Journey through Xizang* was published, with a first print run of a hundred thousand copies. *One Man's Plateau* was reprinted again at the same time, for a total of twenty thousand copies. The two books earned royalties of sixty thousand yuan that year. An Ning repaid the loan of forty thousand. She took the remaining twenty thousand yuan and went to the post office to fill out two remittance slips, one for Yu Xiulan and one for Shen Ping. On both remittance slips, the "Remitter" column read, "A Meadow of Galsang Blossoms."

January to May 2004

West Huixin Street, Beijing

ABOUT THE AUTHOR

DANG YIMIN, born in Fuping, Shaanxi Province, China, is a senior colonel in the Armed Police and a Chinese Writers' Association member. With a postgraduate degree in litigation law, he has authored six literary works, including the critically acclaimed novels *Tibetan Light*, *The Girl Wearing a Bullet Necklace*, *The Stirrings of the Barren Plateau*, and *Journey along the Galsang Road*. His work has earned him several prestigious awards, including the Chinese Writers' Great Red Eagle Literary Award, the Ba Jin Literary Academy Literary Award, and the Fourth Lu Xun Literary Award for outstanding national reportage literature.